FEB 24

W9-BZH-078

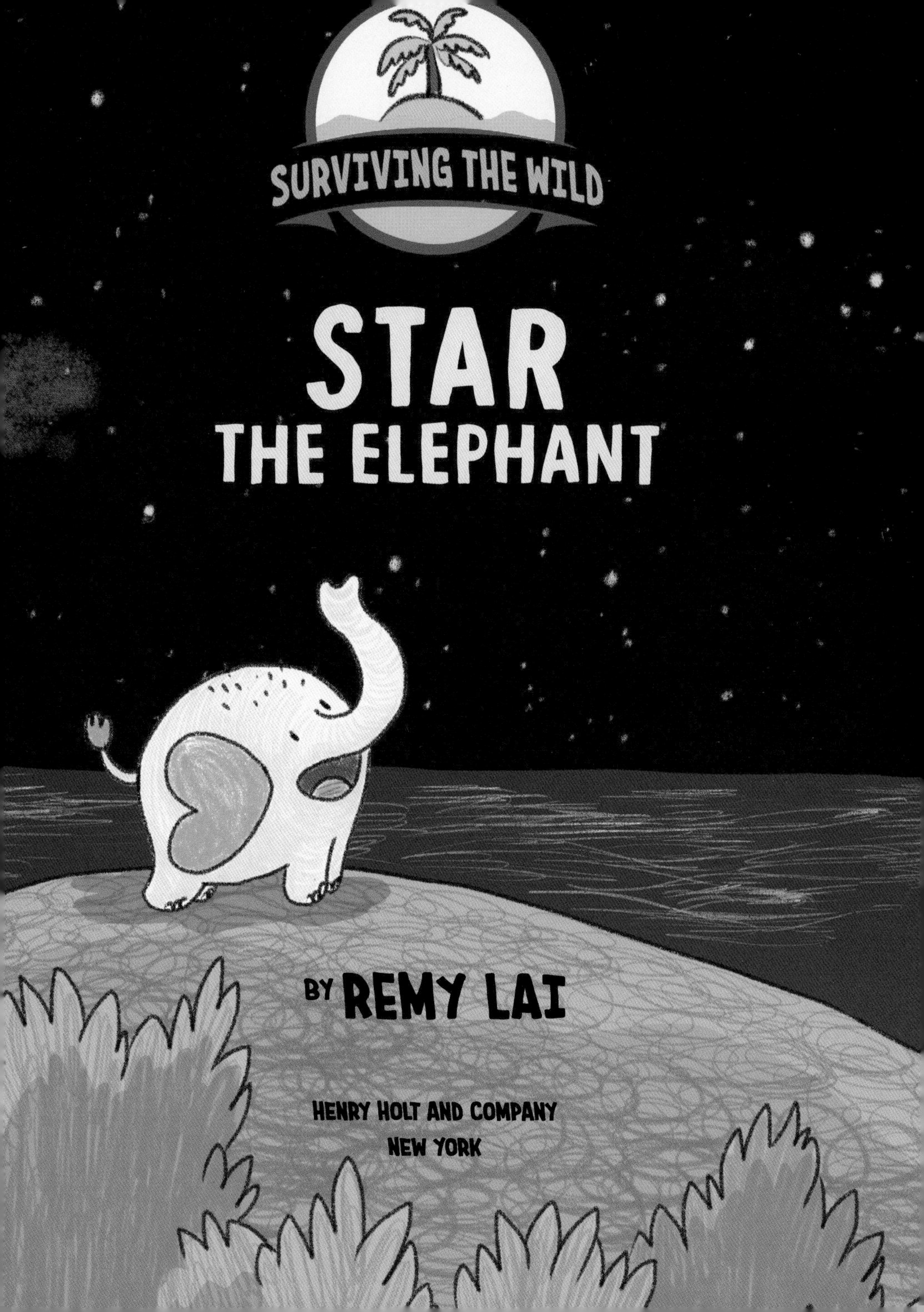

SURVIVING THE WILD

STAR THE ELEPHANT

BY REMY LAI

HENRY HOLT AND COMPANY
NEW YORK

I ACKNOWLEDGE THAT THIS BOOK WAS
WRITTEN AND ILLUSTRATED IN BRISBANE, AUSTRALIA,
ON WHICH THE TURRBAL AND JAGERA PEOPLES ARE THE
TRADITIONAL CUSTODIANS OF THEIR RESPECTIVE LAND.
I PAY MY RESPECT TO THEIR ELDERS,
PAST, PRESENT, AND EMERGING.

HENRY HOLT AND COMPANY, PUBLISHERS SINCE 1866
HENRY HOLT® IS A REGISTERED TRADEMARK OF MACMILLAN PUBLISHING GROUP, LLC
120 BROADWAY, NEW YORK, NY 10271
MACKIDS.COM

OUR BOOKS MAY BE PURCHASED IN BULK FOR PROMOTIONAL, EDUCATIONAL, OR BUSINESS USE.
PLEASE CONTACT YOUR LOCAL BOOKSELLER OR THE MACMILLAN CORPORATE AND
PREMIUM SALES DEPARTMENT AT (800) 221-7945 EXT. 5442
OR BY EMAIL AT MACMILLANSPECIALMARKETS@MACMILLAN.COM.

LIBRARY OF CONGRESS CATALOGING-IN-PUBLICATION DATA IS AVAILABLE.

FIRST EDITION, 2022
DESIGNED BY LISA VEGA
PRINTED IN CHINA BY 1010 PRINTING INTERNATIONAL LIMITED, KWUN TONG, HONG KONG

978-1-250-78499-5 (HARDCOVER)
1 3 5 7 9 10 8 6 4 2

THE YOUNG PEOPLE—THEY CARE!
—SIR DAVID ATTENBOROUGH

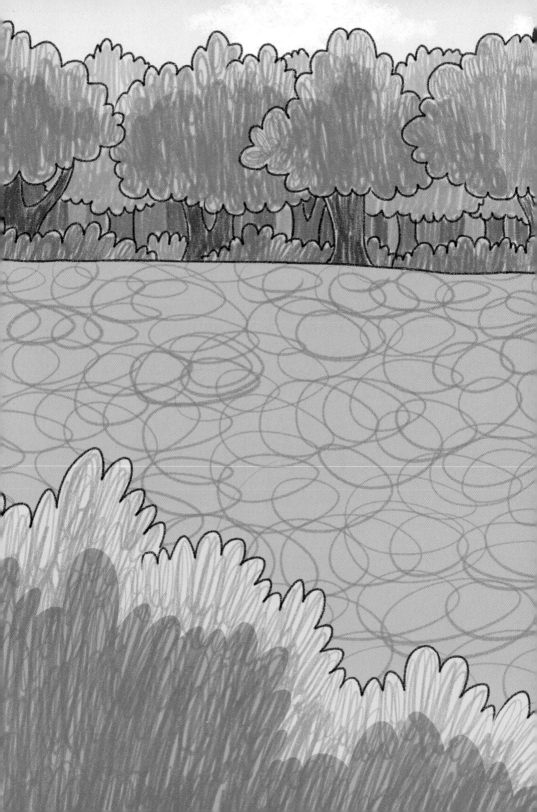

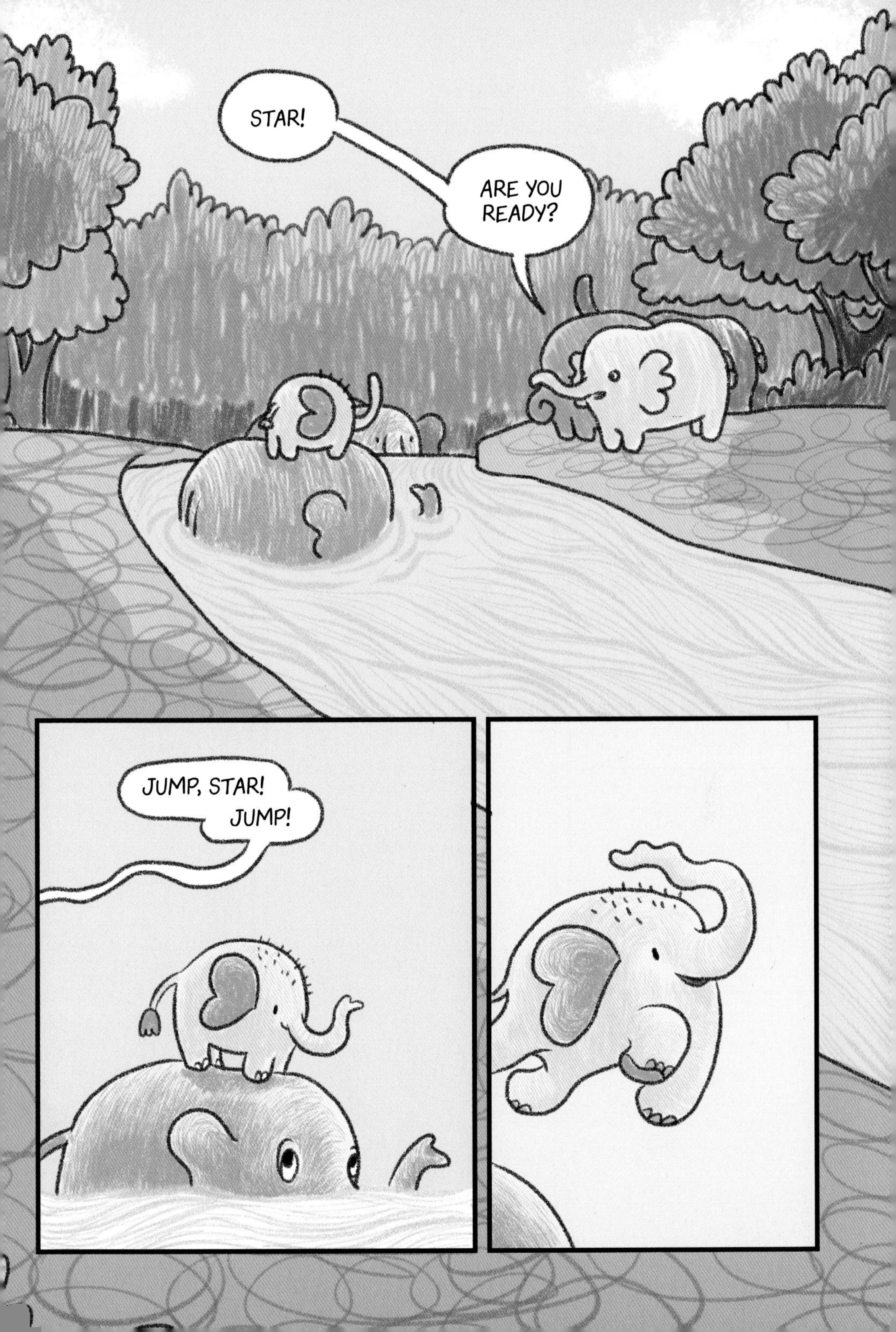
STAR!
ARE YOU READY?
JUMP, STAR! JUMP!

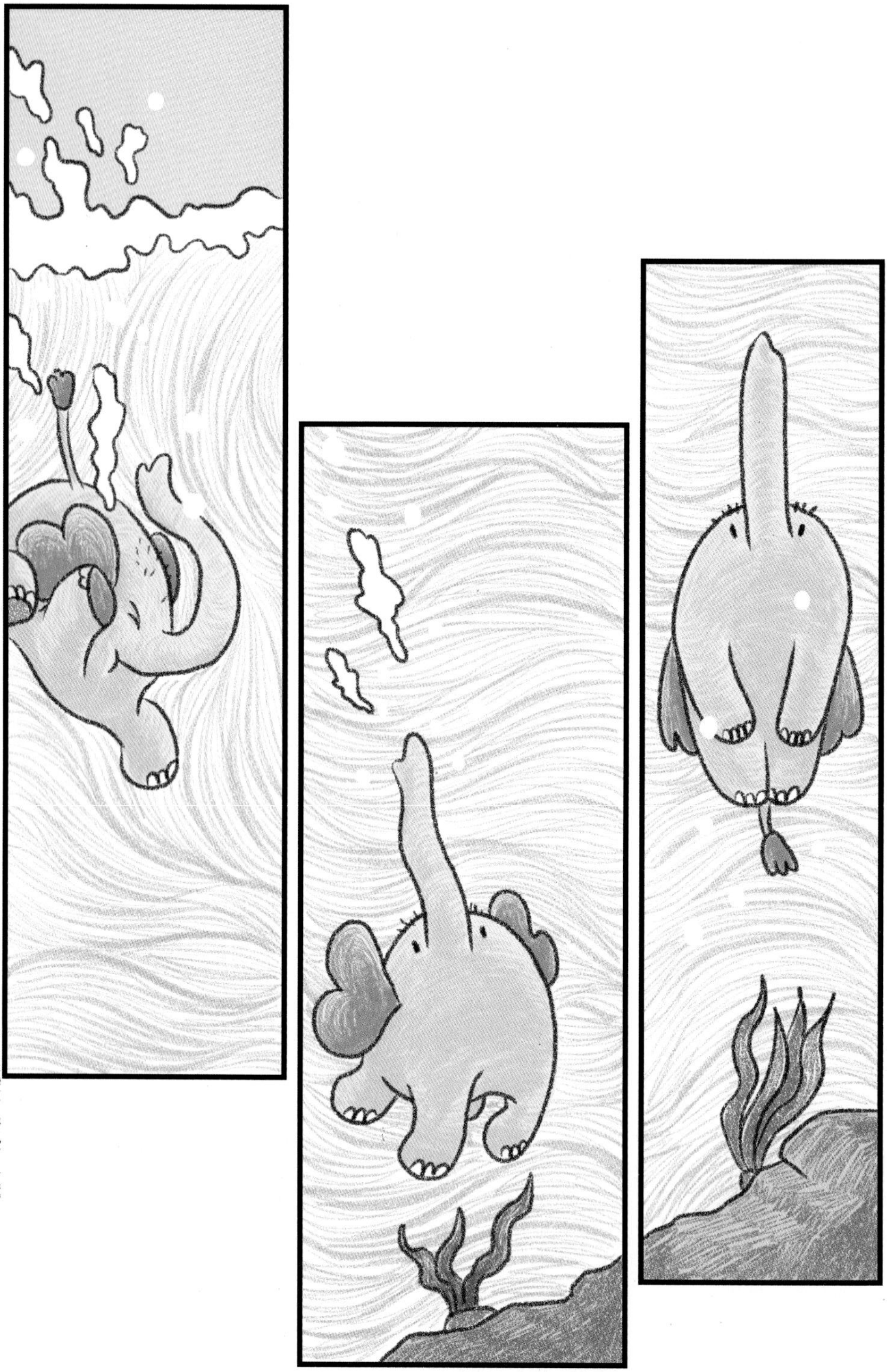

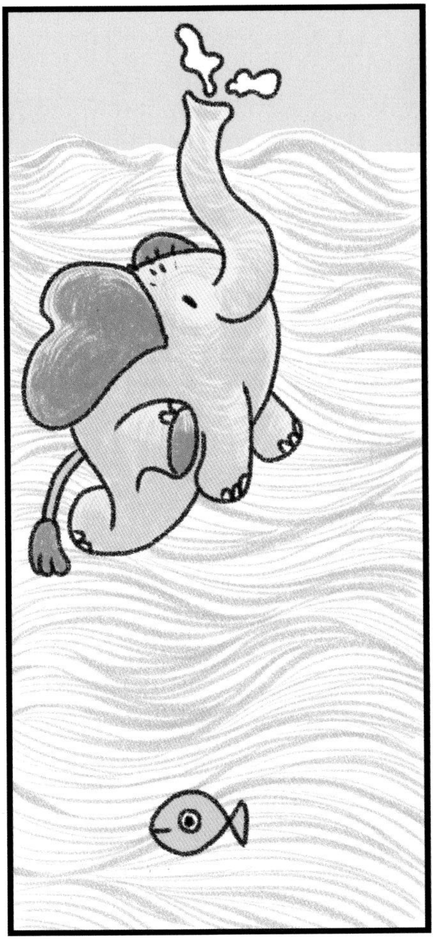

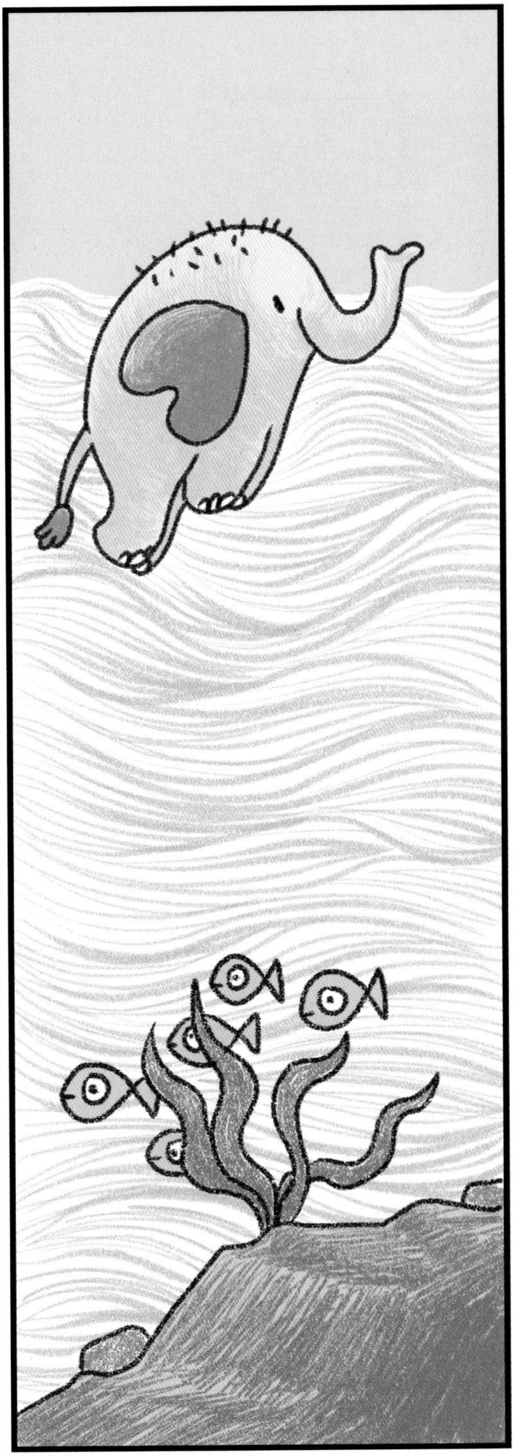

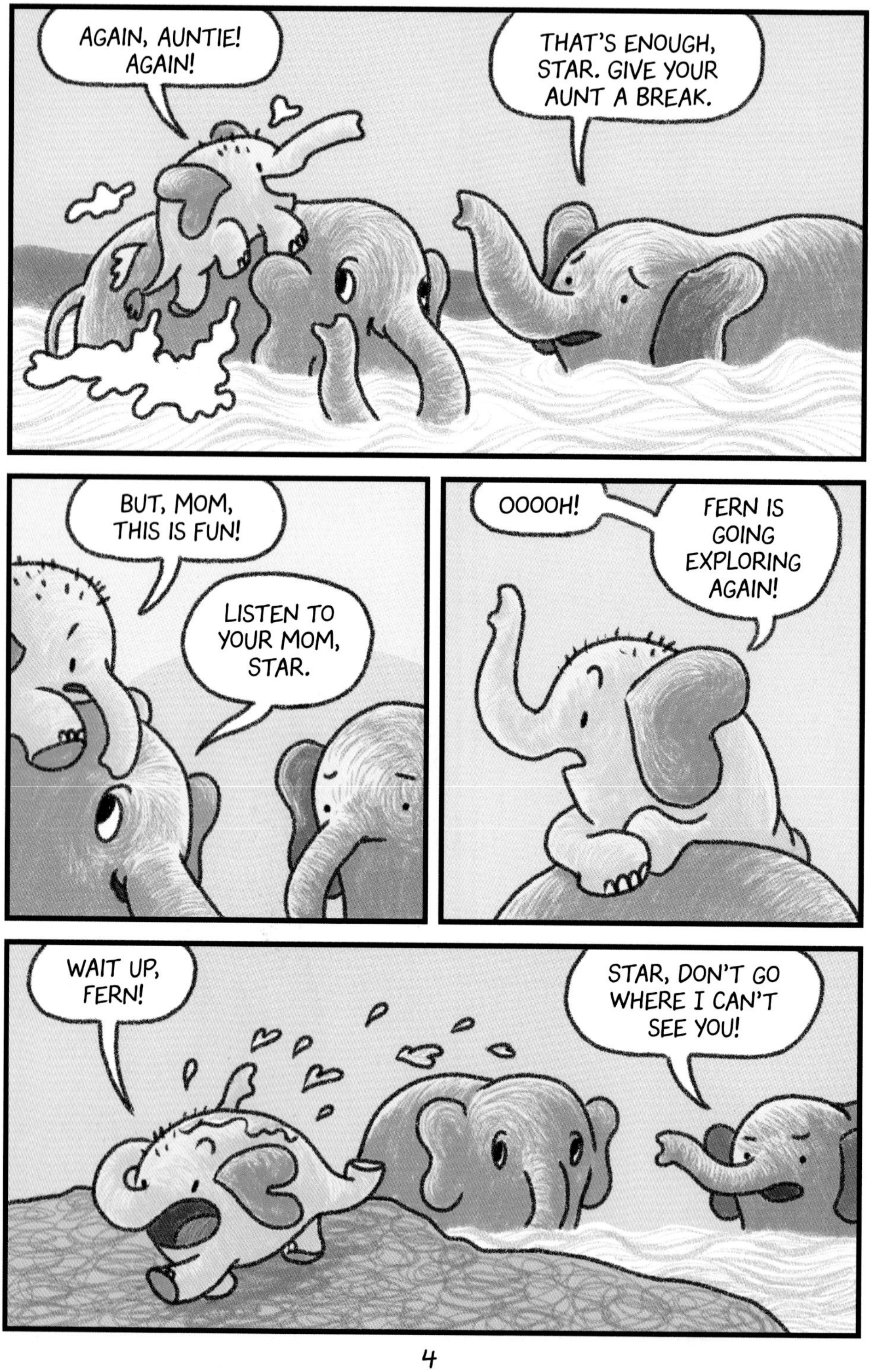
AGAIN, AUNTIE! AGAIN!
THAT'S ENOUGH, STAR. GIVE YOUR AUNT A BREAK.
BUT, MOM, THIS IS FUN!
LISTEN TO YOUR MOM, STAR.
OOOOH!
FERN IS GOING EXPLORING AGAIN!
WAIT UP, FERN!
STAR, DON'T GO WHERE I CAN'T SEE YOU!

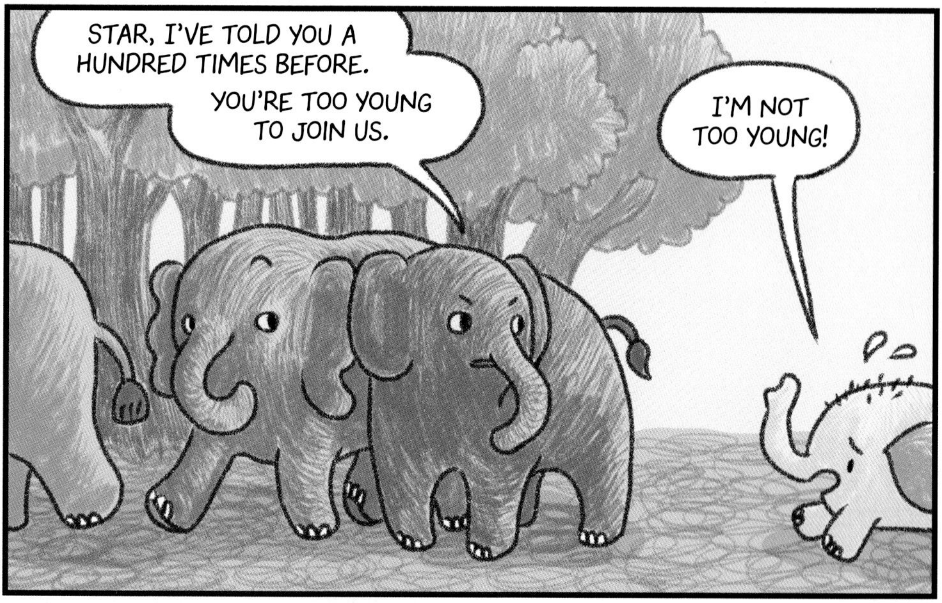
STAR, I'VE TOLD YOU A HUNDRED TIMES BEFORE.
YOU'RE TOO YOUNG TO JOIN US.
I'M NOT TOO YOUNG!

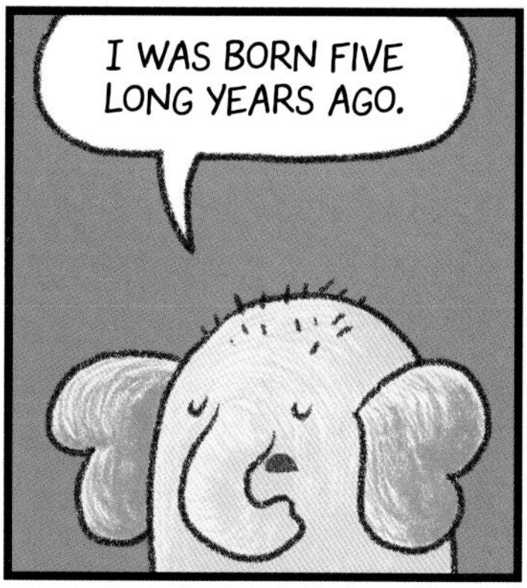
I WAS BORN FIVE LONG YEARS AGO.

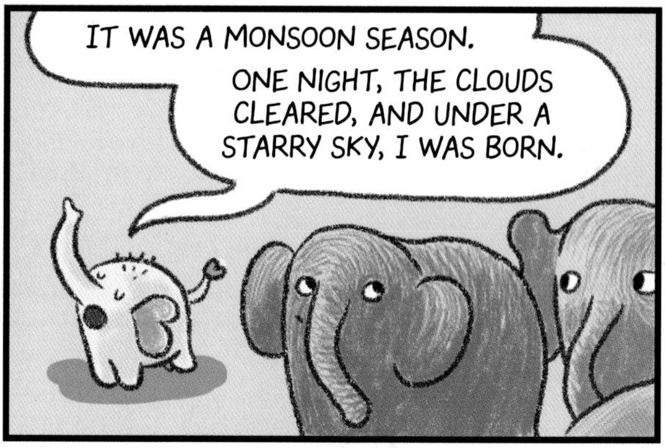
IT WAS A MONSOON SEASON.
ONE NIGHT, THE CLOUDS CLEARED, AND UNDER A STARRY SKY, I WAS BORN.

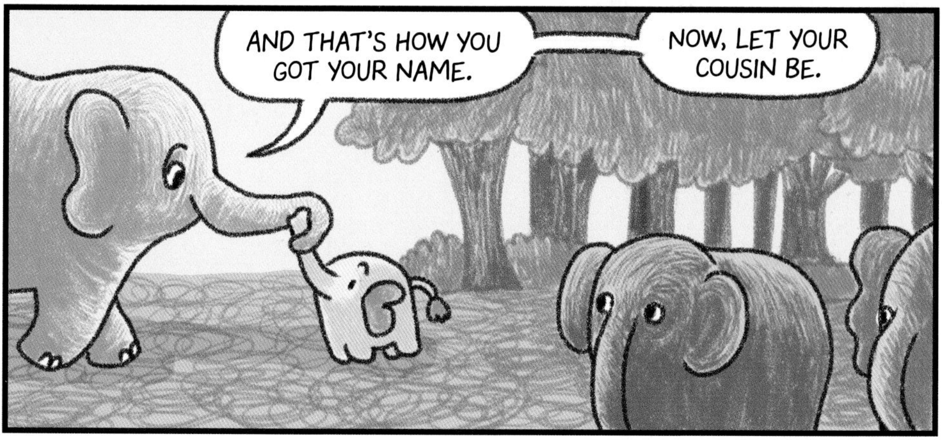
AND THAT'S HOW YOU GOT YOUR NAME.
NOW, LET YOUR COUSIN BE.

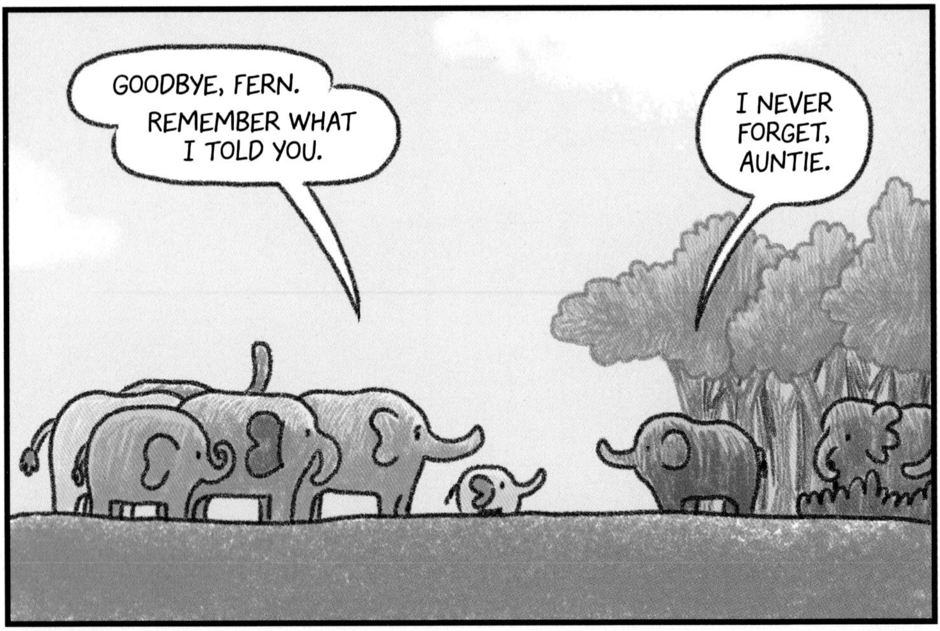
GOODBYE, FERN. REMEMBER WHAT I TOLD YOU.
I NEVER FORGET, AUNTIE.

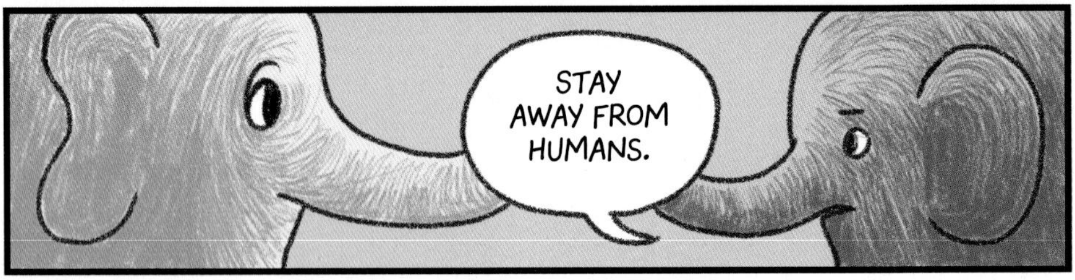
STAY AWAY FROM HUMANS.

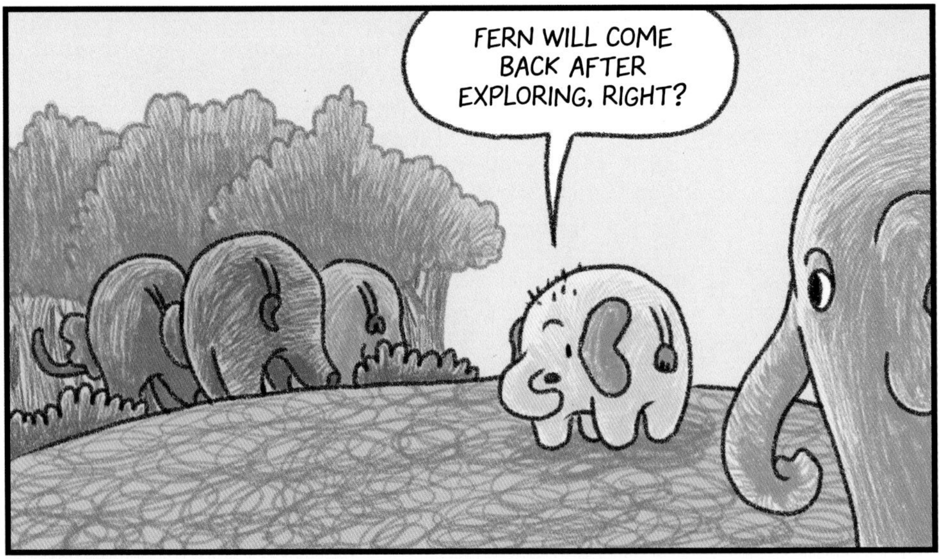
FERN WILL COME BACK AFTER EXPLORING, RIGHT?

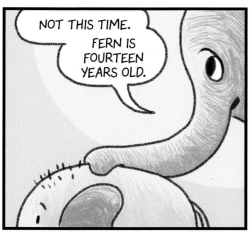

NOT THIS TIME. FERN IS FOURTEEN YEARS OLD.

HE'S READY TO FIND A HERD OF HIS OWN. ONE DAY YOU WILL DO THE SAME.

I'M NEVER LEAVING YOU AND MOM!

DON'T FRET. YOU WON'T HAVE TO WORRY ABOUT THAT UNTIL YOU'RE FERN'S AGE.

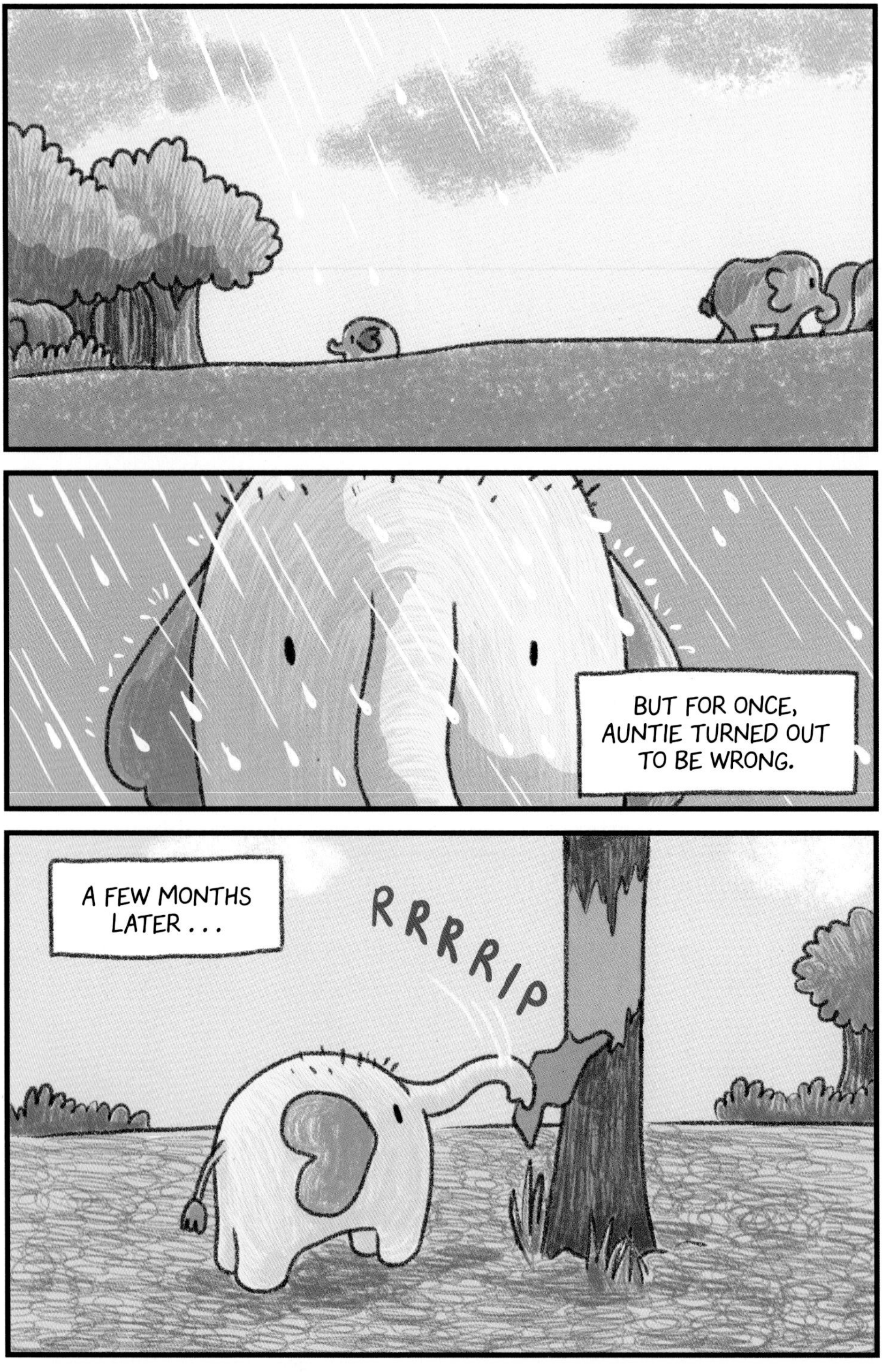
BUT FOR ONCE, AUNTIE TURNED OUT TO BE WRONG.
A FEW MONTHS LATER . . .
RRRRRIP

NOM
NOM
NOM

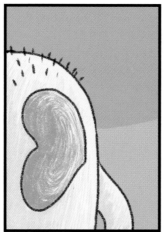

THERE ARE NO MORE TEAK TREES WITH BARK!

MOM!

THE ONLY GRASSES LEFT IN THIS AREA ARE THE KINDS WE DON'T EAT.

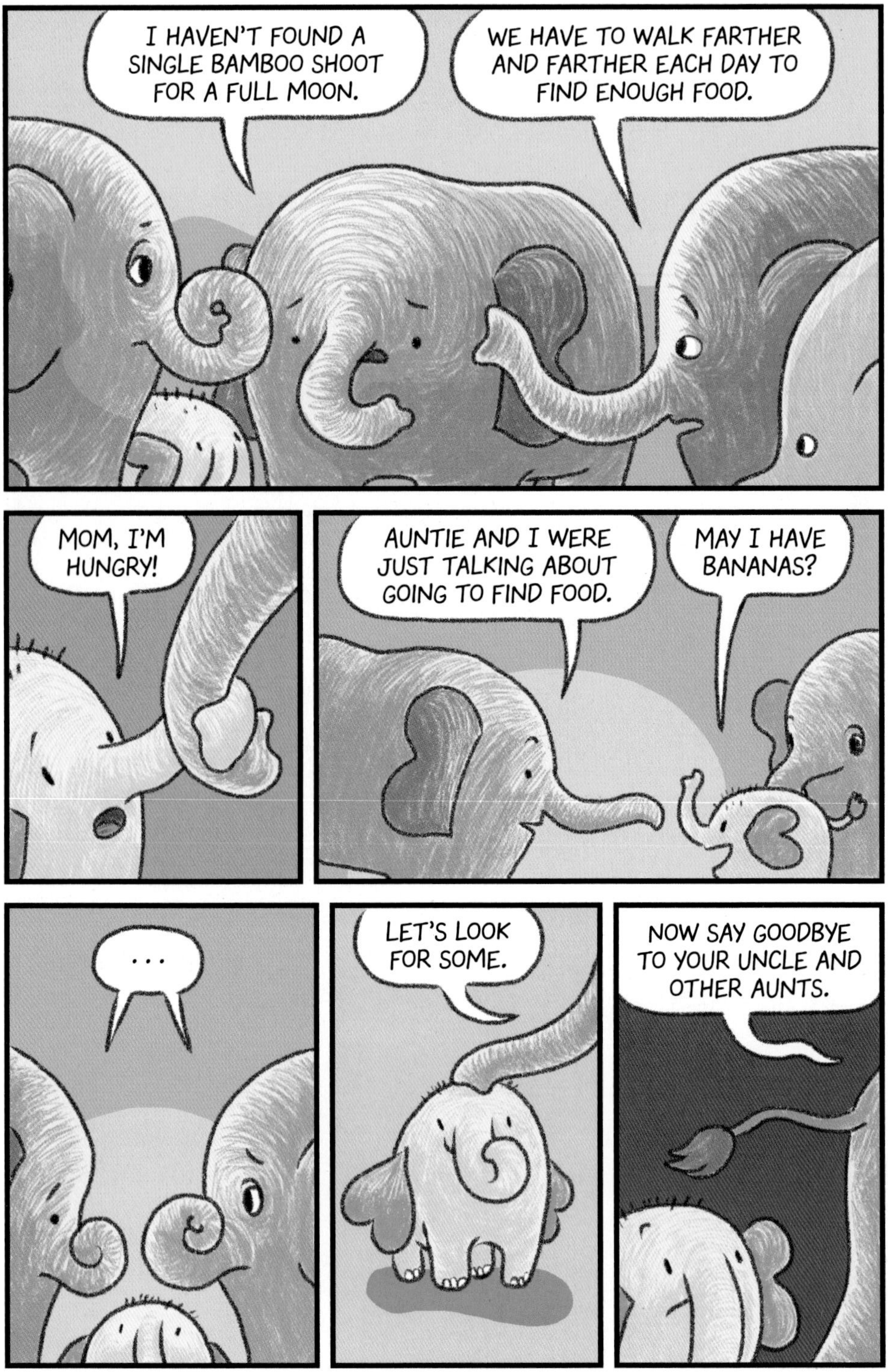
I HAVEN'T FOUND A SINGLE BAMBOO SHOOT FOR A FULL MOON.
WE HAVE TO WALK FARTHER AND FARTHER EACH DAY TO FIND ENOUGH FOOD.
MOM, I'M HUNGRY!
AUNTIE AND I WERE JUST TALKING ABOUT GOING TO FIND FOOD.
MAY I HAVE BANANAS?
. . .
LET'S LOOK FOR SOME.
NOW SAY GOODBYE TO YOUR UNCLE AND OTHER AUNTS.

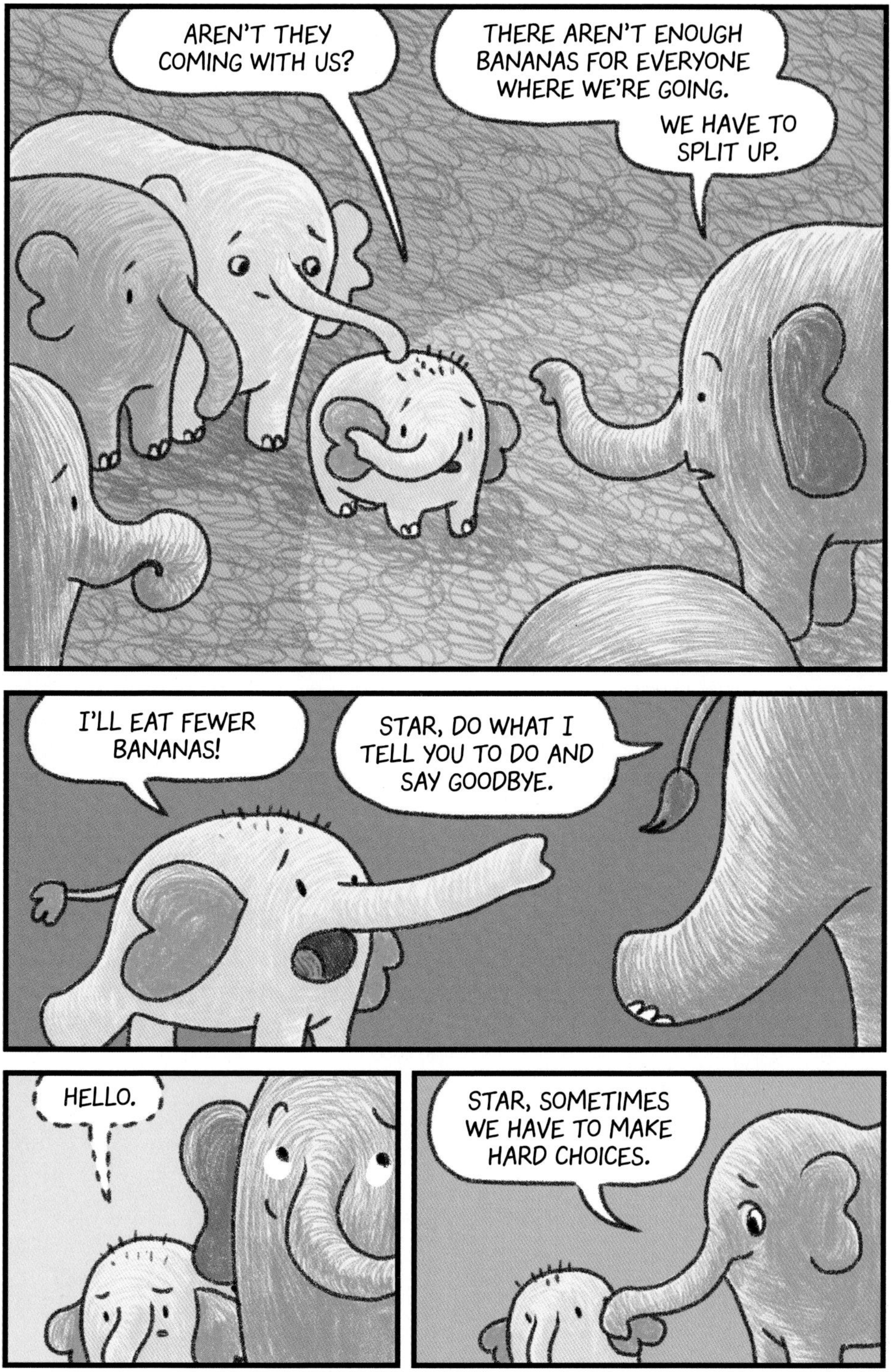
AREN'T THEY COMING WITH US?
THERE AREN'T ENOUGH BANANAS FOR EVERYONE WHERE WE'RE GOING.
WE HAVE TO SPLIT UP.
I'LL EAT FEWER BANANAS!
STAR, DO WHAT I TELL YOU TO DO AND SAY GOODBYE.
HELLO.
STAR, SOMETIMES WE HAVE TO MAKE HARD CHOICES.

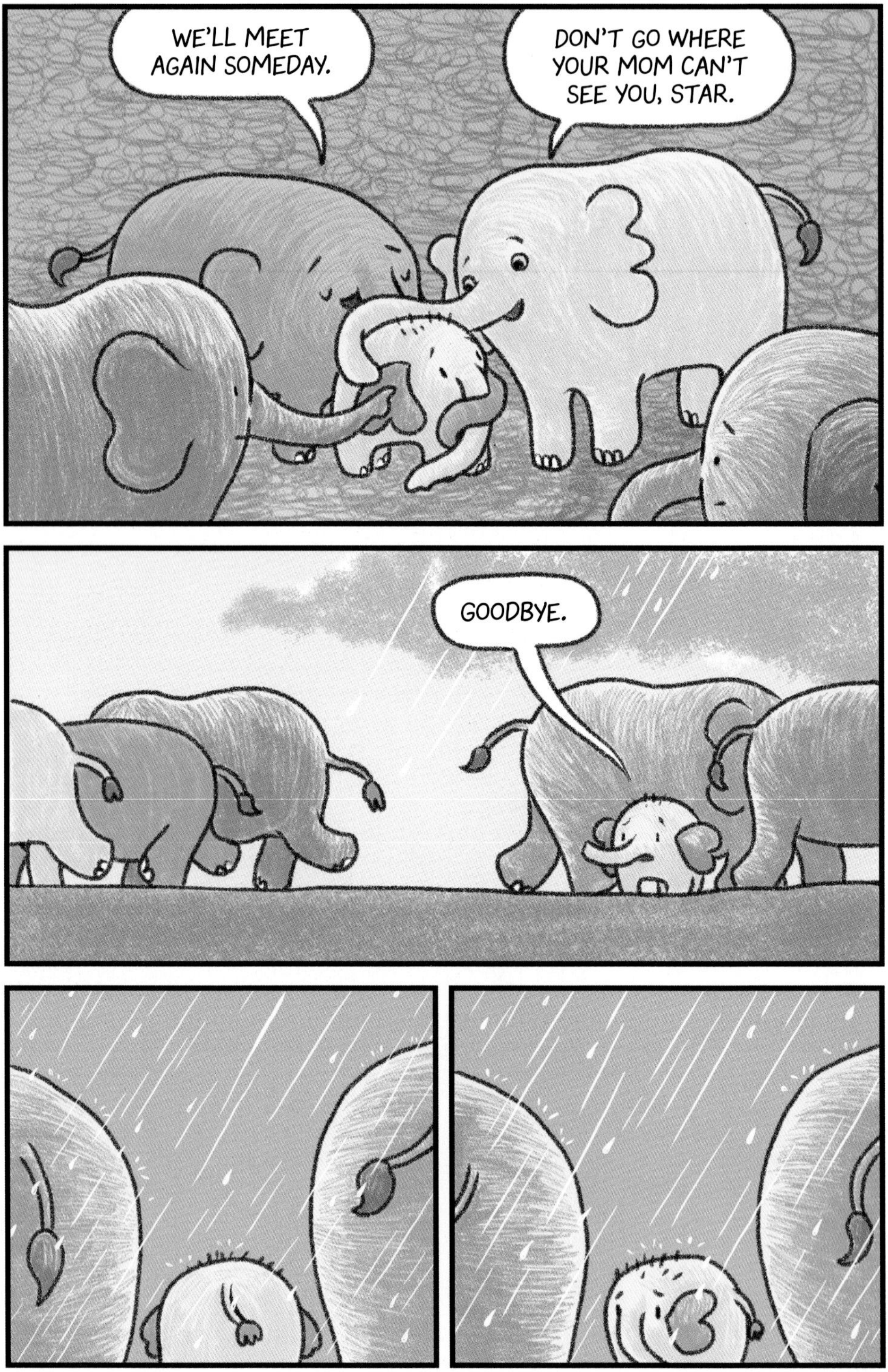
WE'LL MEET AGAIN SOMEDAY.
DON'T GO WHERE YOUR MOM CAN'T SEE YOU, STAR.
GOODBYE.

BANANANANA!

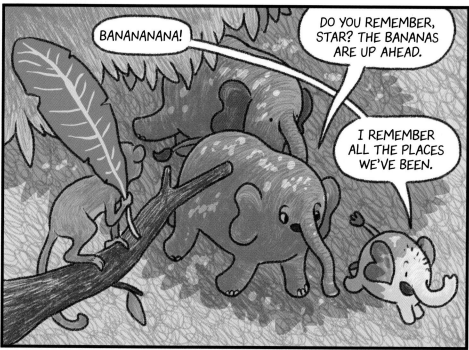

BANANANANA!

DO YOU REMEMBER, STAR? THE BANANAS ARE UP AHEAD.

I REMEMBER ALL THE PLACES WE'VE BEEN.

OUR HOME!

?

!

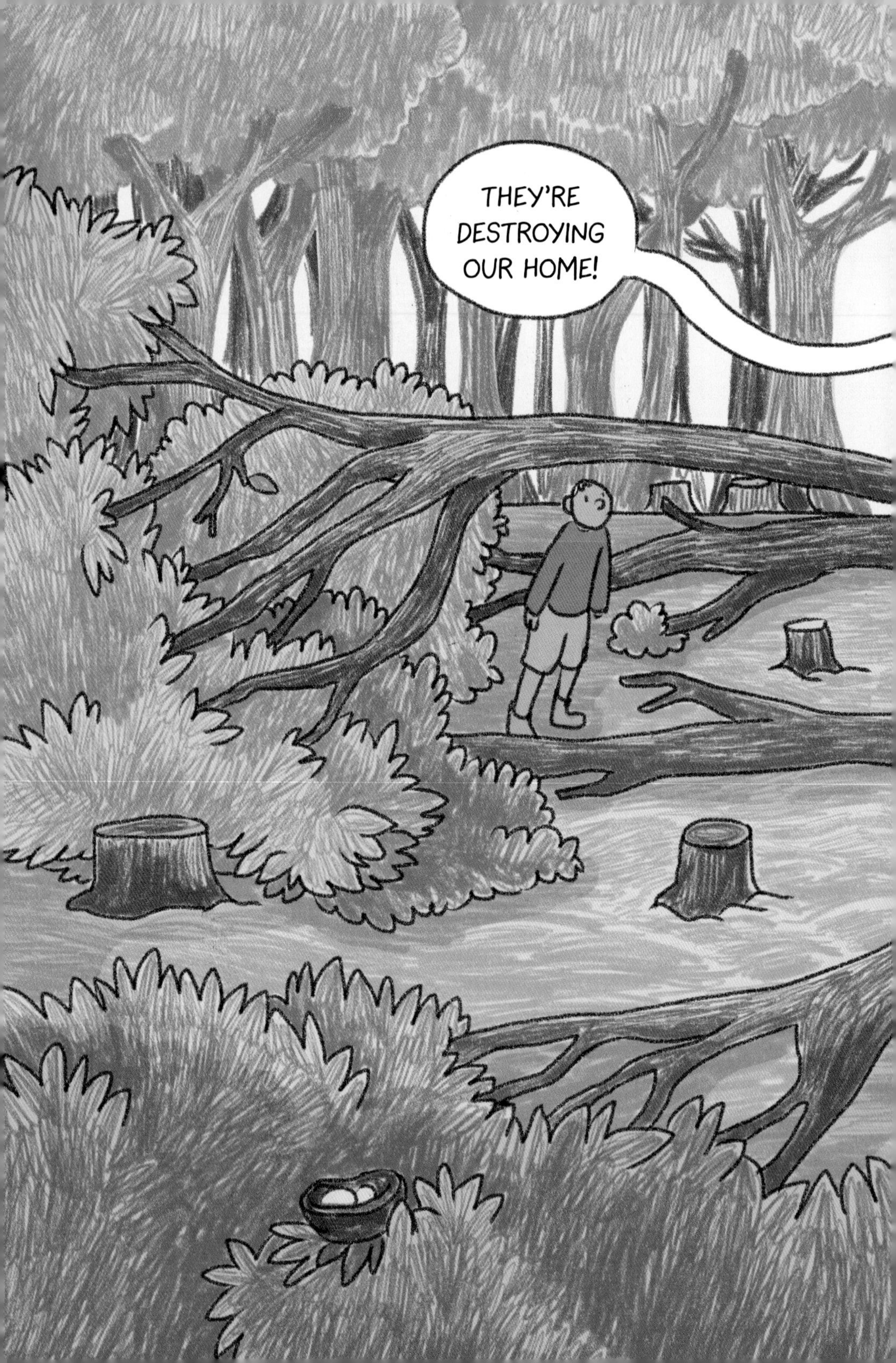
THEY'RE DESTROYING OUR HOME!

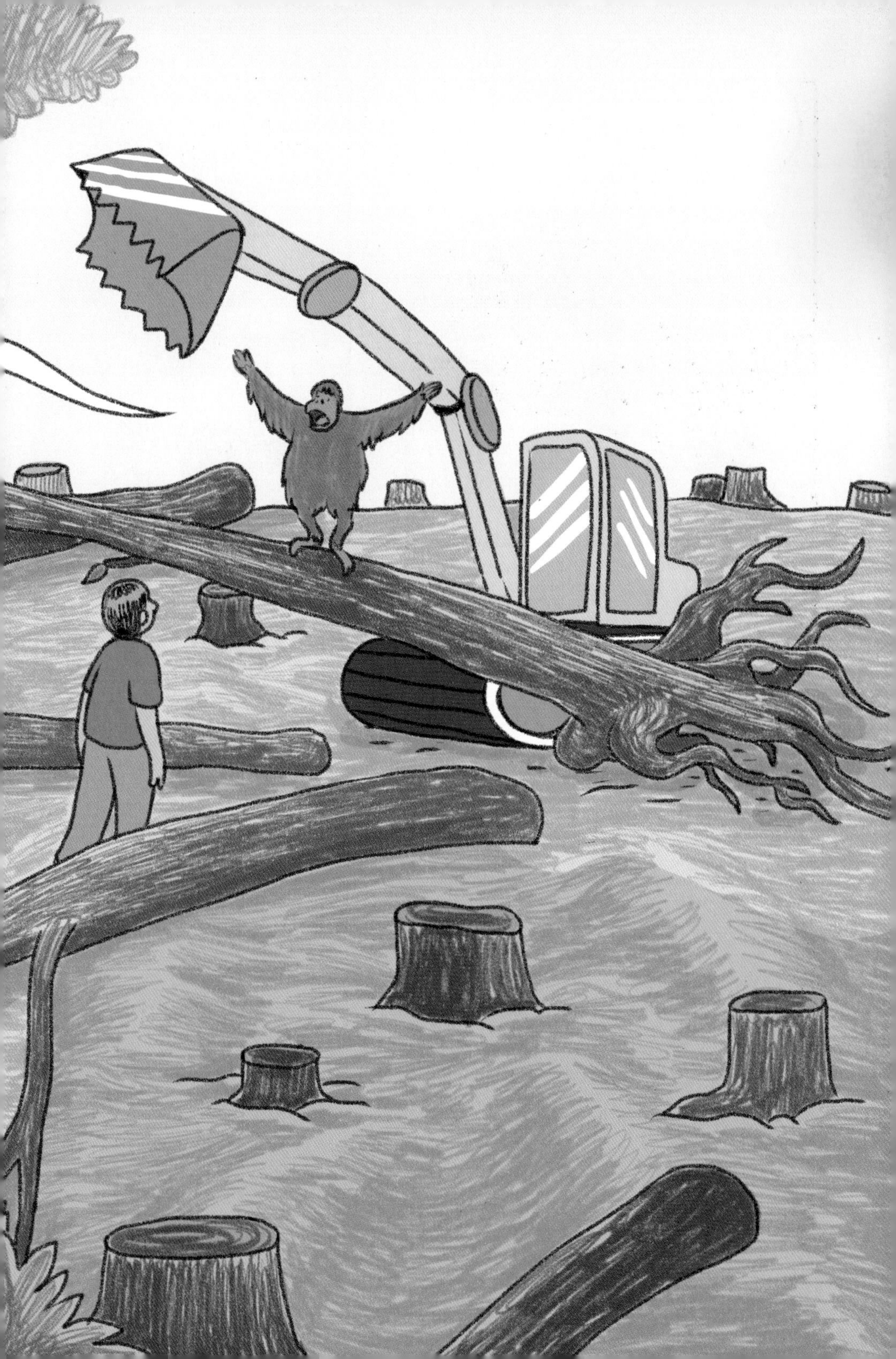

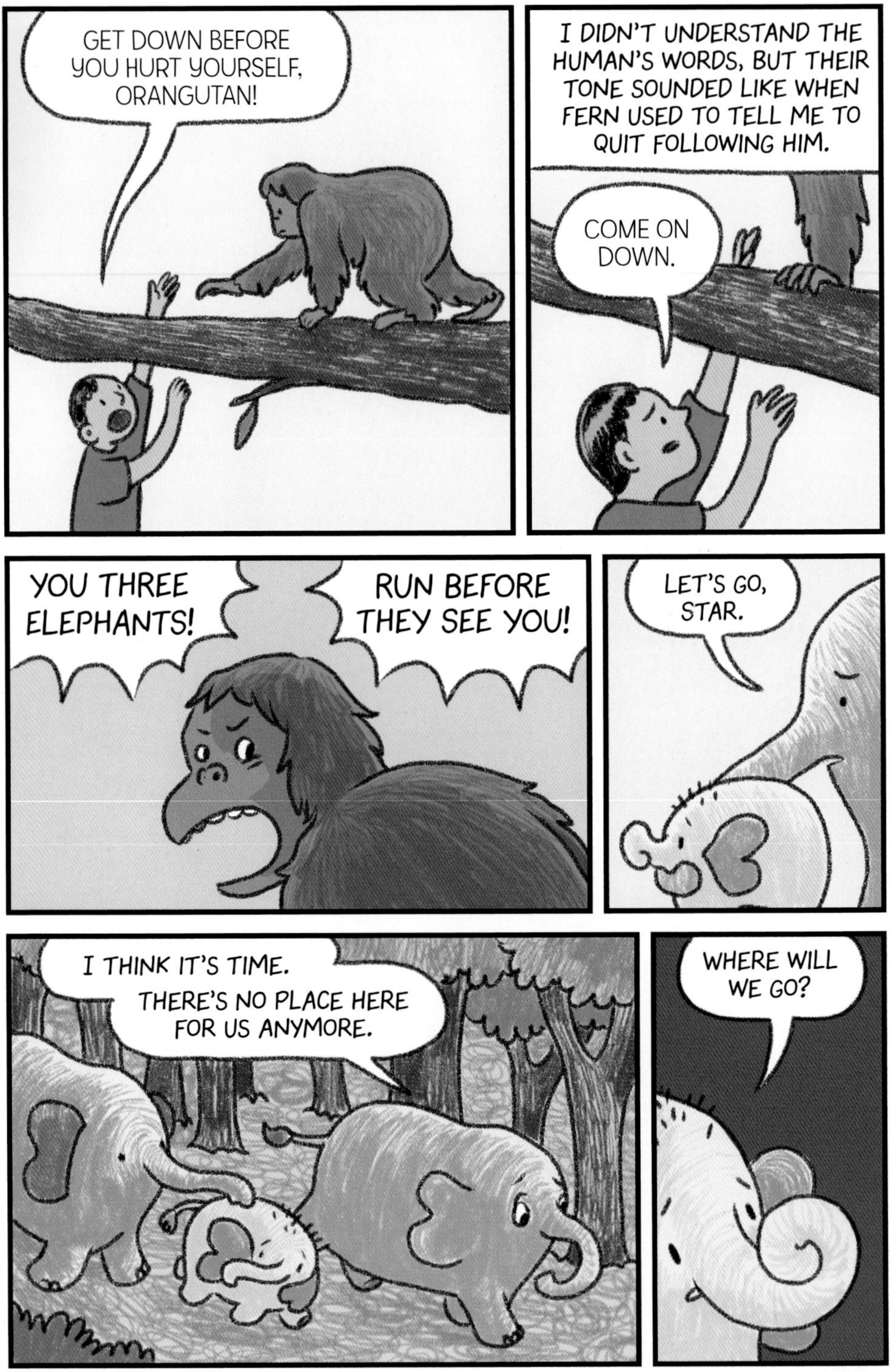
GET DOWN BEFORE YOU HURT YOURSELF, ORANGUTAN!
I DIDN'T UNDERSTAND THE HUMAN'S WORDS, BUT THEIR TONE SOUNDED LIKE WHEN FERN USED TO TELL ME TO QUIT FOLLOWING HIM.
COME ON DOWN.
YOU THREE ELEPHANTS!
RUN BEFORE THEY SEE YOU!
LET'S GO, STAR.
I THINK IT'S TIME.
THERE'S NO PLACE HERE FOR US ANYMORE.
WHERE WILL WE GO?

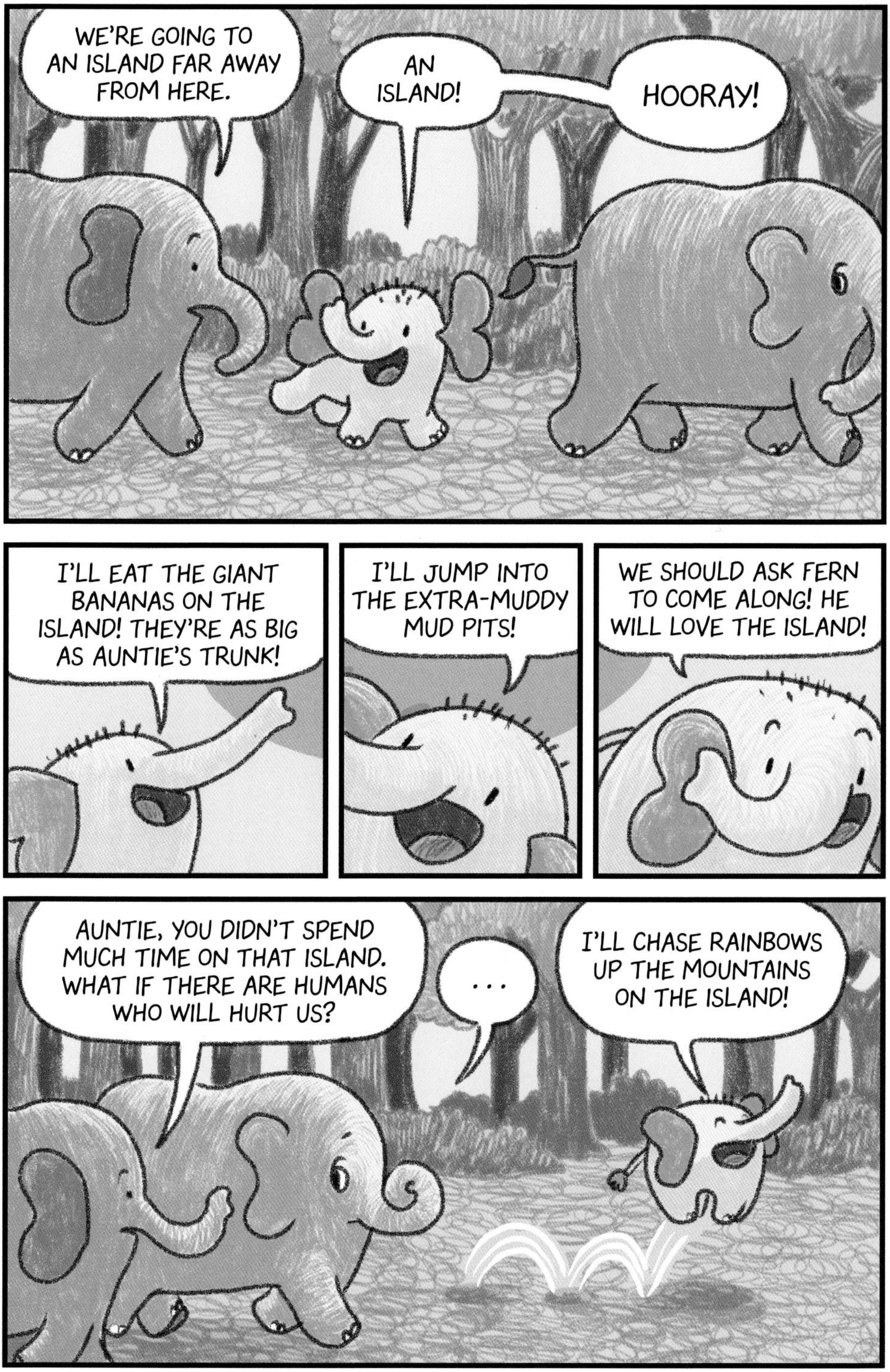
WE'RE GOING TO AN ISLAND FAR AWAY FROM HERE.
AN ISLAND!
HOORAY!
I'LL EAT THE GIANT BANANAS ON THE ISLAND! THEY'RE AS BIG AS AUNTIE'S TRUNK!
I'LL JUMP INTO THE EXTRA-MUDDY MUD PITS!
WE SHOULD ASK FERN TO COME ALONG! HE WILL LOVE THE ISLAND!
AUNTIE, YOU DIDN'T SPEND MUCH TIME ON THAT ISLAND. WHAT IF THERE ARE HUMANS WHO WILL HURT US?
. . .
I'LL CHASE RAINBOWS UP THE MOUNTAINS ON THE ISLAND!

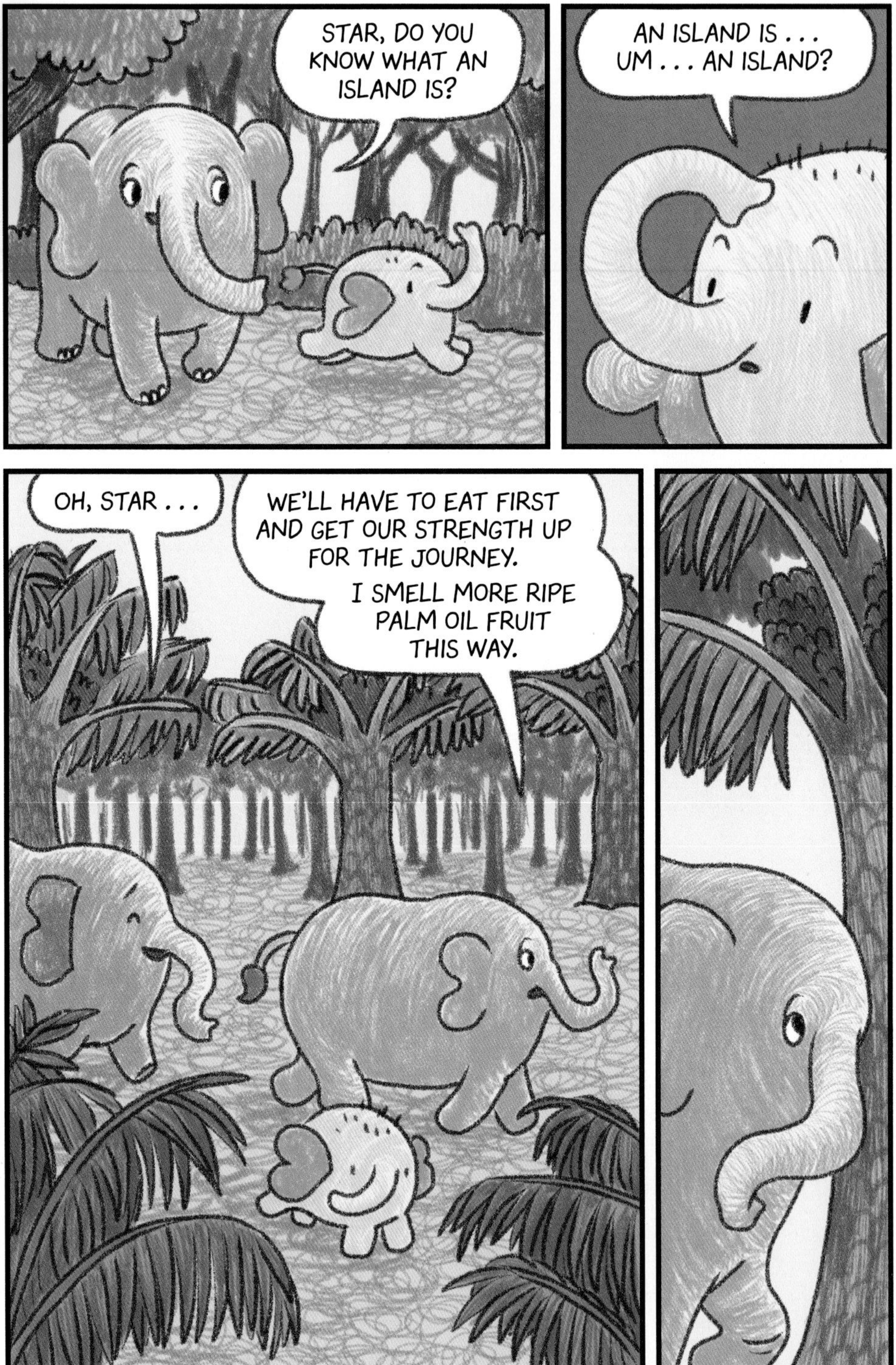
STAR, DO YOU KNOW WHAT AN ISLAND IS?
AN ISLAND IS . . . UM . . . AN ISLAND?
OH, STAR . . .
WE'LL HAVE TO EAT FIRST AND GET OUR STRENGTH UP FOR THE JOURNEY.
I SMELL MORE RIPE PALM OIL FRUIT THIS WAY.

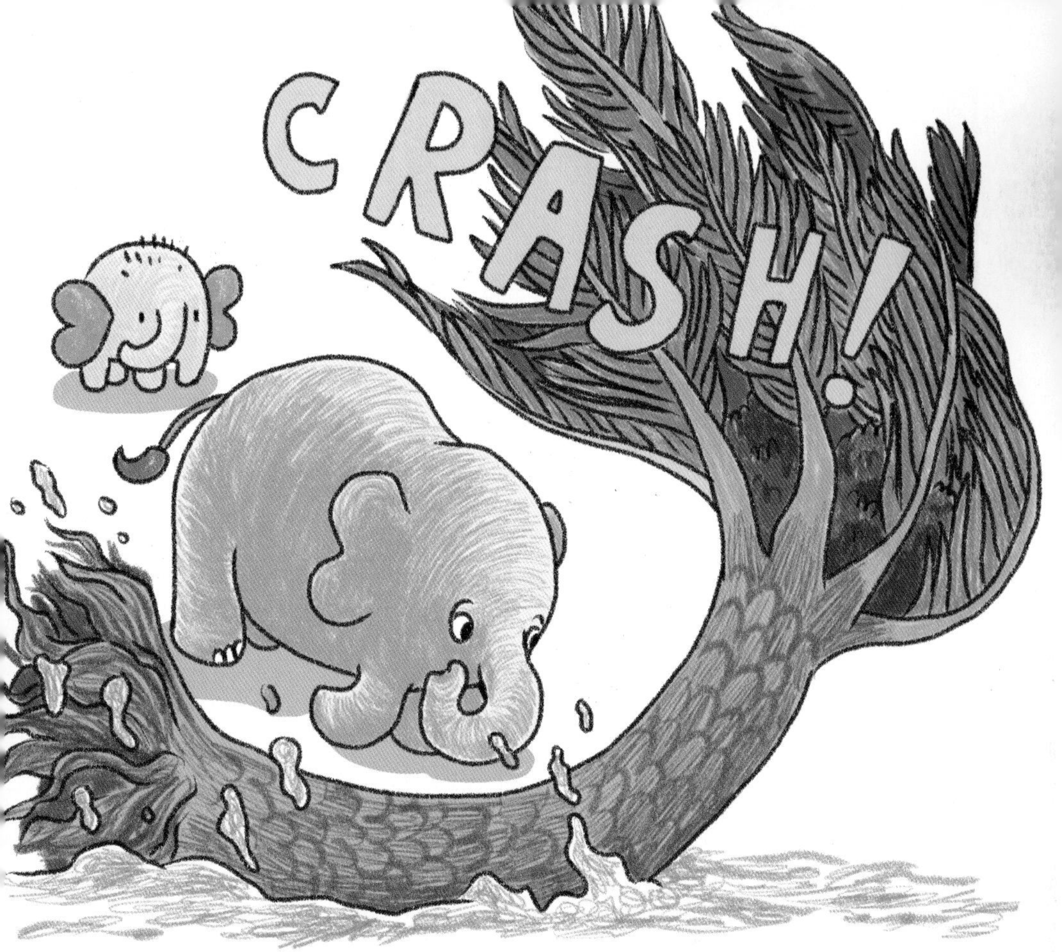
CRASH!

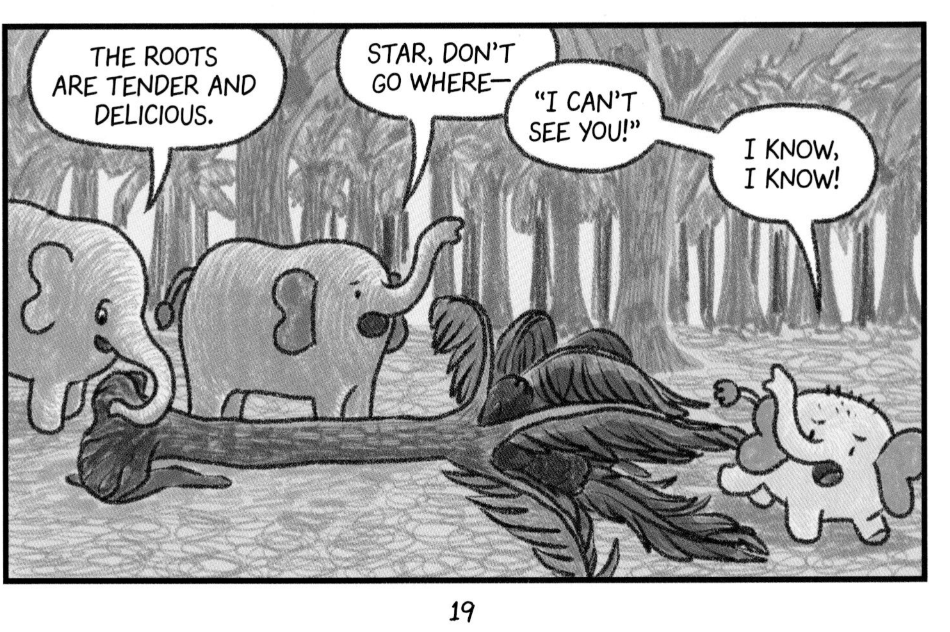
THE ROOTS ARE TENDER AND DELICIOUS.
STAR, DON'T GO WHERE—
"I CAN'T SEE YOU!"
I KNOW, I KNOW!

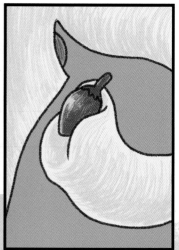

PHRREE·EEEE!

DON'T EAT OUR FRUIT! DON'T DESTROY OUR CROPS!

PHREE

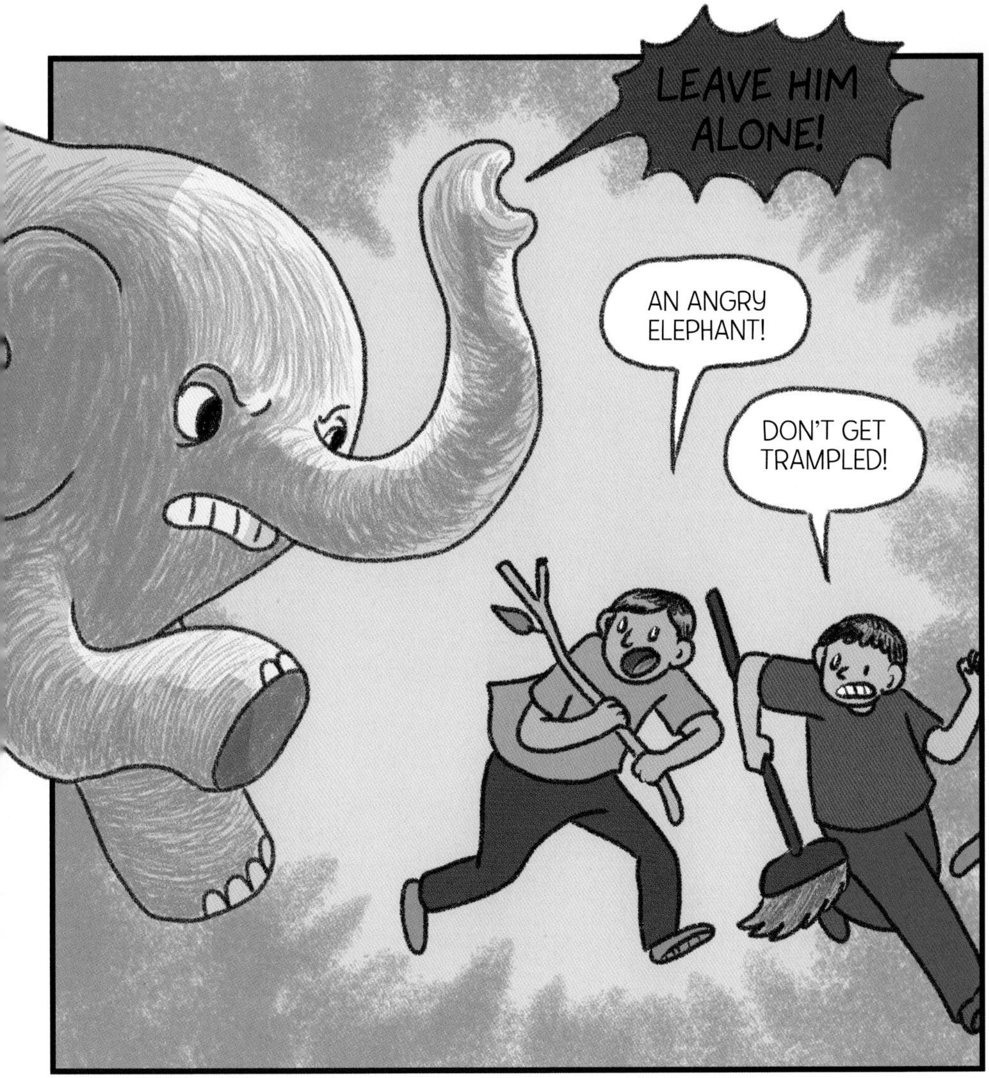
LEAVE HIM ALONE!
AN ANGRY ELEPHANT!
DON'T GET TRAMPLED!

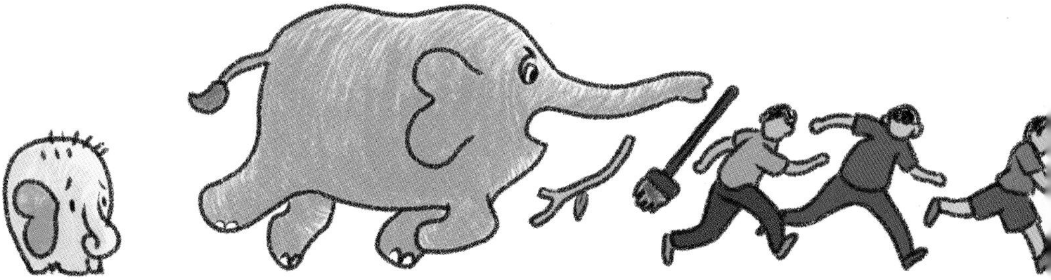

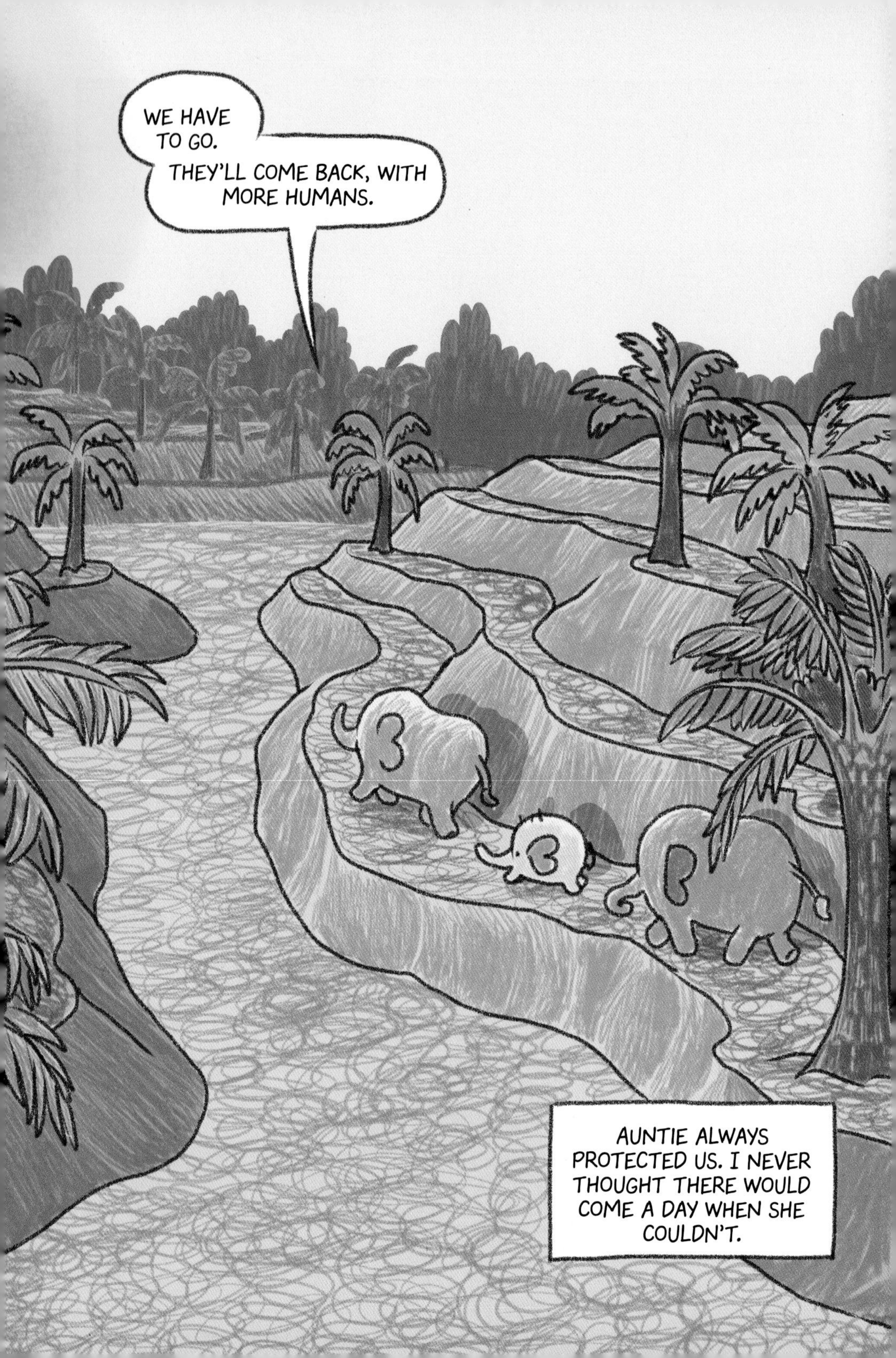
WE HAVE TO GO.
THEY'LL COME BACK, WITH MORE HUMANS.
AUNTIE ALWAYS PROTECTED US. I NEVER THOUGHT THERE WOULD COME A DAY WHEN SHE COULDN'T.

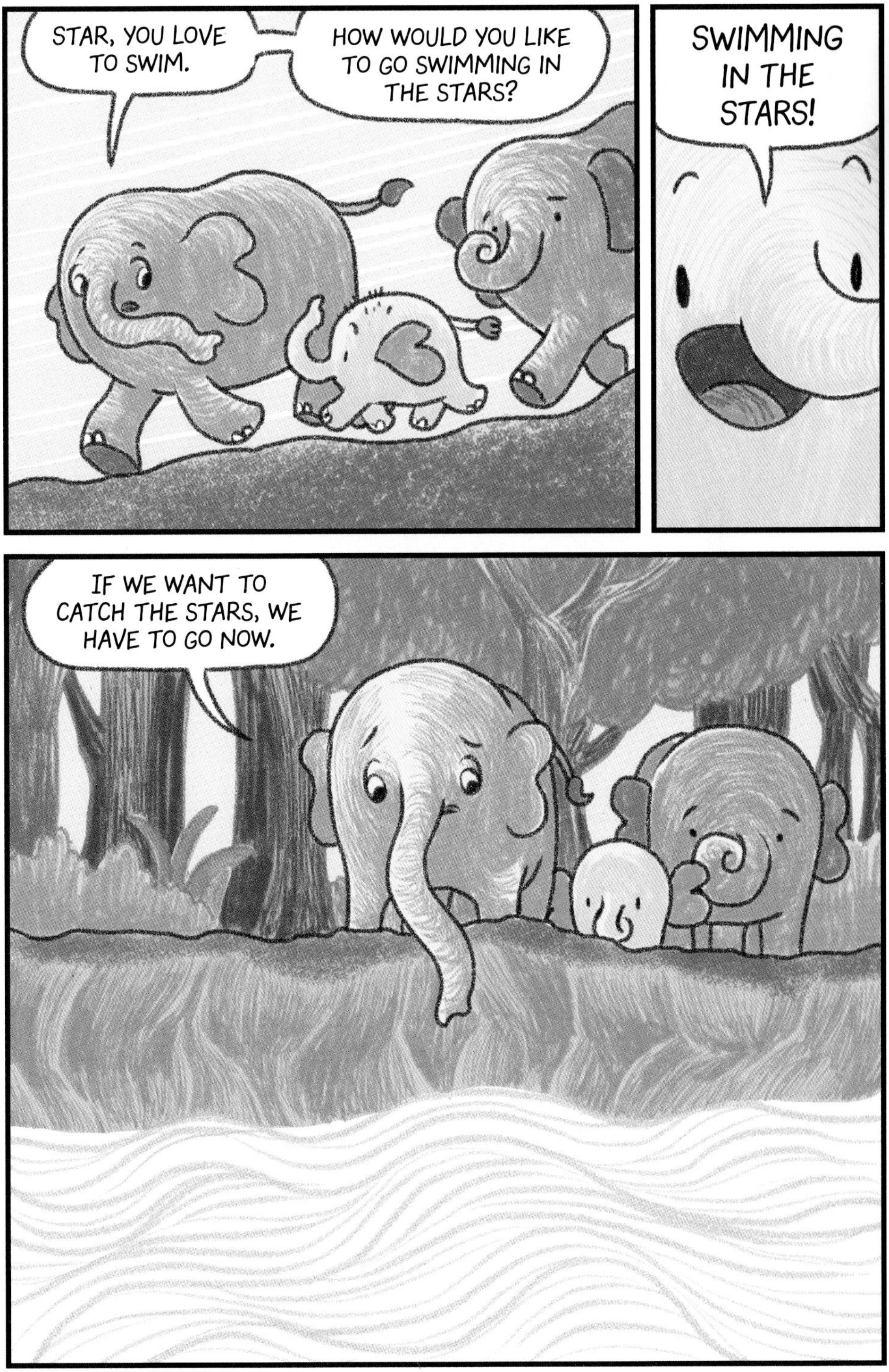
STAR, YOU LOVE TO SWIM.
HOW WOULD YOU LIKE TO GO SWIMMING IN THE STARS?
SWIMMING IN THE STARS!
IF WE WANT TO CATCH THE STARS, WE HAVE TO GO NOW.

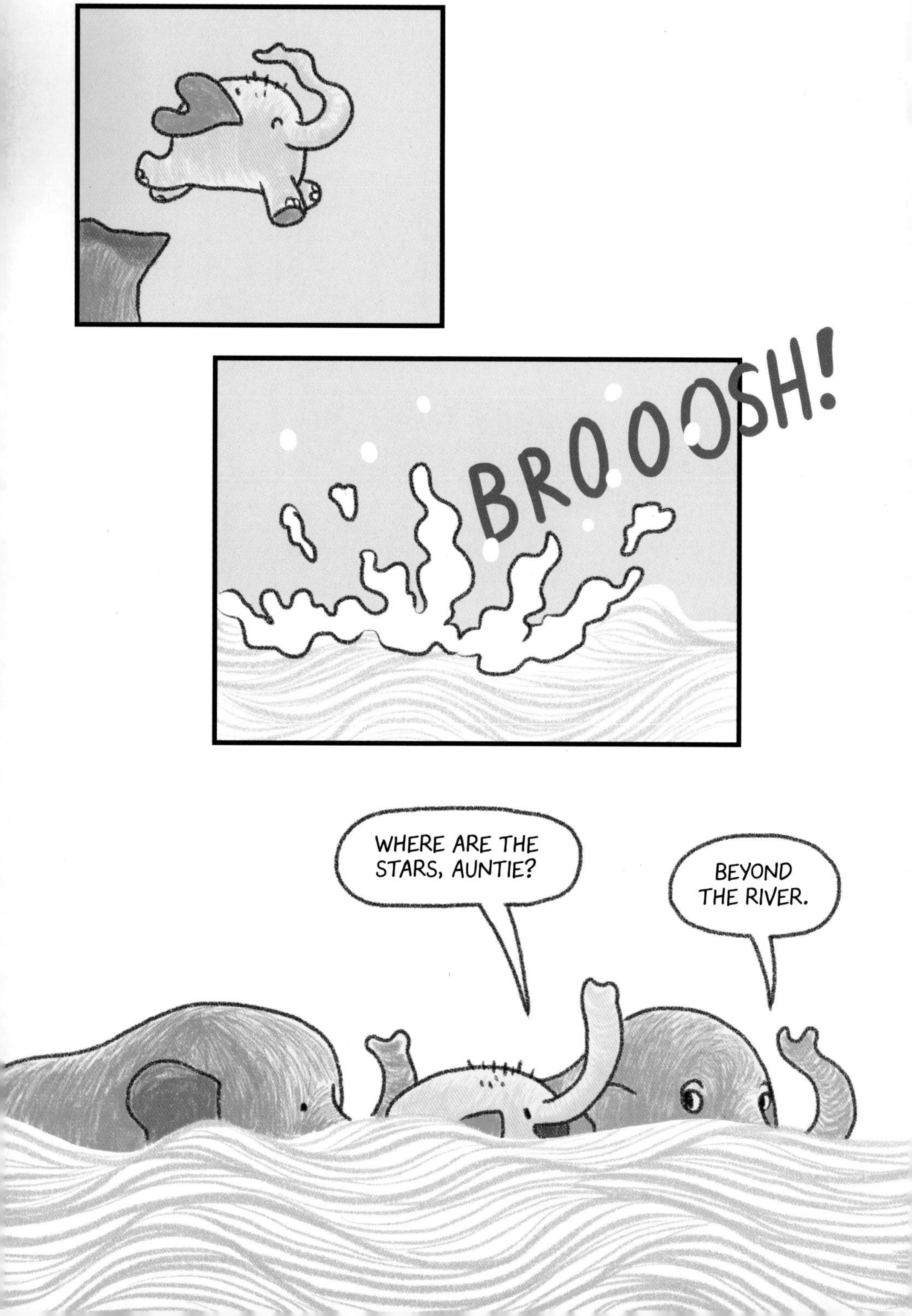
BROOOSH!
WHERE ARE THE STARS, AUNTIE?
BEYOND THE RIVER.

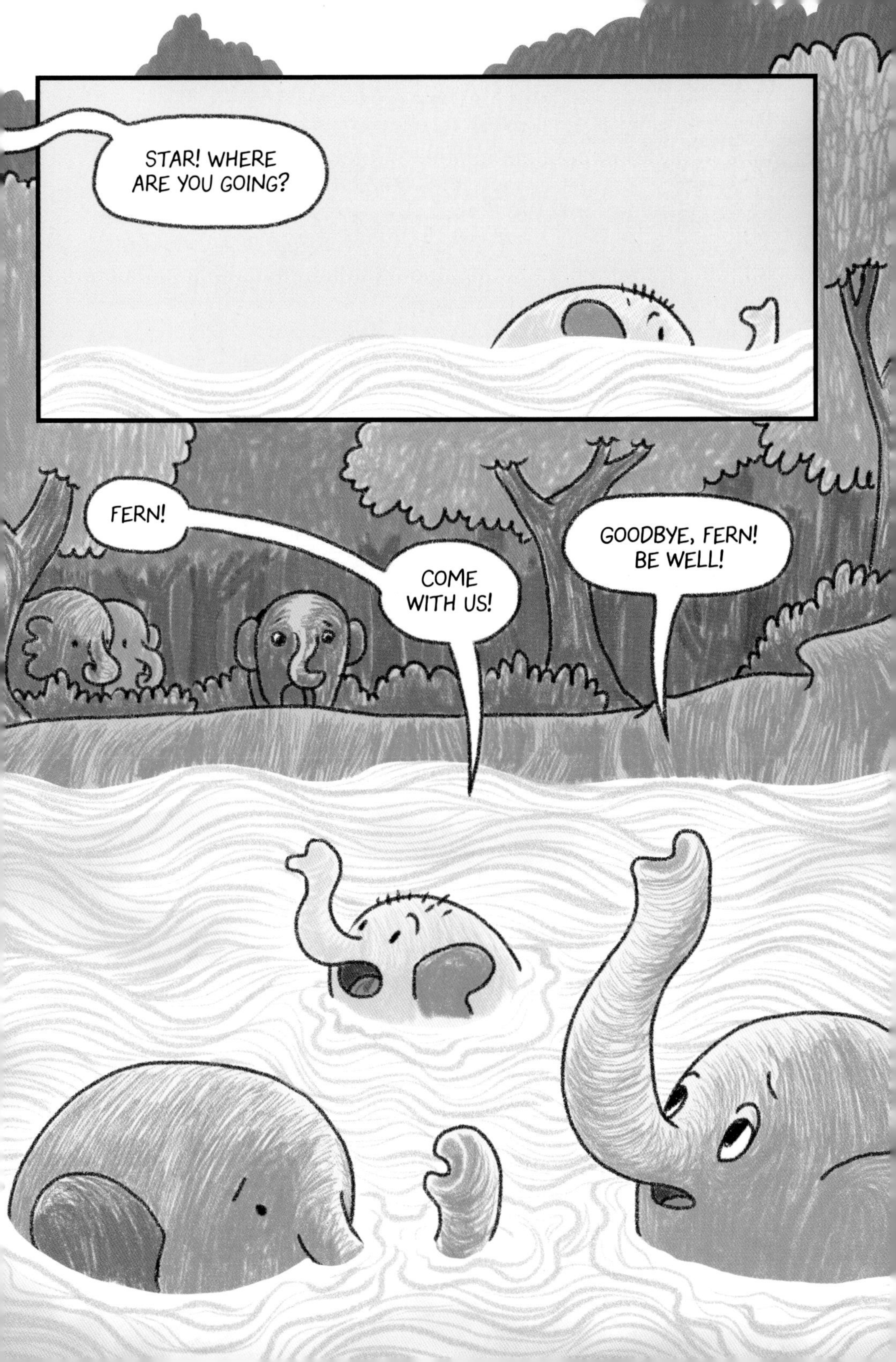
STAR! WHERE ARE YOU GOING?
FERN!
COME WITH US!
GOODBYE, FERN! BE WELL!

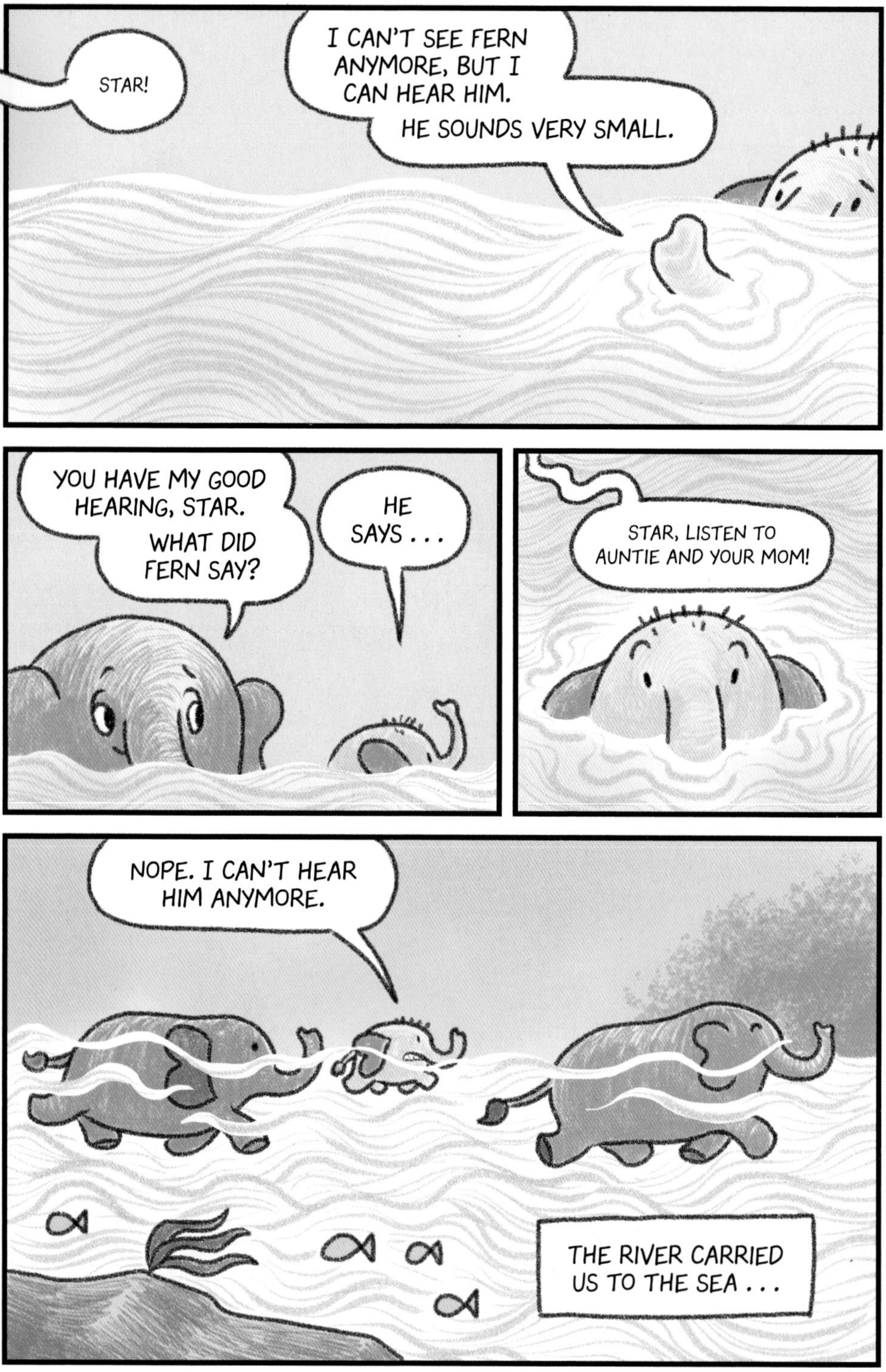
STAR!
I CAN'T SEE FERN ANYMORE, BUT I CAN HEAR HIM.
HE SOUNDS VERY SMALL.
YOU HAVE MY GOOD HEARING, STAR.
WHAT DID FERN SAY?
HE SAYS . . .
STAR, LISTEN TO AUNTIE AND YOUR MOM!
NOPE. I CAN'T HEAR HIM ANYMORE.
THE RIVER CARRIED US TO THE SEA . . .

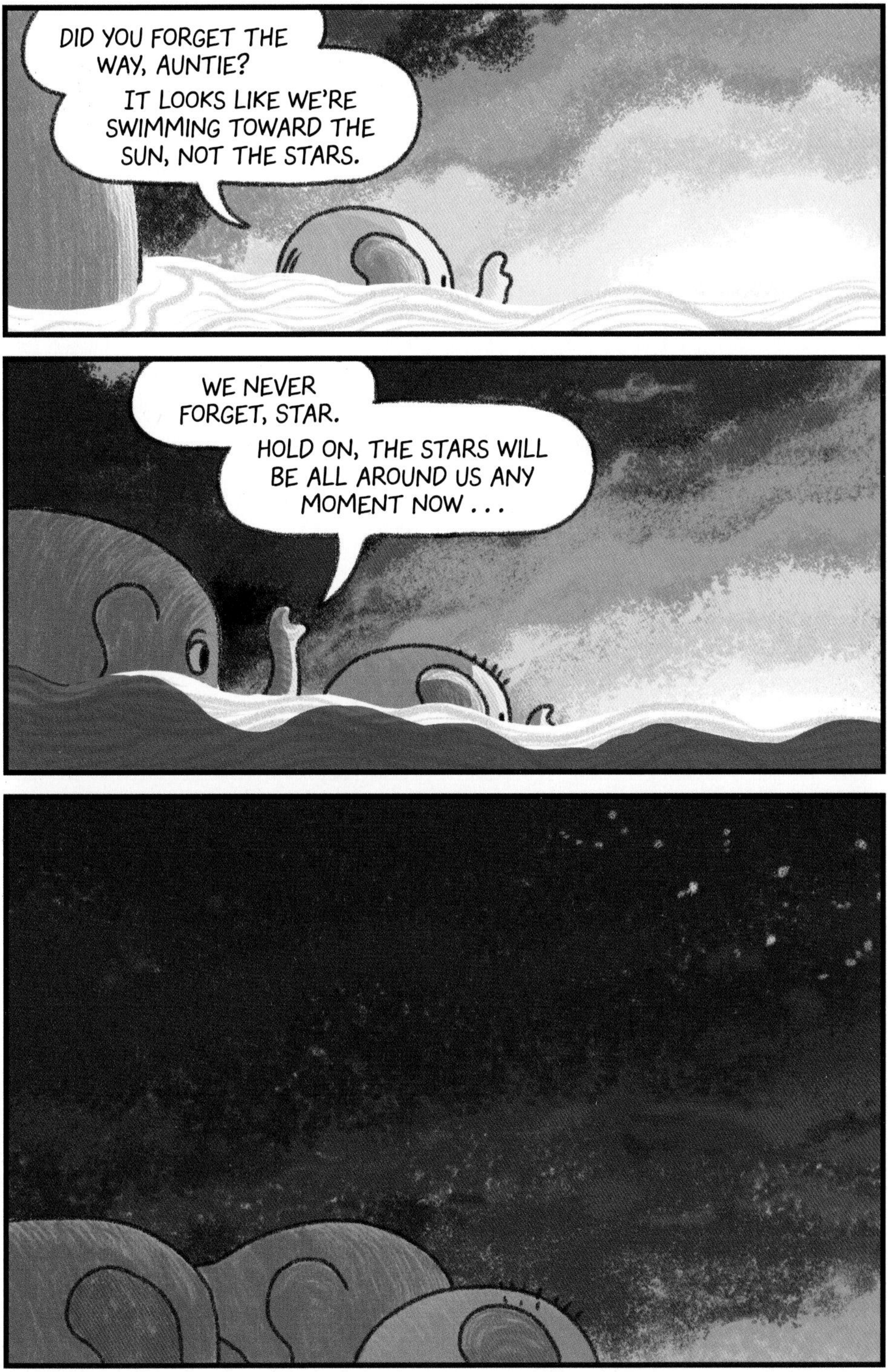
DID YOU FORGET THE WAY, AUNTIE?
IT LOOKS LIKE WE'RE SWIMMING TOWARD THE SUN, NOT THE STARS.
WE NEVER FORGET, STAR.
HOLD ON, THE STARS WILL BE ALL AROUND US ANY MOMENT NOW . . .

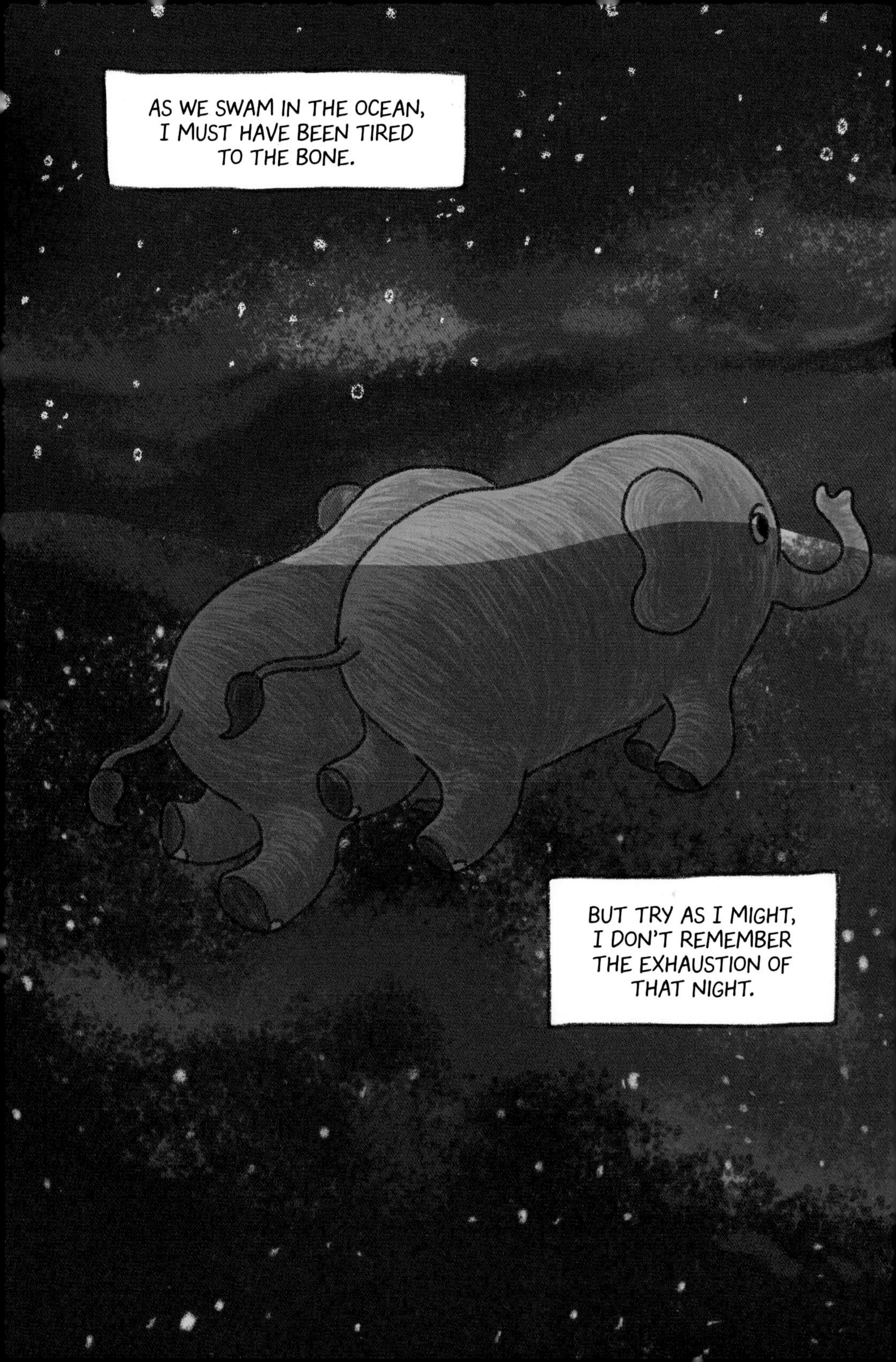
AS WE SWAM IN THE OCEAN, I MUST HAVE BEEN TIRED TO THE BONE.
BUT TRY AS I MIGHT, I DON'T REMEMBER THE EXHAUSTION OF THAT NIGHT.

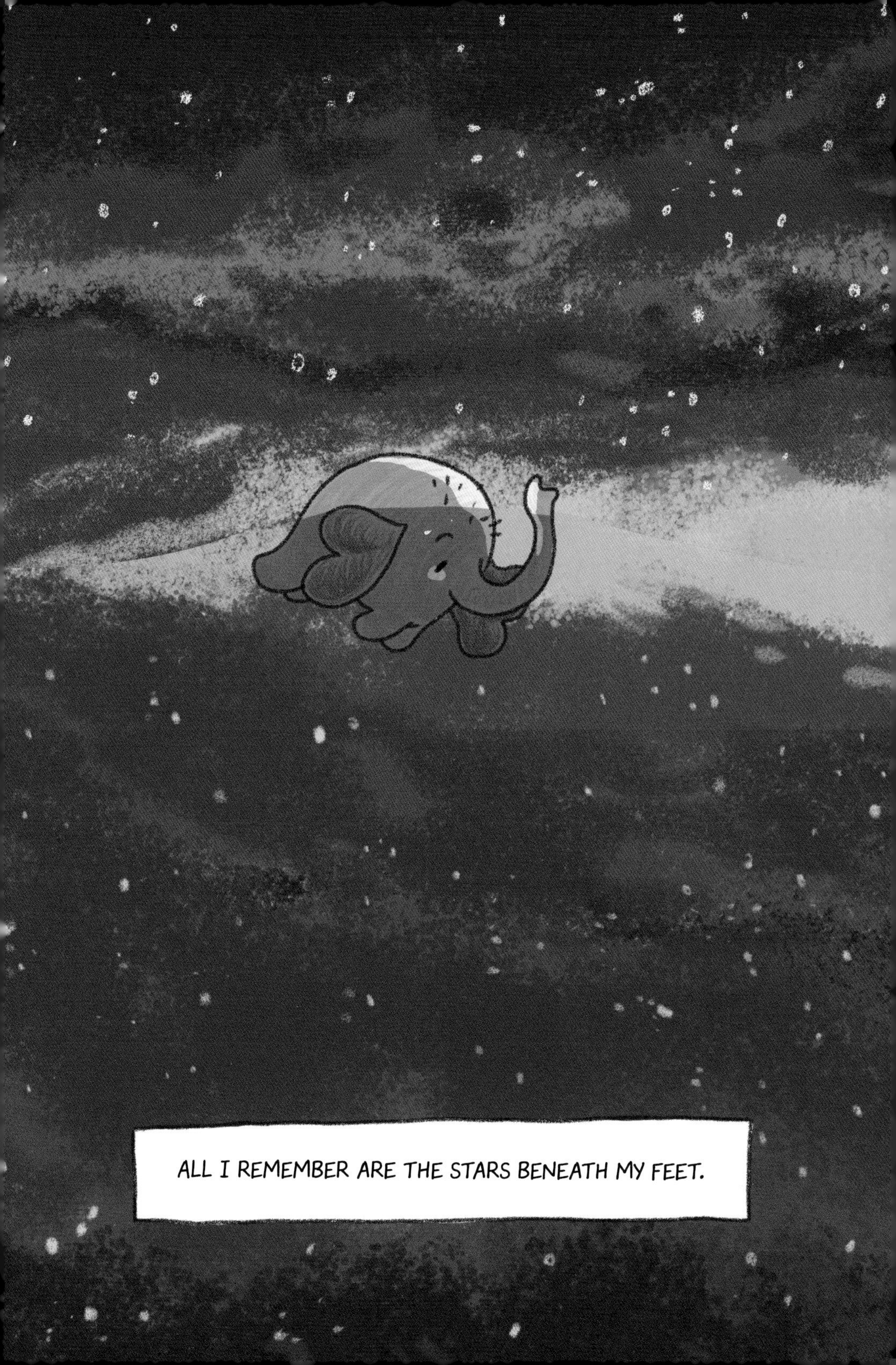
ALL I REMEMBER ARE THE STARS BENEATH MY FEET.

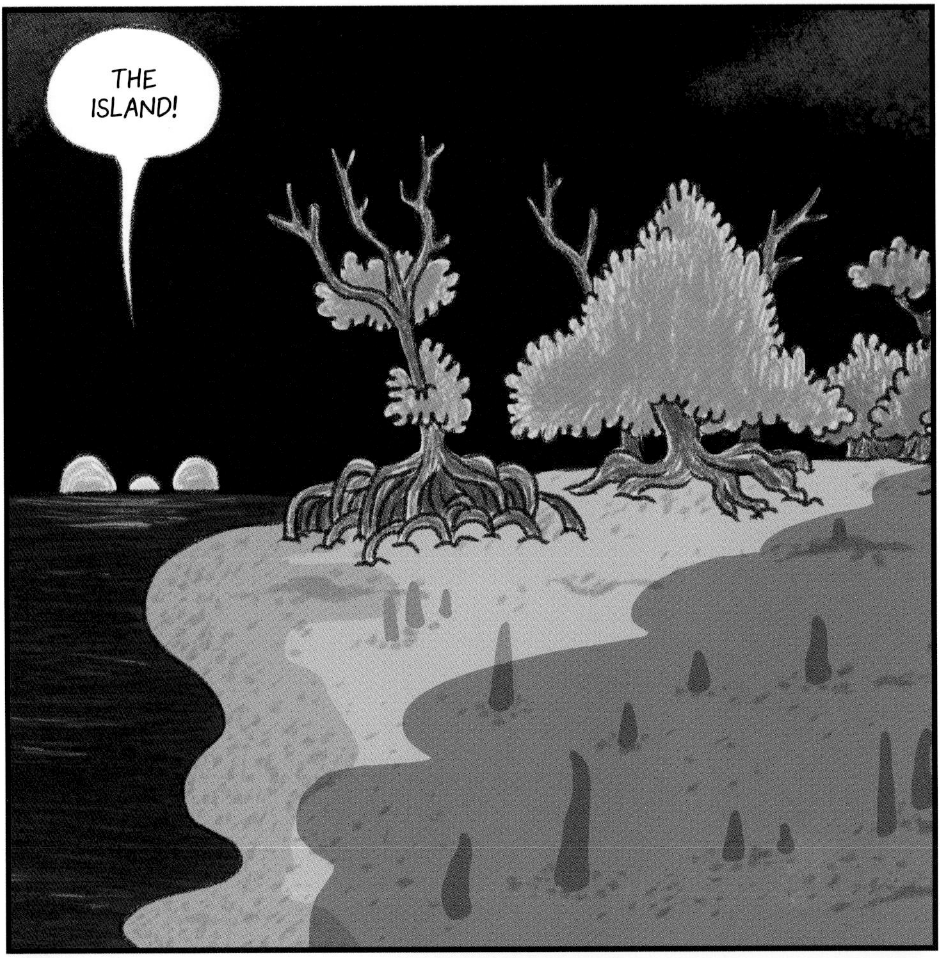
THE ISLAND!

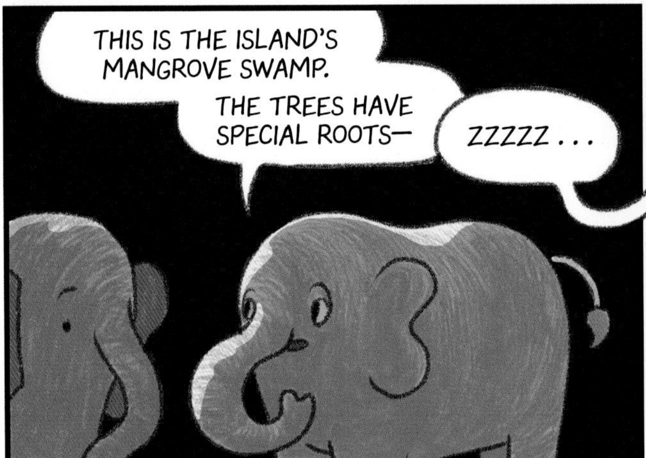
THIS IS THE ISLAND'S MANGROVE SWAMP.
THE TREES HAVE SPECIAL ROOTS—
ZZZZZ . . .

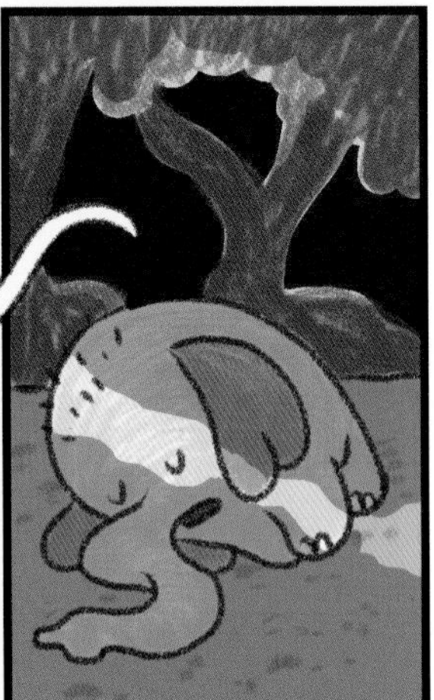

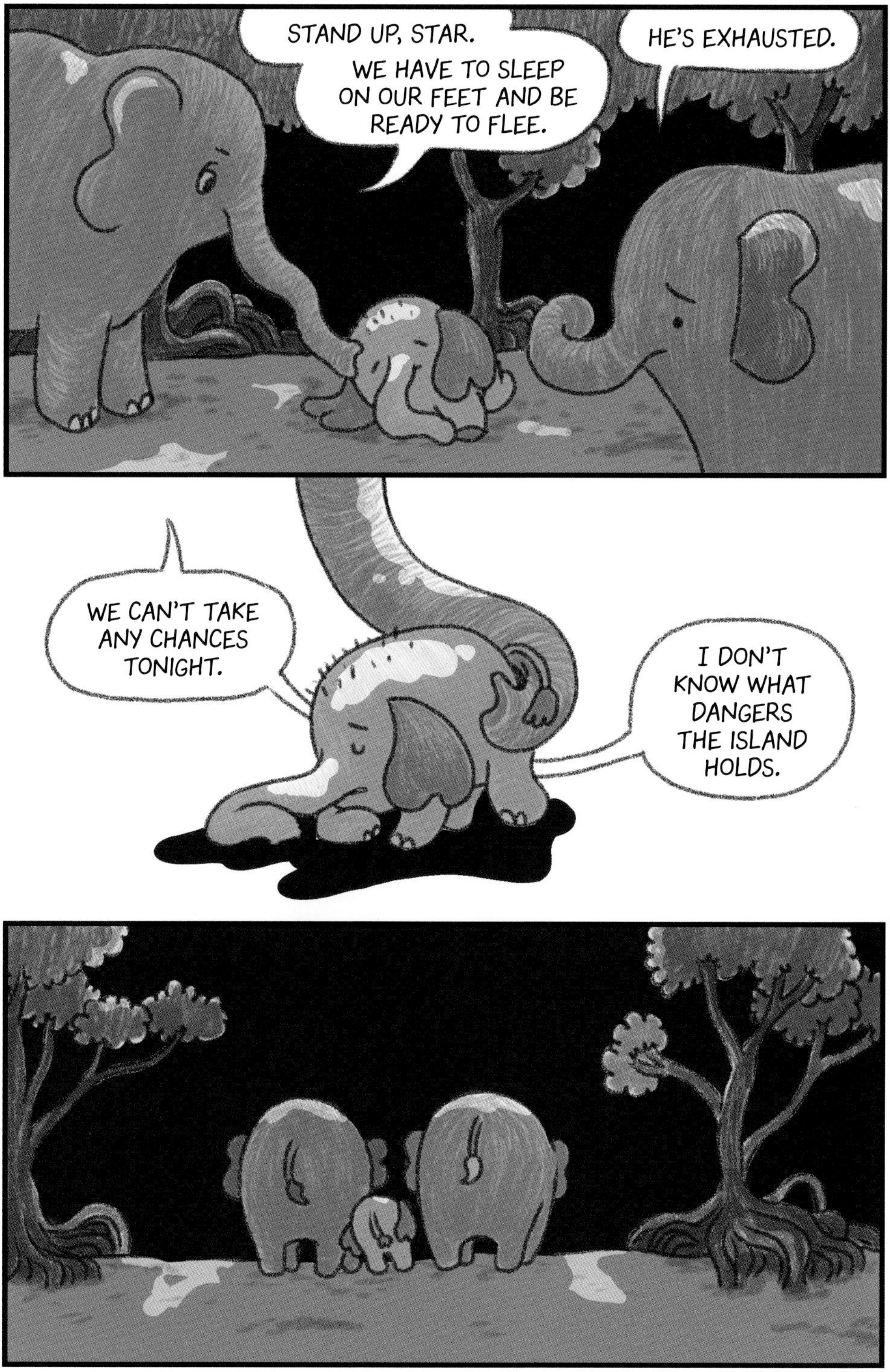
STAND UP, STAR.
WE HAVE TO SLEEP ON OUR FEET AND BE READY TO FLEE.
HE'S EXHAUSTED.
WE CAN'T TAKE ANY CHANCES TONIGHT.
I DON'T KNOW WHAT DANGERS THE ISLAND HOLDS.

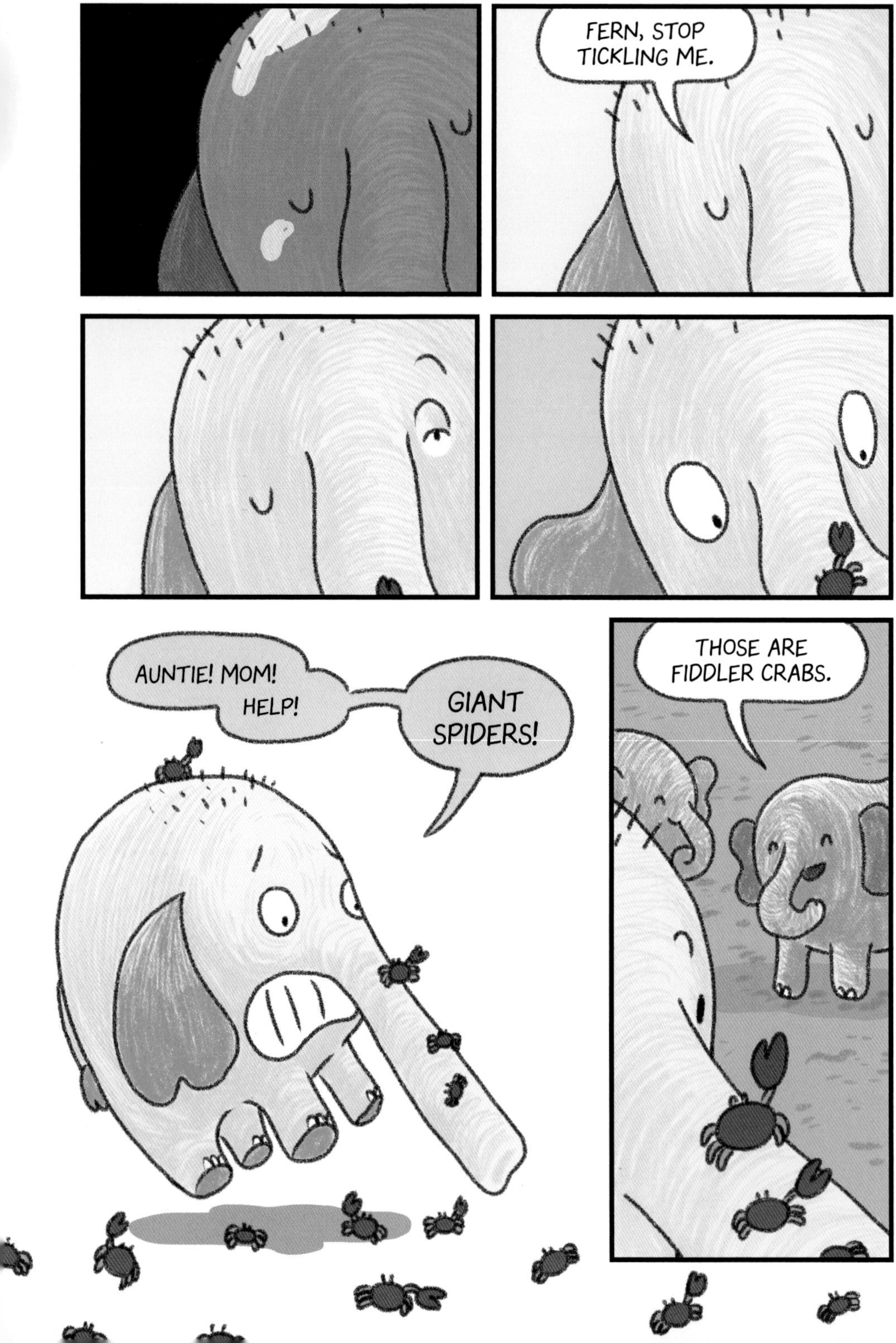
FERN, STOP TICKLING ME.
AUNTIE! MOM! HELP!
GIANT SPIDERS!
THOSE ARE FIDDLER CRABS.

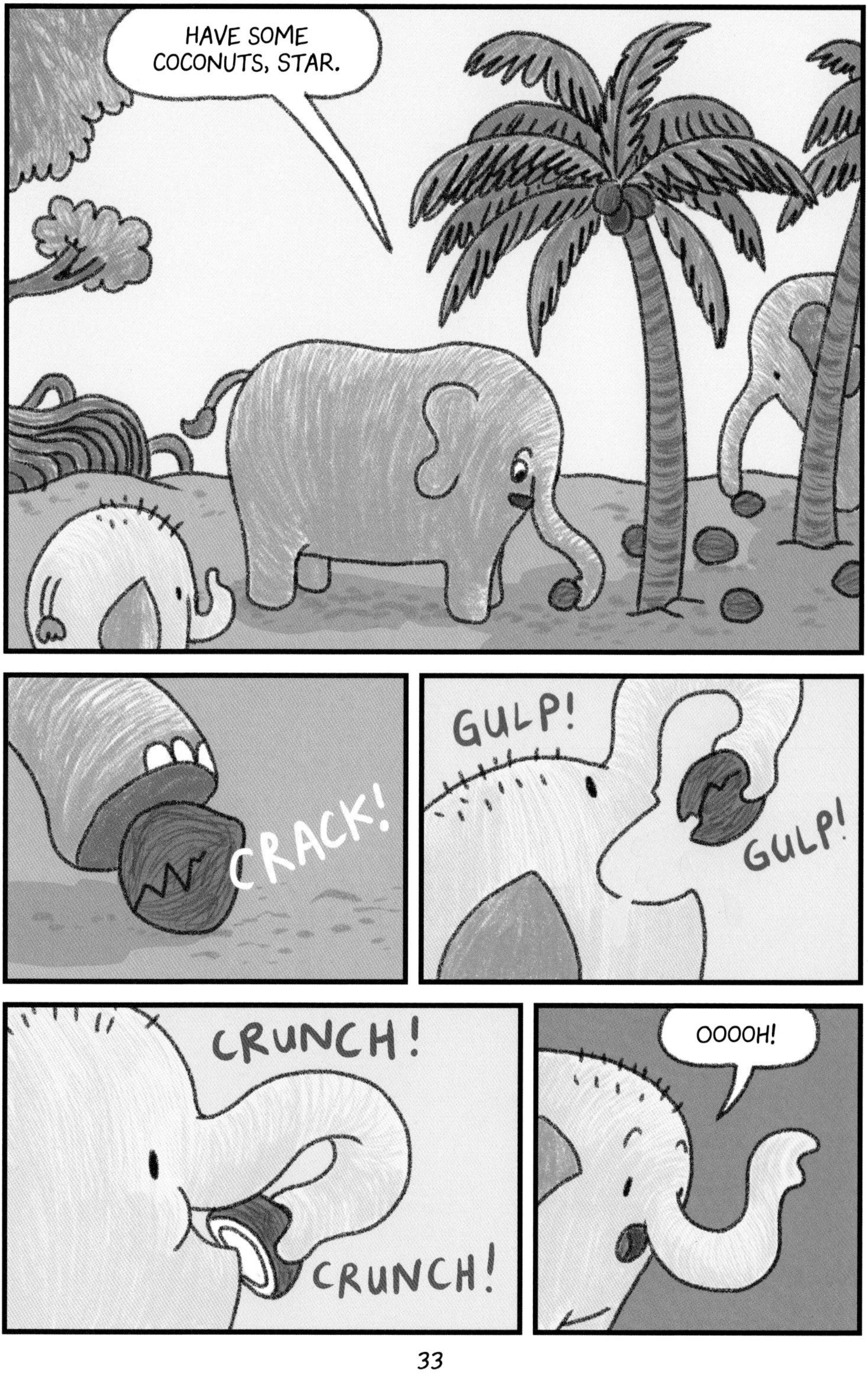
HAVE SOME COCONUTS, STAR.
CRACK!
GULP!
GULP!
CRUNCH!
CRUNCH!
OOOOH!

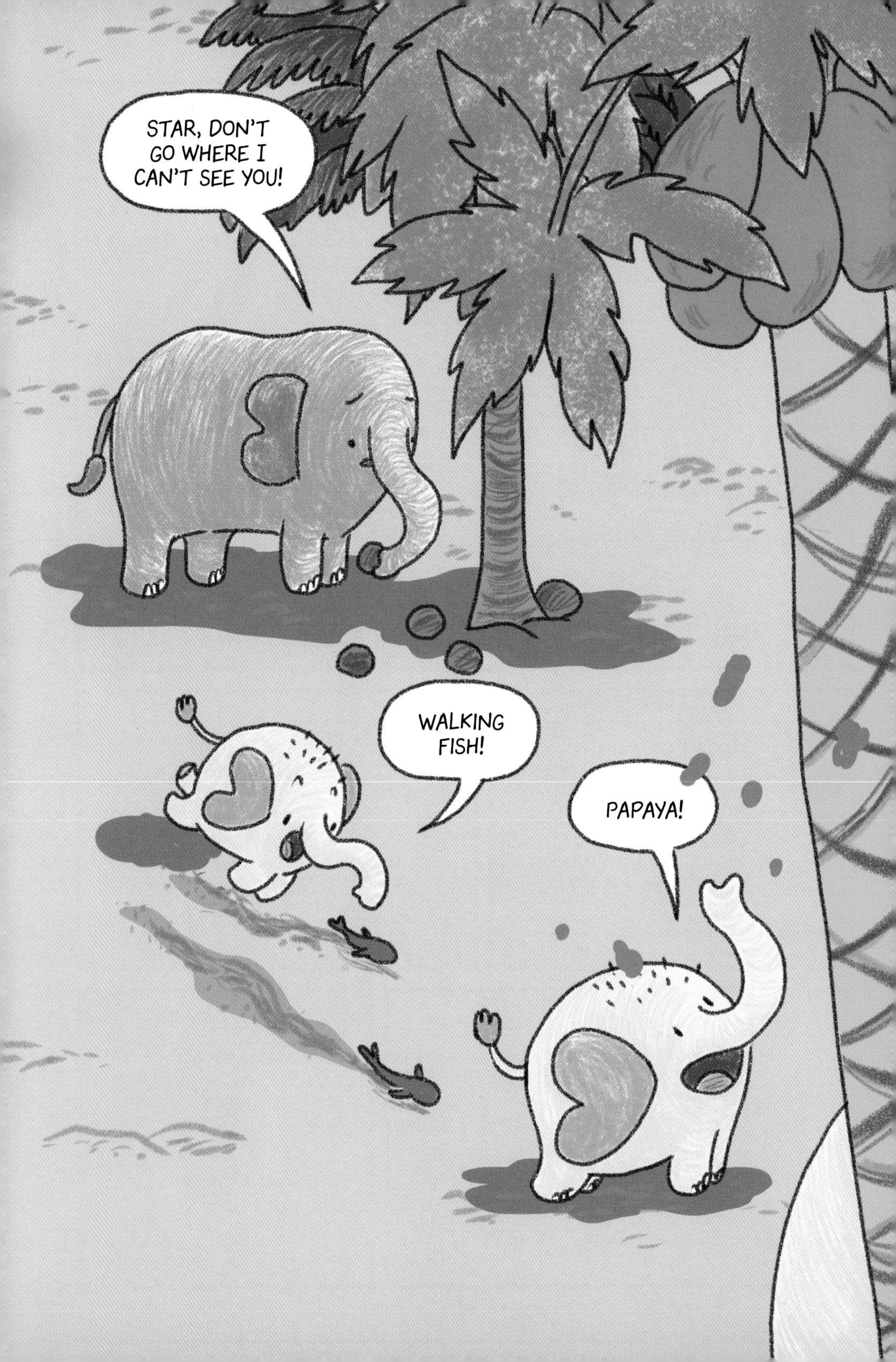
STAR, DON'T GO WHERE I CAN'T SEE YOU!
WALKING FISH!
PAPAYA!

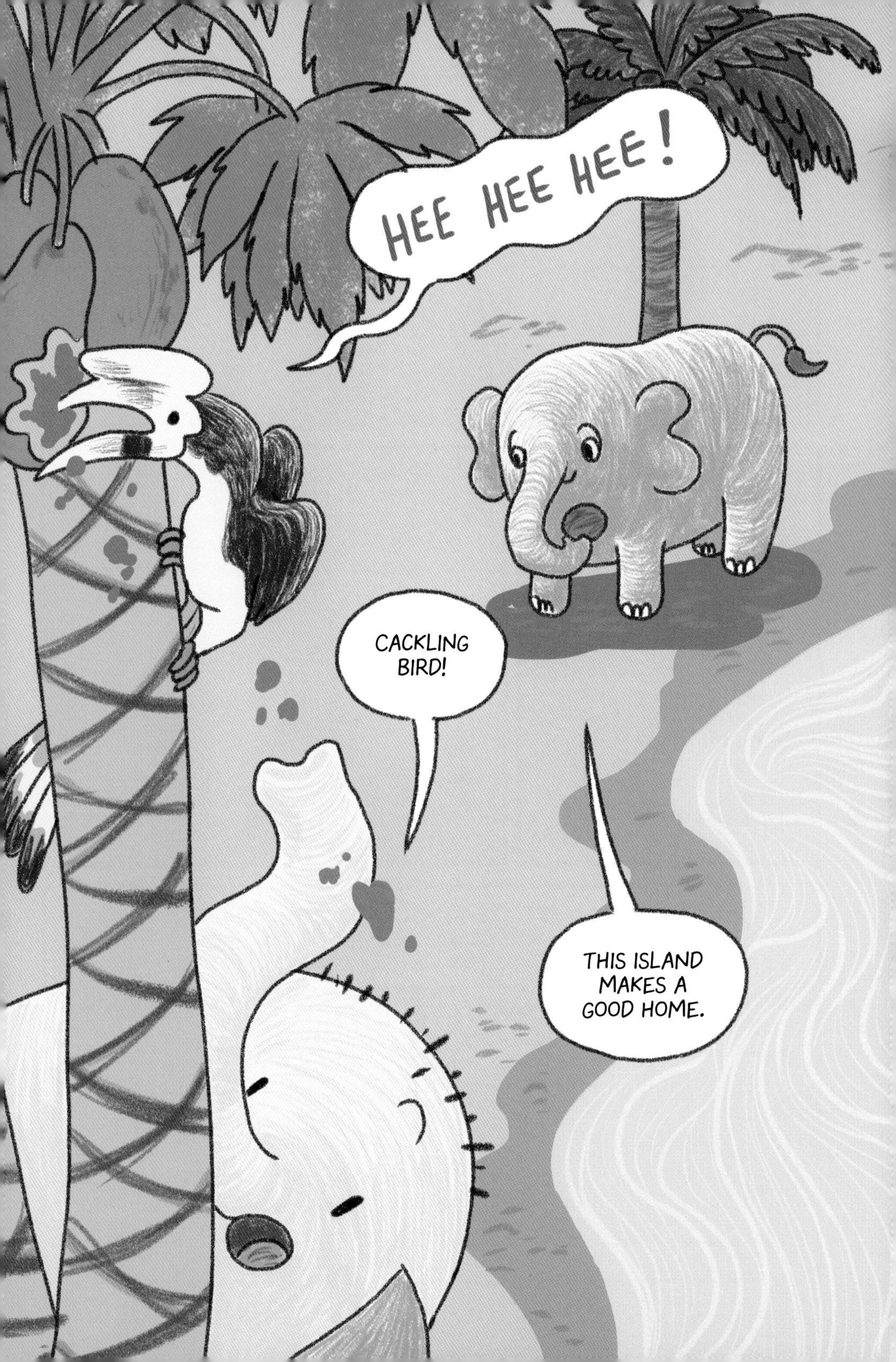
HEE HEE HEE!
CACKLING BIRD!
THIS ISLAND MAKES A GOOD HOME.

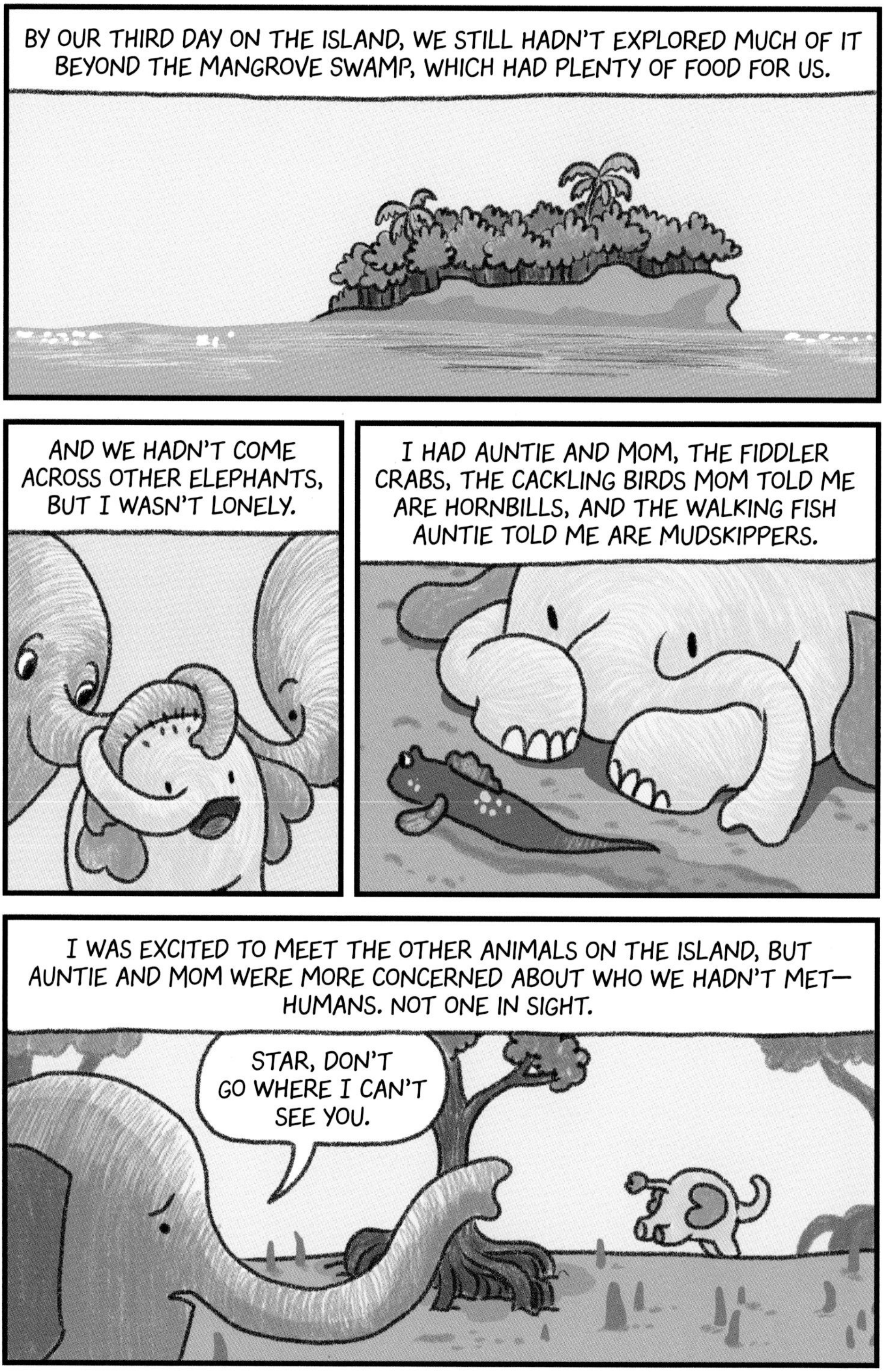
BY OUR THIRD DAY ON THE ISLAND, WE STILL HADN'T EXPLORED MUCH OF IT BEYOND THE MANGROVE SWAMP, WHICH HAD PLENTY OF FOOD FOR US.
AND WE HADN'T COME ACROSS OTHER ELEPHANTS, BUT I WASN'T LONELY.
I HAD AUNTIE AND MOM, THE FIDDLER CRABS, THE CACKLING BIRDS MOM TOLD ME ARE HORNBILLS, AND THE WALKING FISH AUNTIE TOLD ME ARE MUDSKIPPERS.
I WAS EXCITED TO MEET THE OTHER ANIMALS ON THE ISLAND, BUT AUNTIE AND MOM WERE MORE CONCERNED ABOUT WHO WE HADN'T MET—HUMANS. NOT ONE IN SIGHT.
STAR, DON'T GO WHERE I CAN'T SEE YOU.

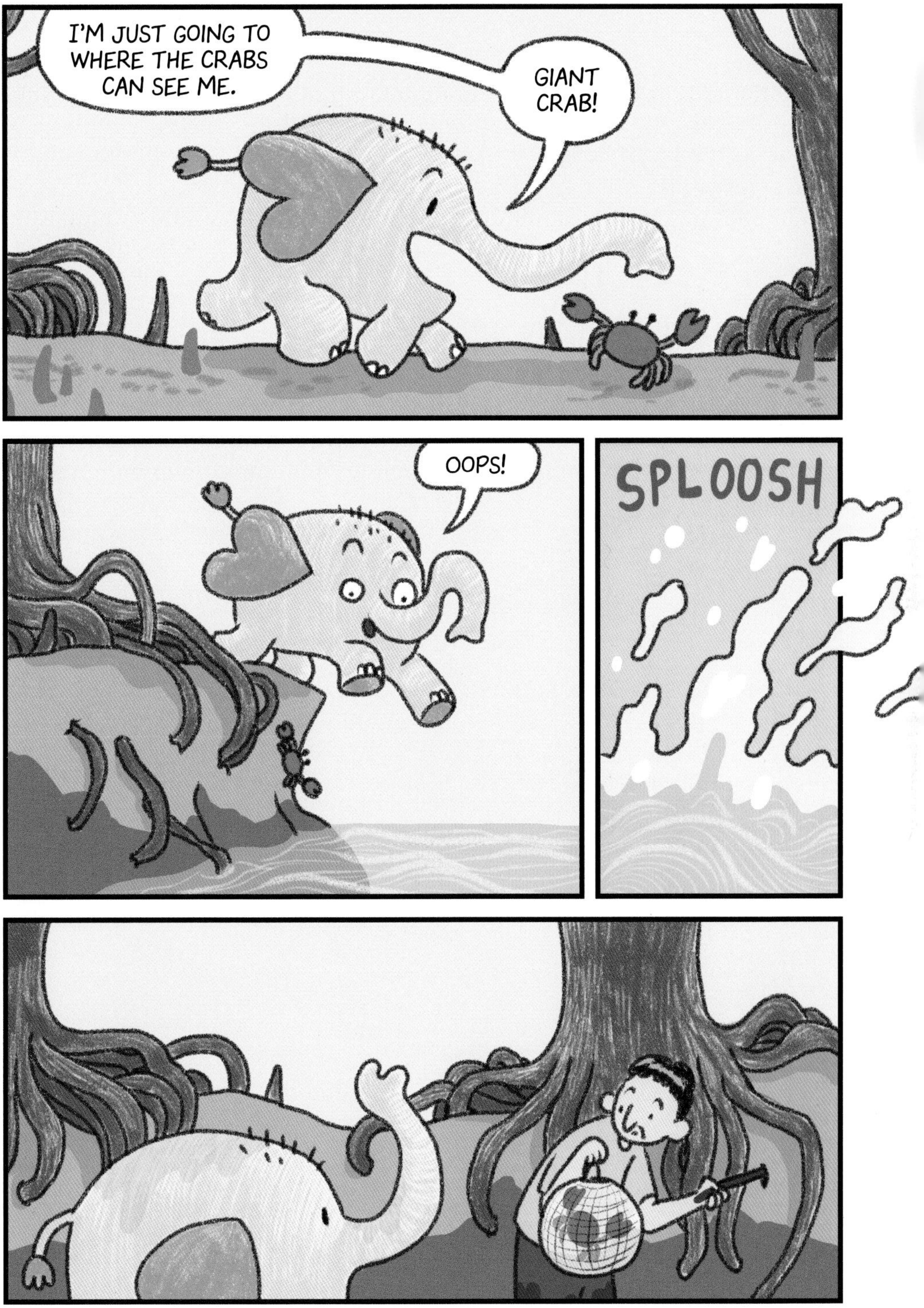
I'M JUST GOING TO WHERE THE CRABS CAN SEE ME.
GIANT CRAB!
OOPS!
SPLOOSH

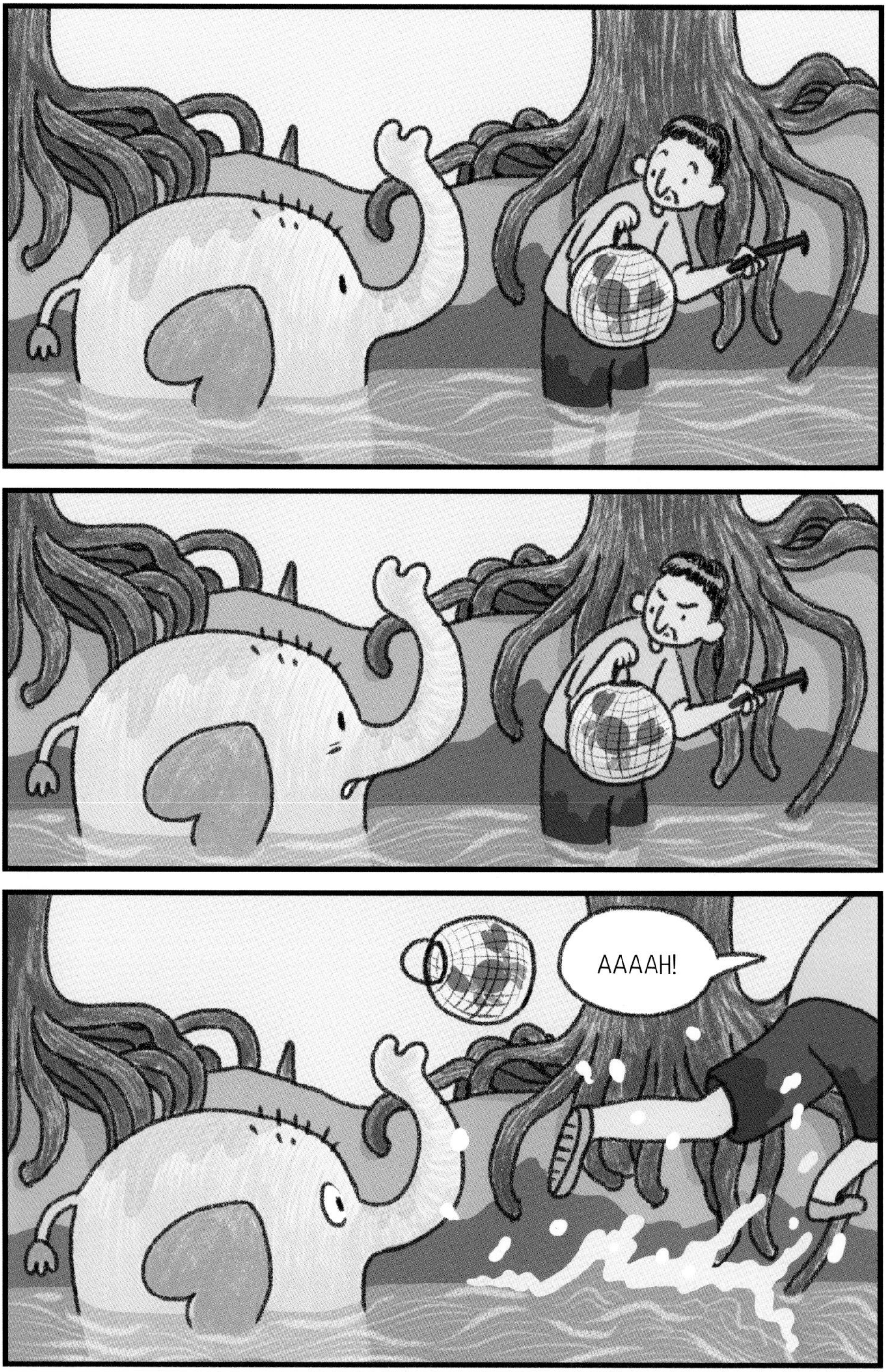
AAAAH!

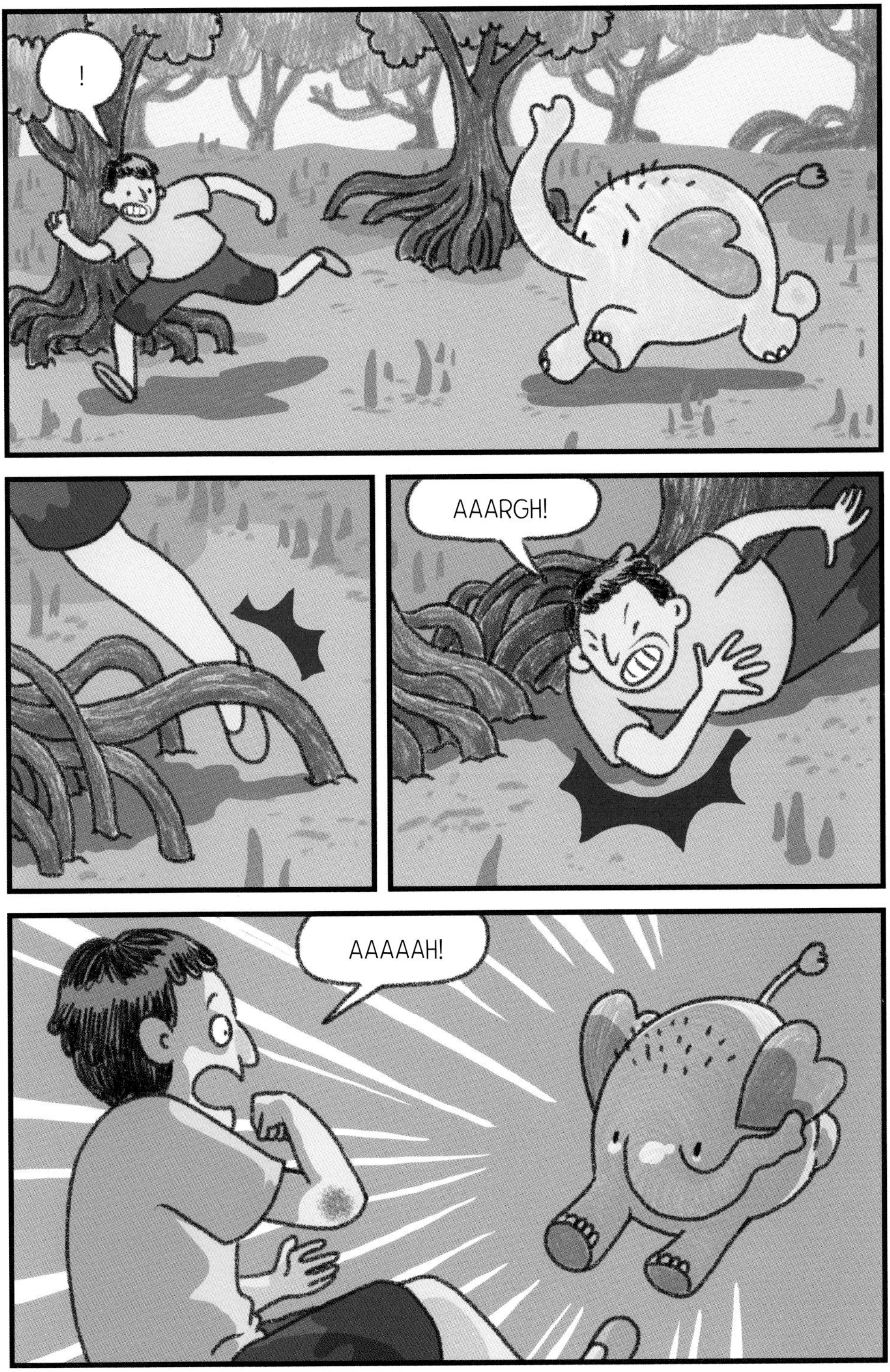
!
AAARGH!
AAAAAH!

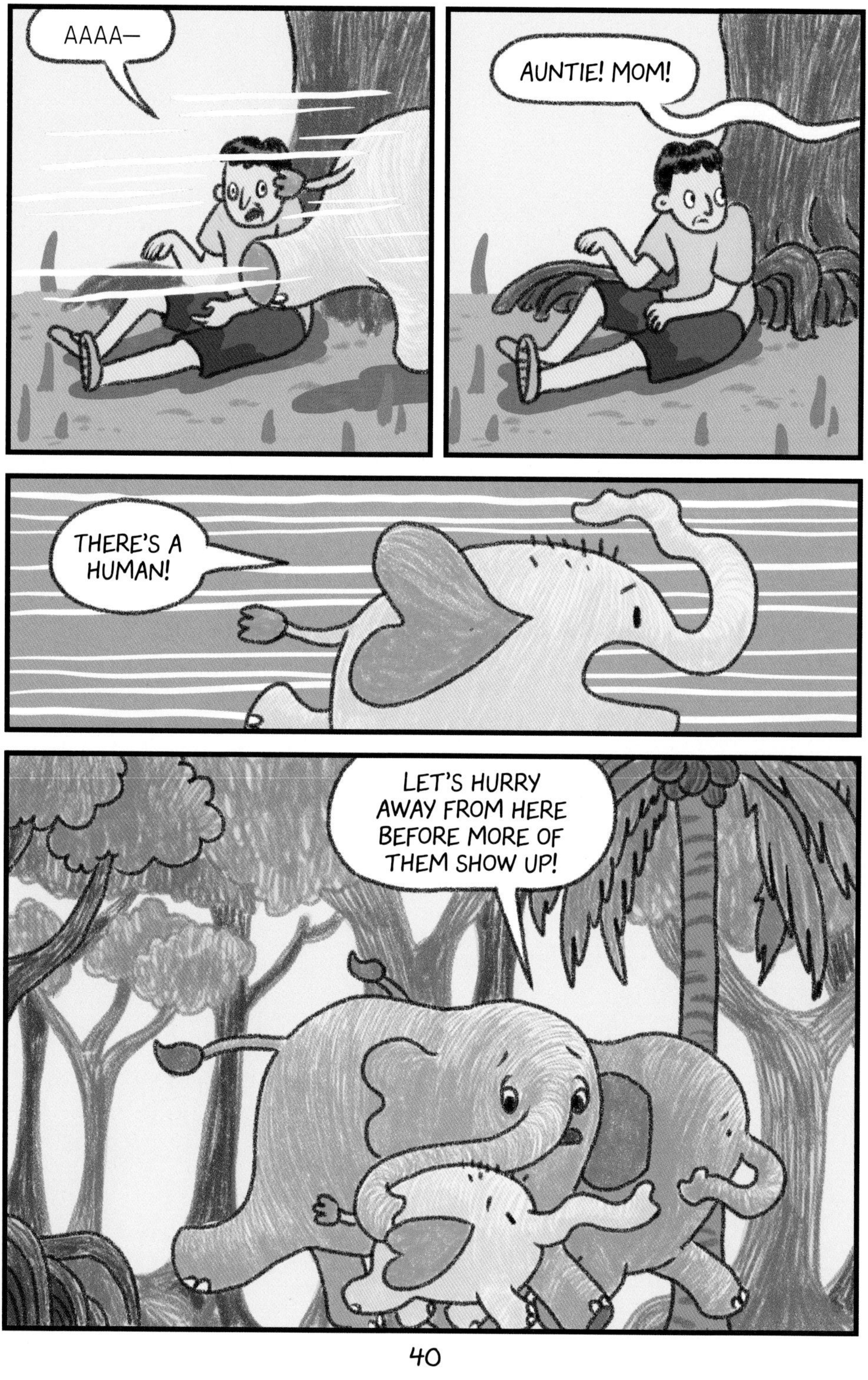
AAAA—
AUNTIE! MOM!
THERE'S A HUMAN!
LET'S HURRY AWAY FROM HERE BEFORE MORE OF THEM SHOW UP!

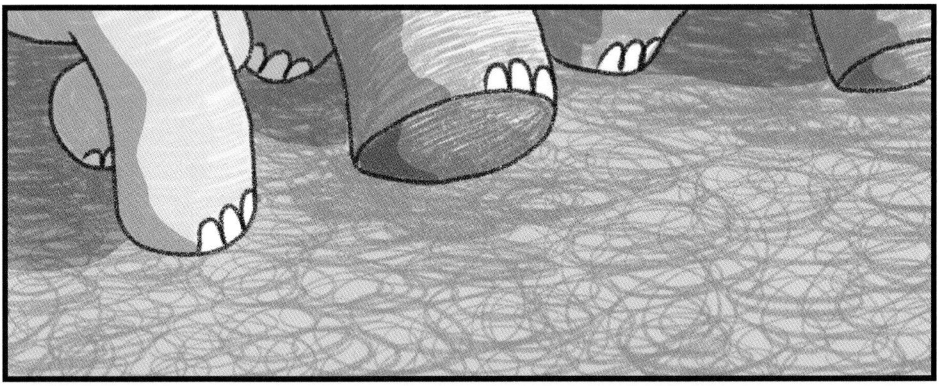

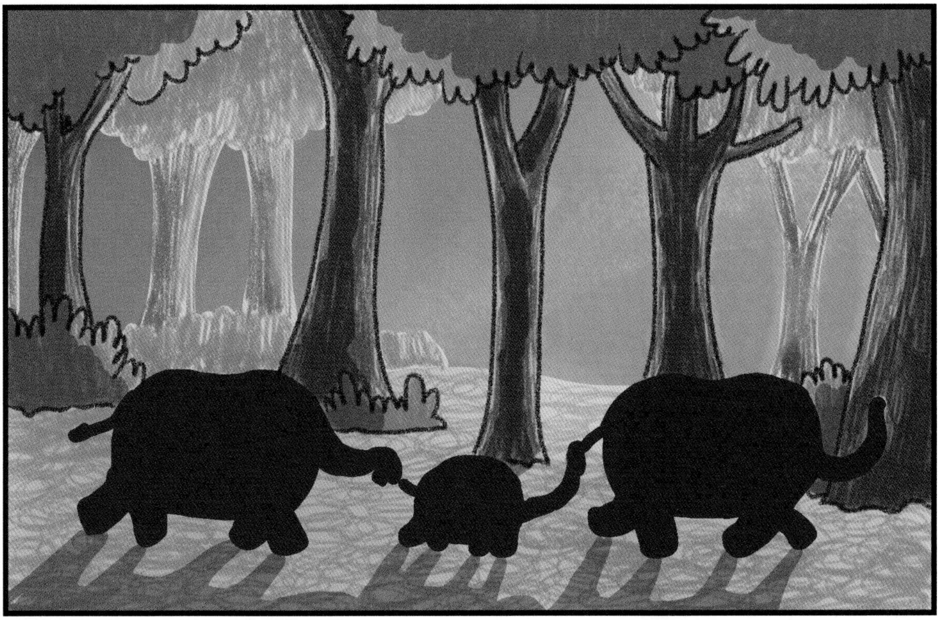

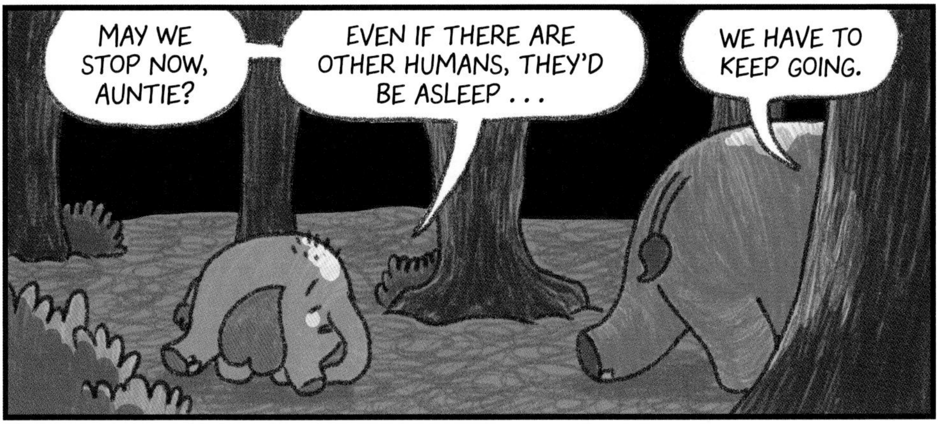
MAY WE STOP NOW, AUNTIE?
EVEN IF THERE ARE OTHER HUMANS, THEY'D BE ASLEEP . . .
WE HAVE TO KEEP GOING.

HMM?

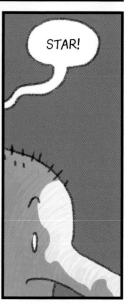

STAR!

I TOLD YOU NOT TO GO WHERE I CAN'T SEE YOU!

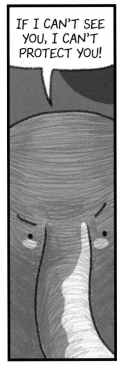

IF I CAN'T SEE YOU, I CAN'T PROTECT YOU!

I'M SORRY, MOM.

HUMANS ARE EVERYWHERE.

NO MATTER WHERE WE GO.

THE QUESTION IS HOW MANY HUMANS ARE ON THIS ISLAND?

AND WHAT WILL THEY DO WHEN THEY FIND US?

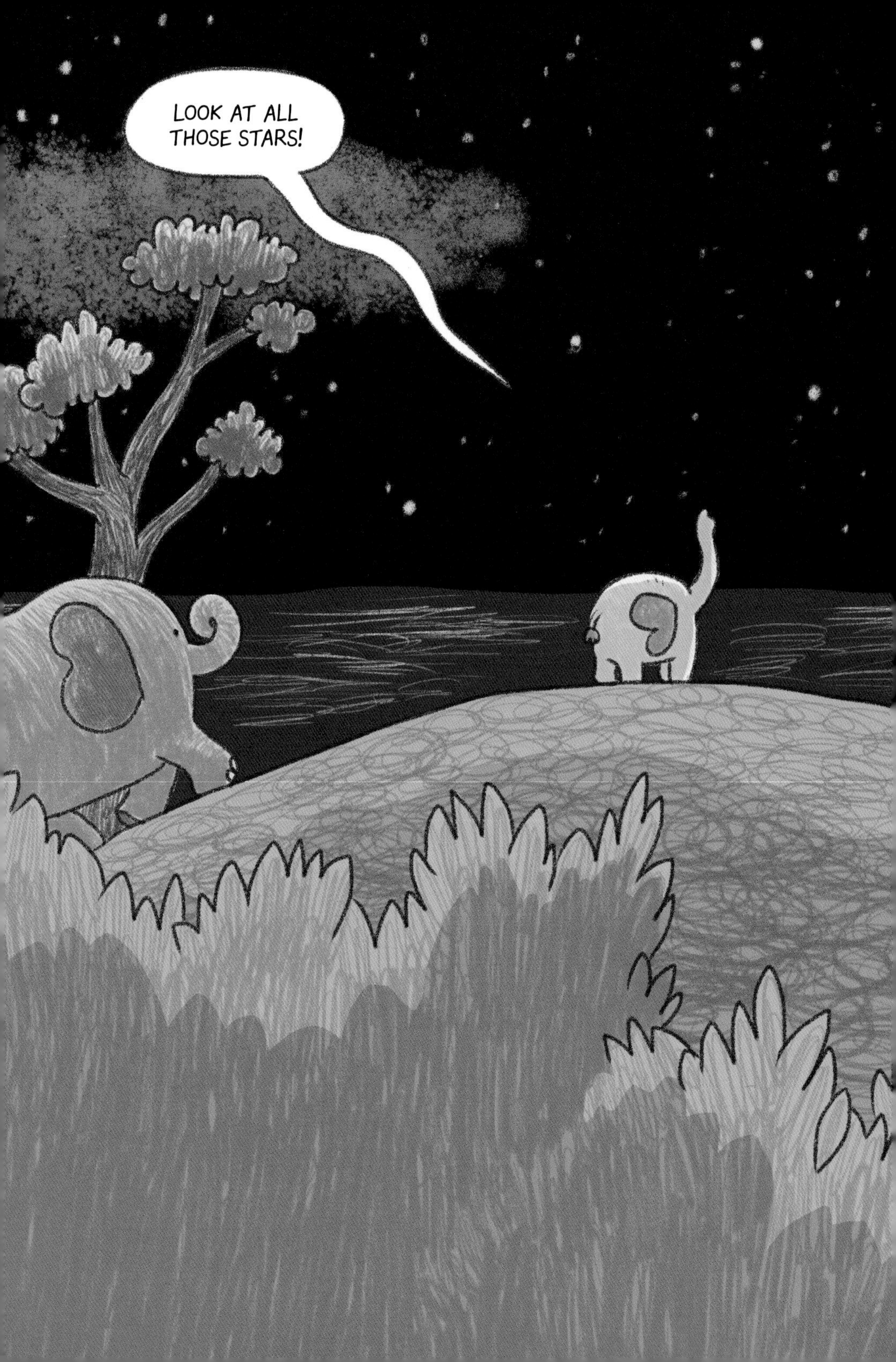
LOOK AT ALL THOSE STARS!

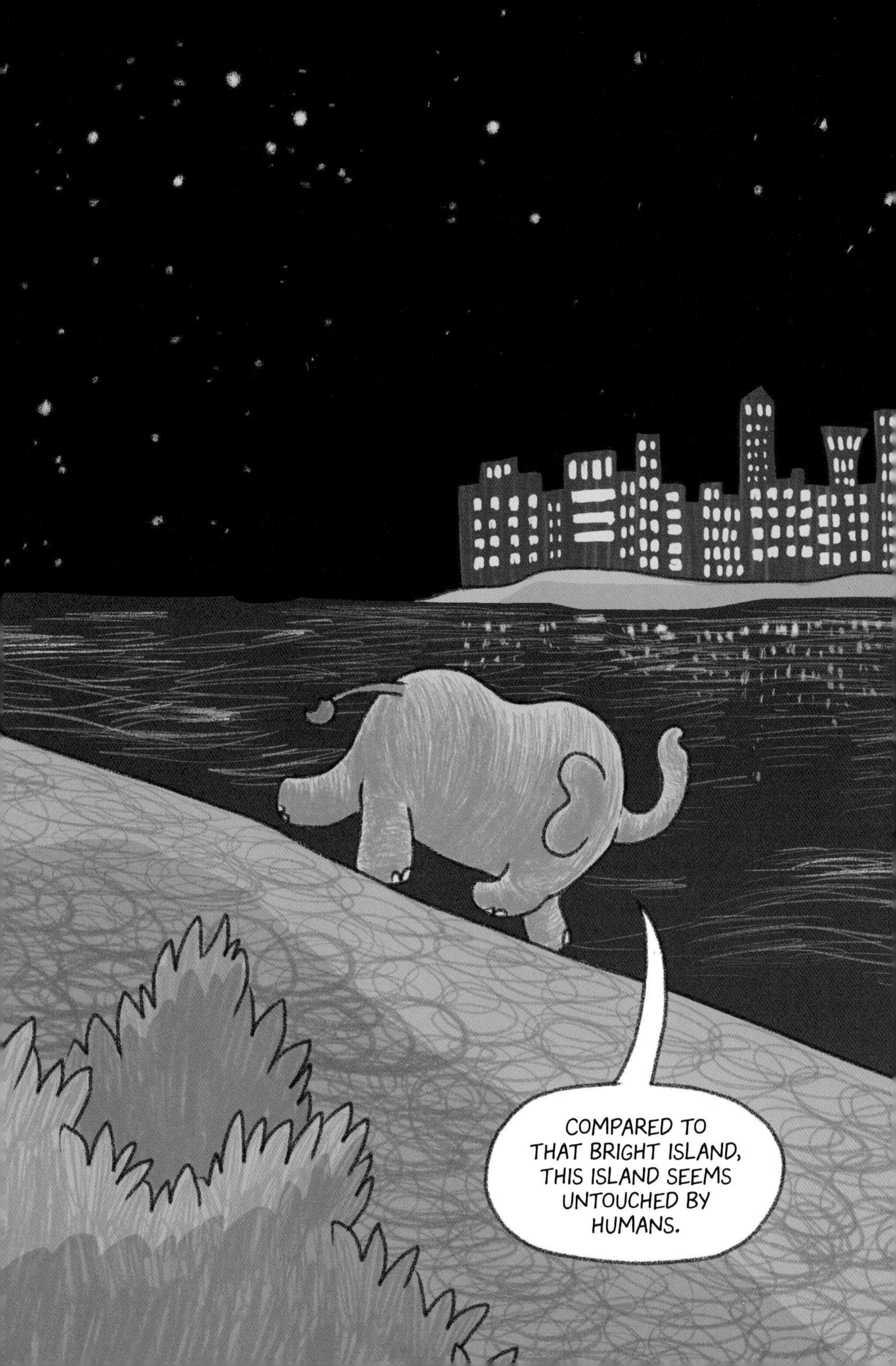
COMPARED TO THAT BRIGHT ISLAND, THIS ISLAND SEEMS UNTOUCHED BY HUMANS.

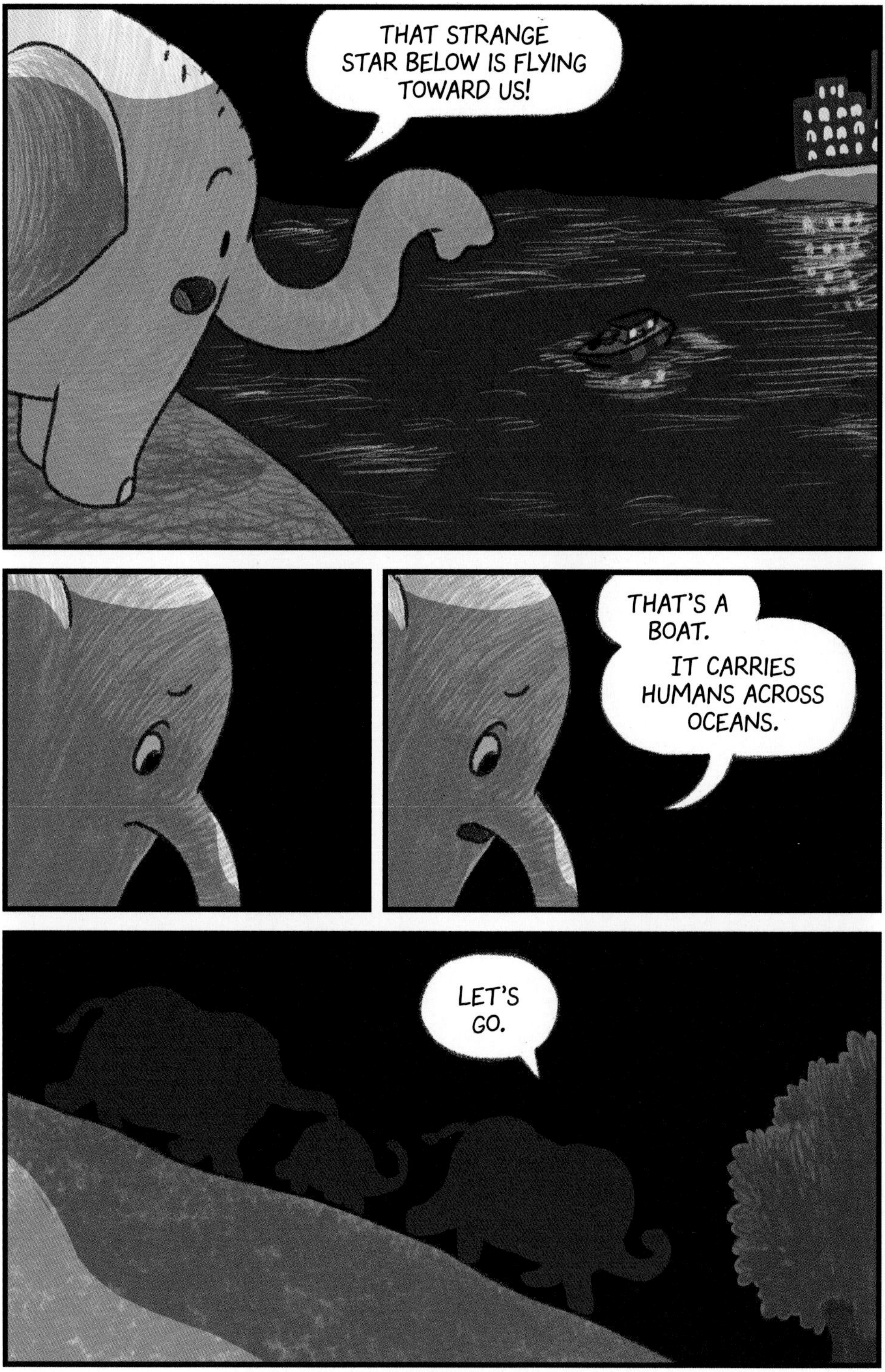
THAT STRANGE STAR BELOW IS FLYING TOWARD US!
THAT'S A BOAT.
IT CARRIES HUMANS ACROSS OCEANS.
LET'S GO.

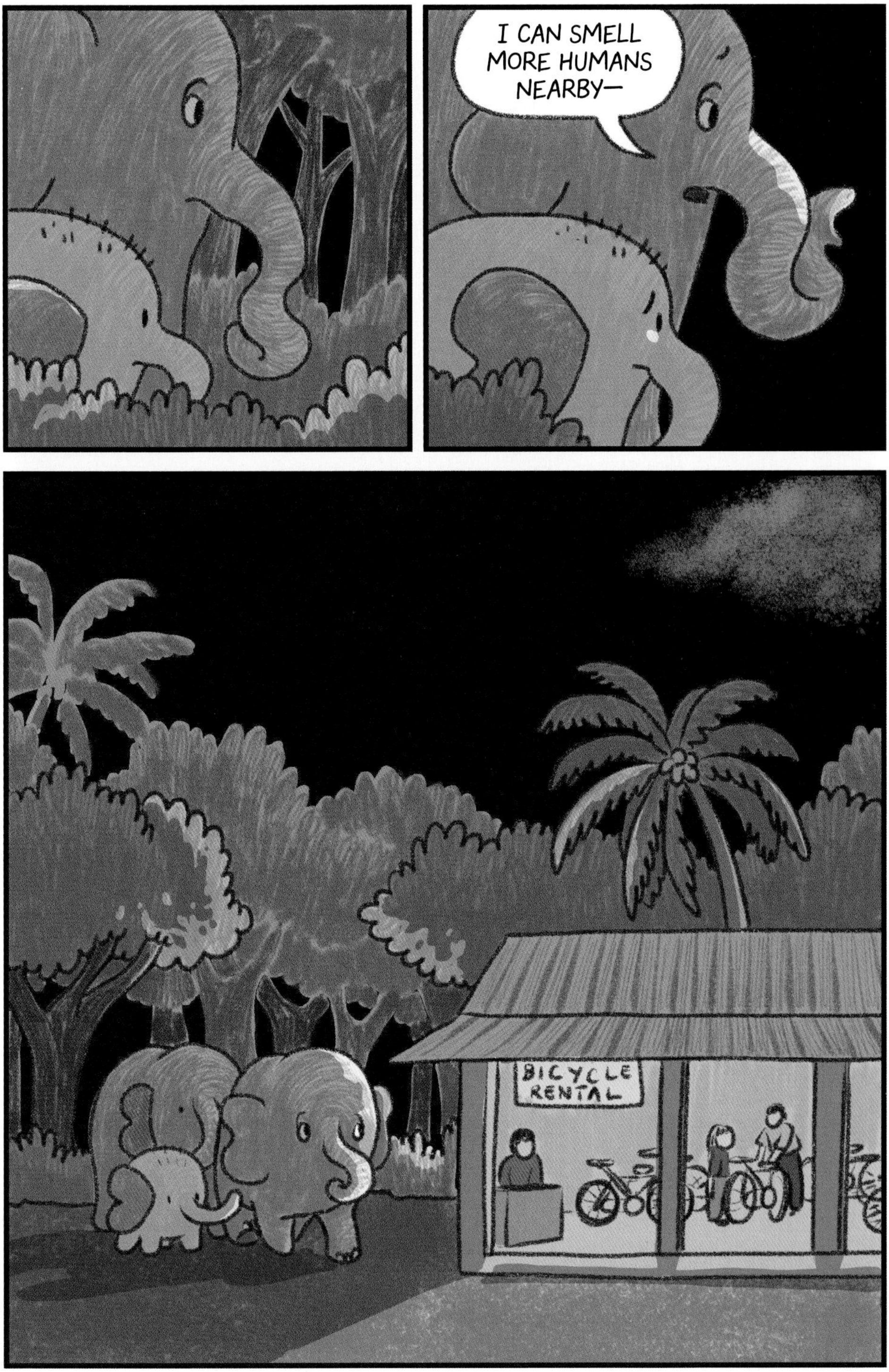
I CAN SMELL MORE HUMANS NEARBY—
BICYCLE RENTAL

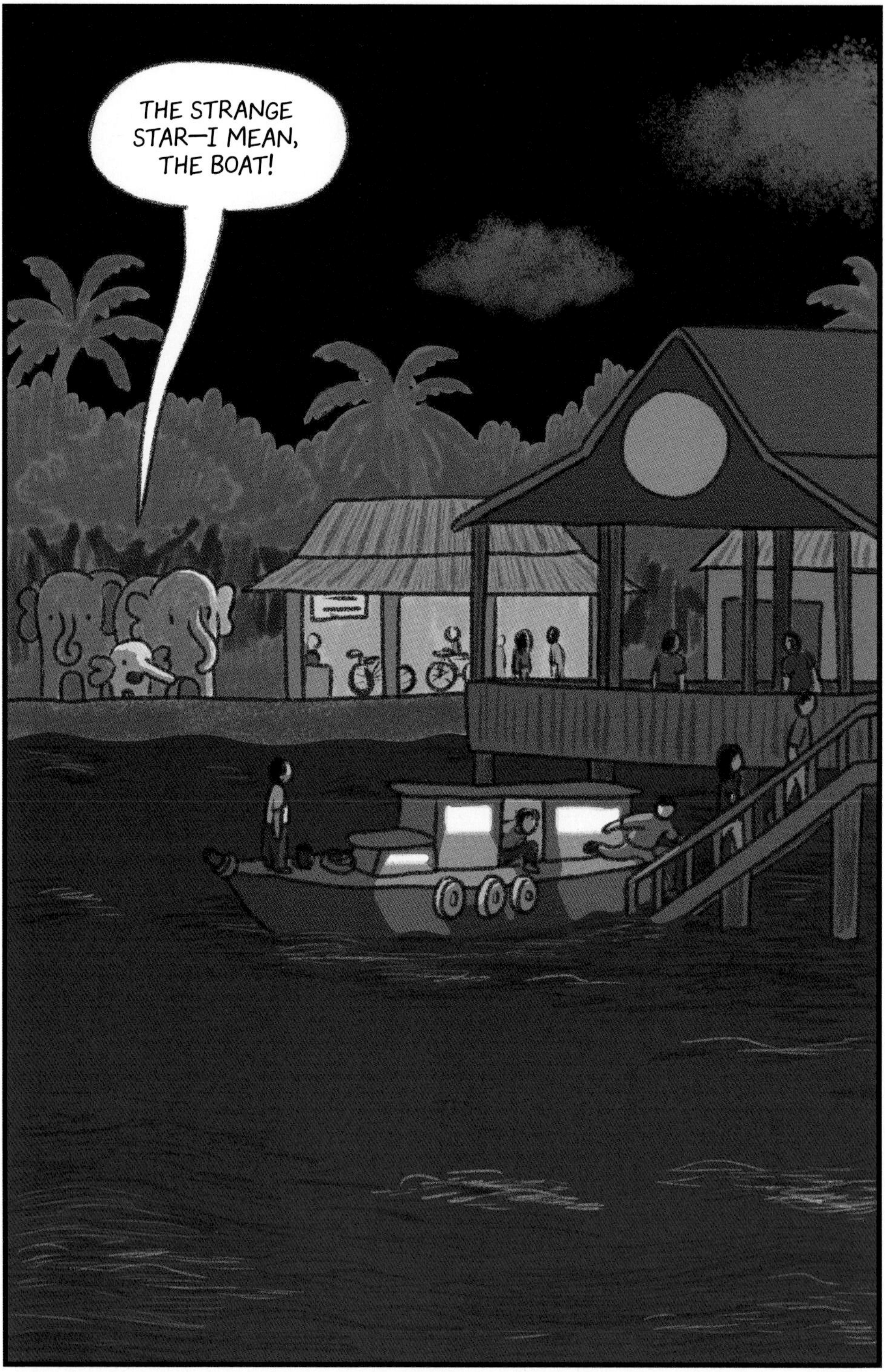
THE STRANGE STAR—I MEAN, THE BOAT!

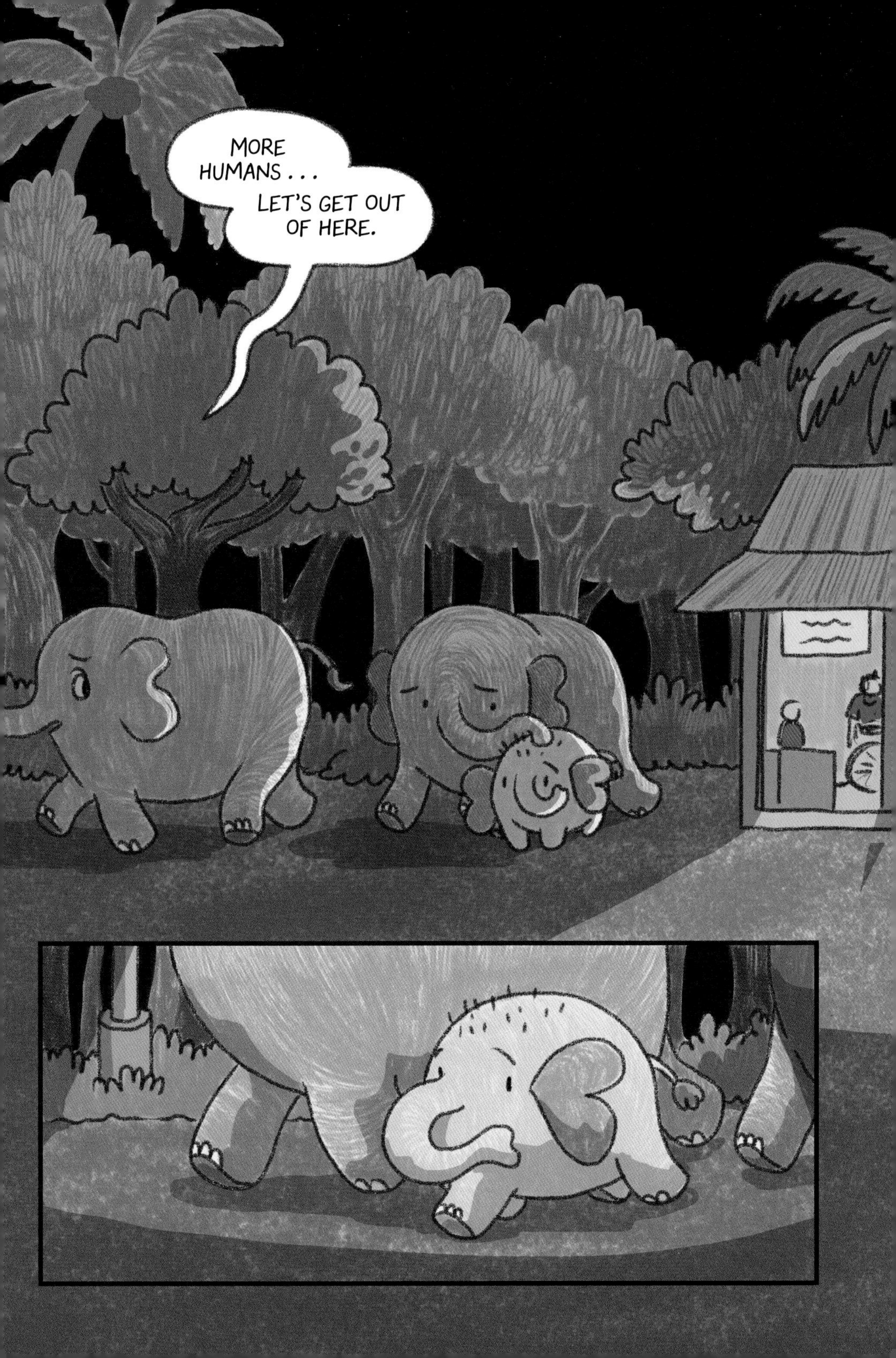
MORE HUMANS . . .
LET'S GET OUT OF HERE.

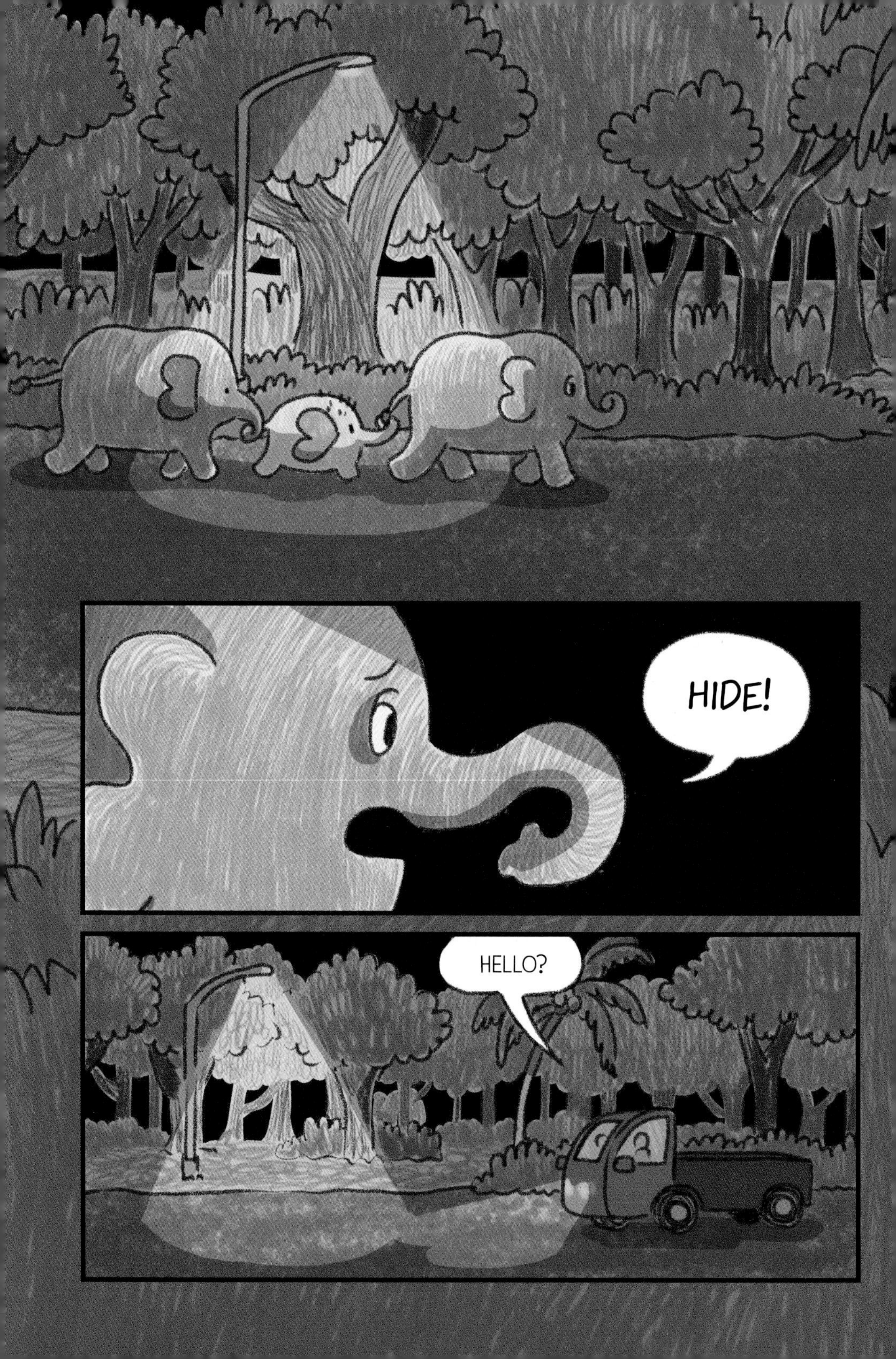
HIDE!
HELLO?

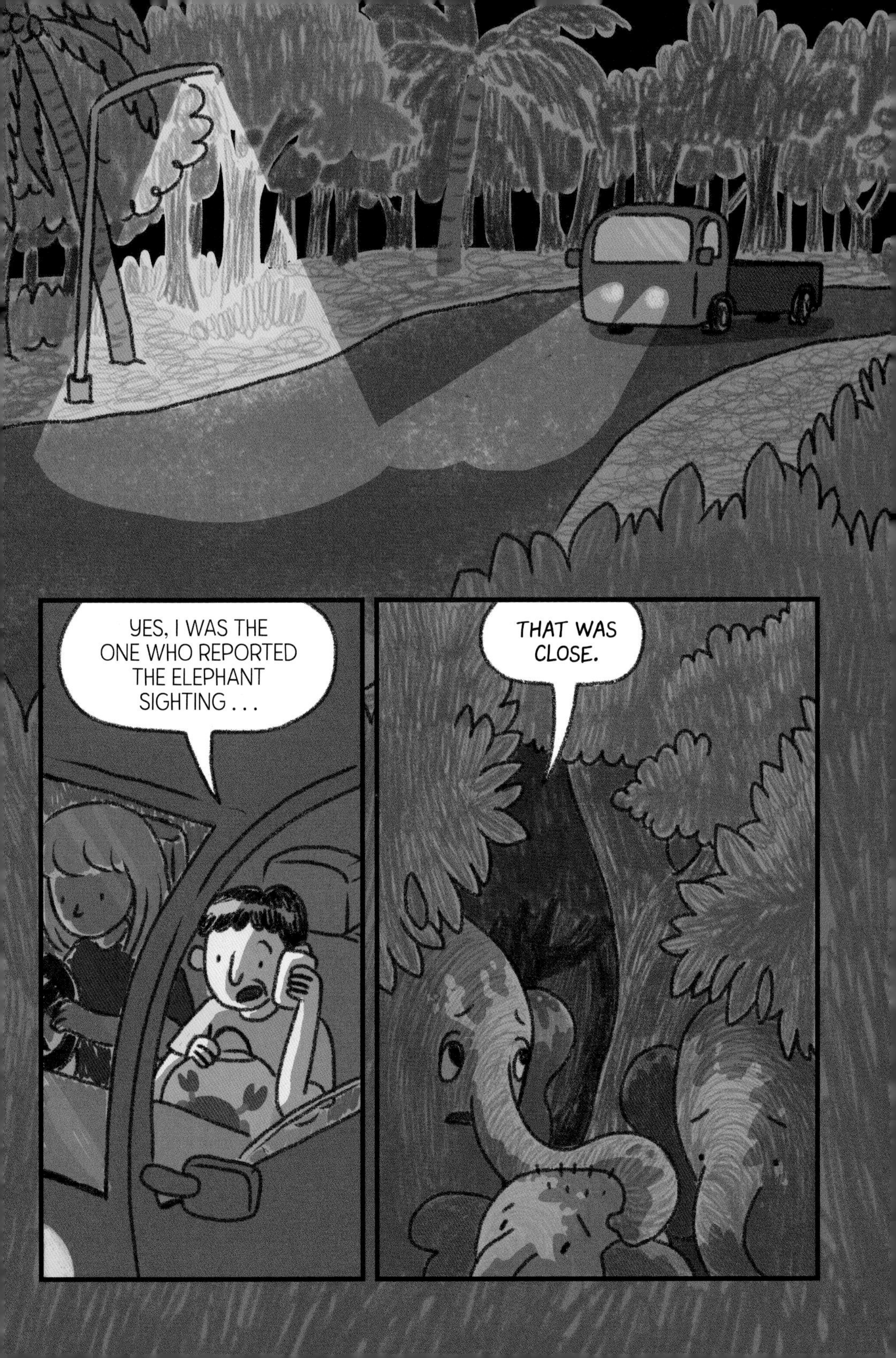
YES, I WAS THE ONE WHO REPORTED THE ELEPHANT SIGHTING . . .
THAT WAS CLOSE.

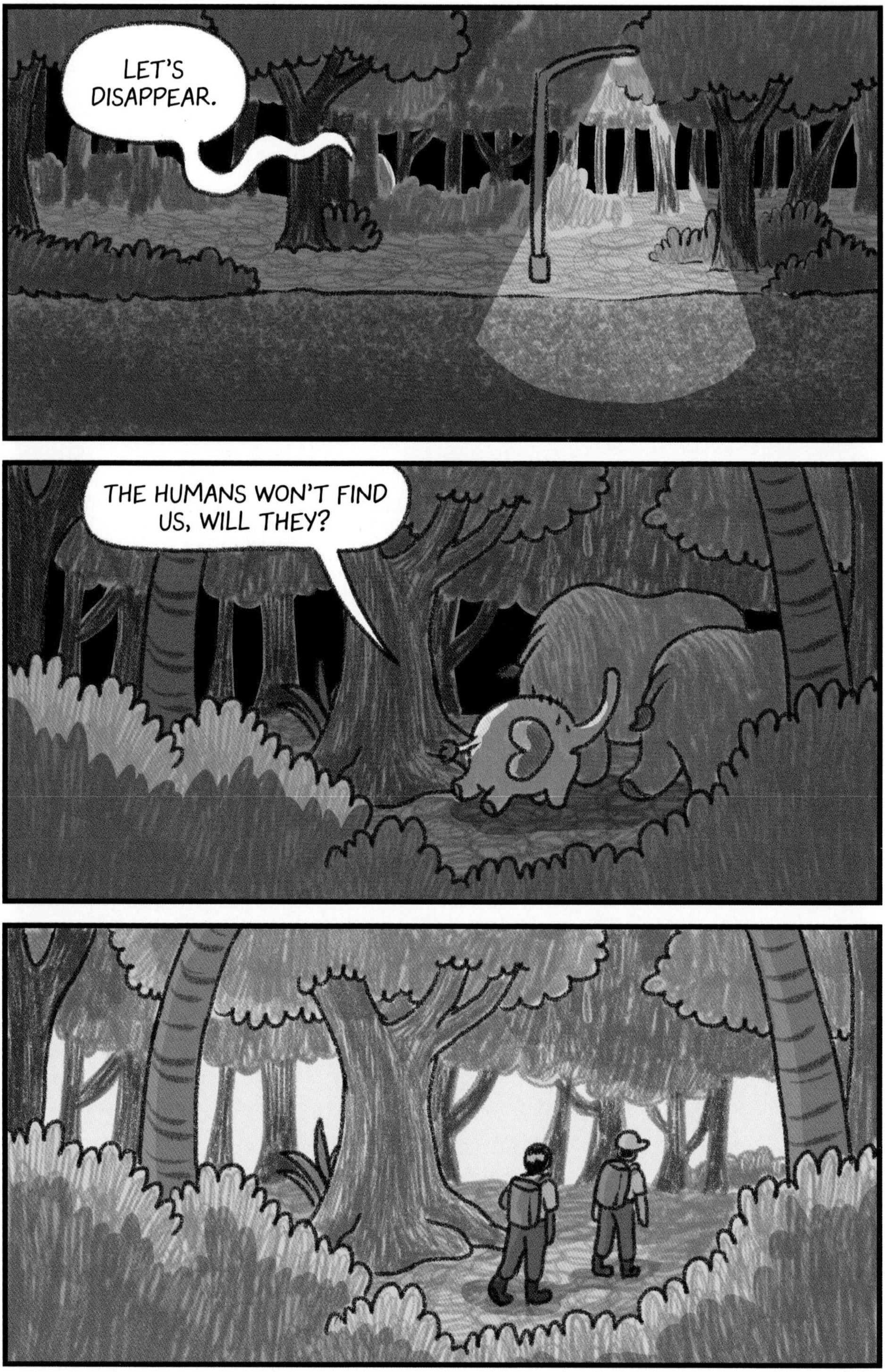
LET'S DISAPPEAR.
THE HUMANS WON'T FIND US, WILL THEY?

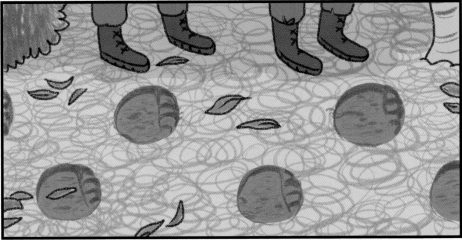

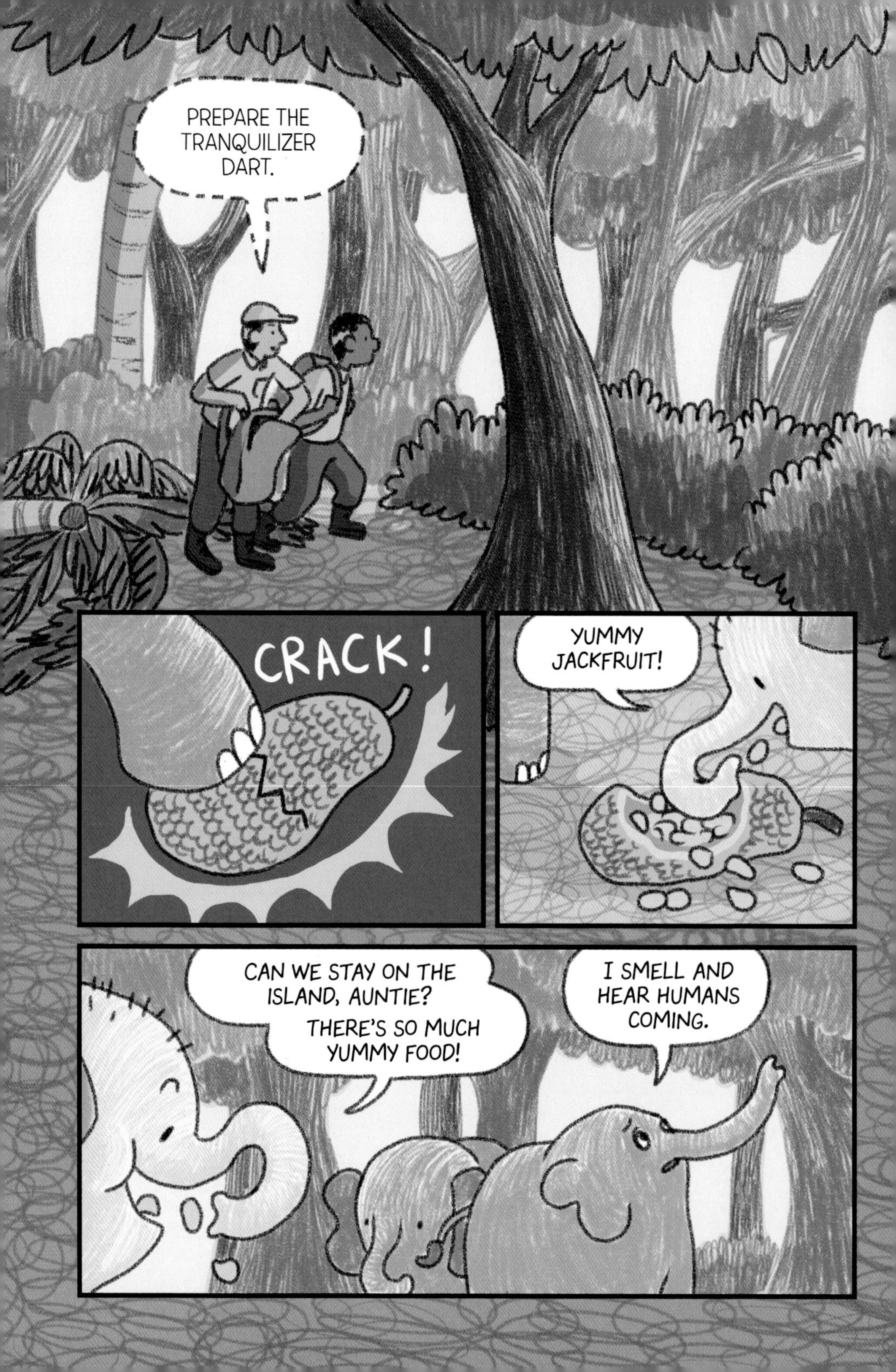
PREPARE THE TRANQUILIZER DART.
CRACK!
YUMMY JACKFRUIT!
CAN WE STAY ON THE ISLAND, AUNTIE?
THERE'S SO MUCH YUMMY FOOD!
I SMELL AND HEAR HUMANS COMING.

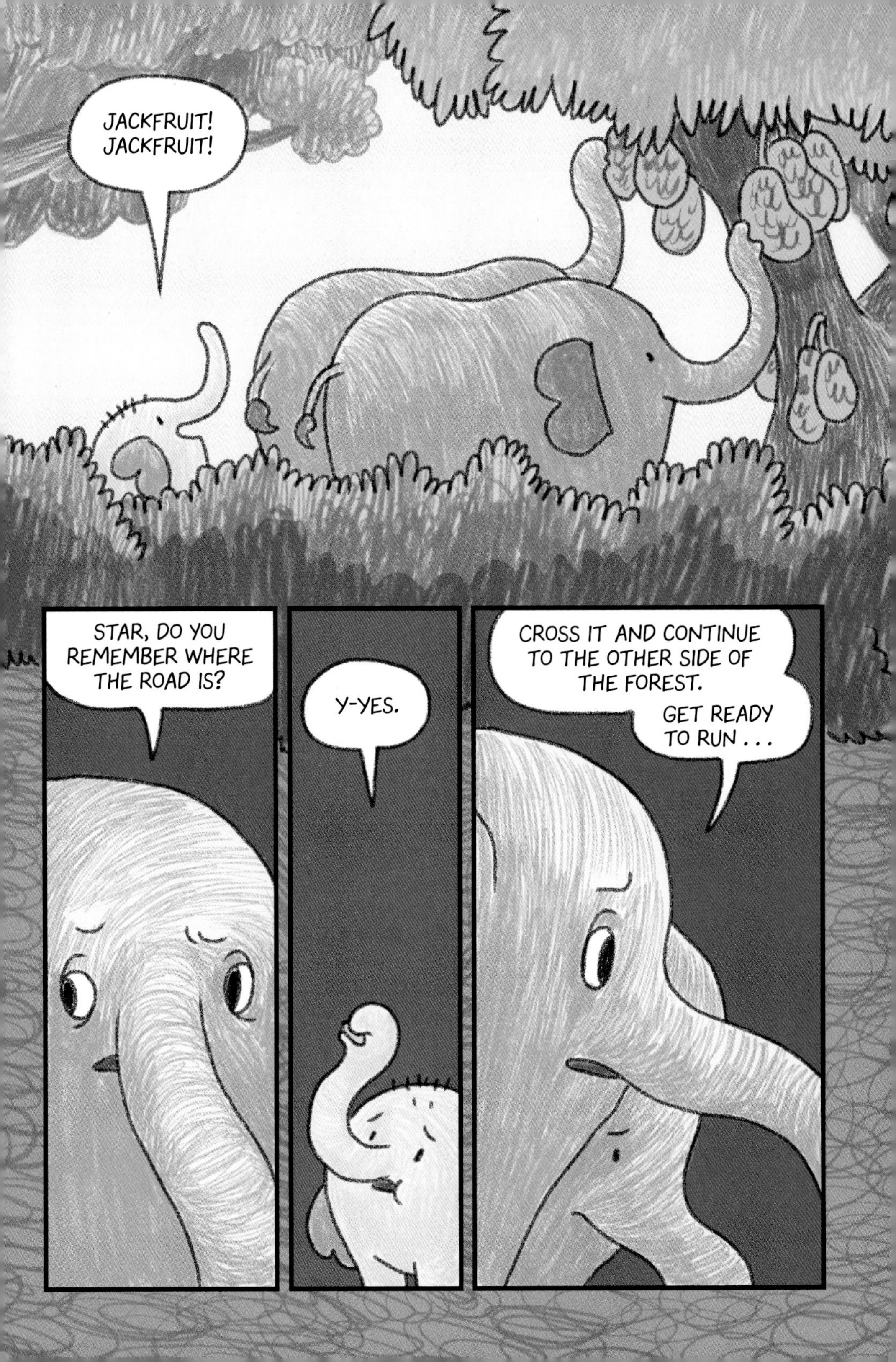
JACKFRUIT! JACKFRUIT!
STAR, DO YOU REMEMBER WHERE THE ROAD IS?
Y-YES.
CROSS IT AND CONTINUE TO THE OTHER SIDE OF THE FOREST.
GET READY TO RUN . . .

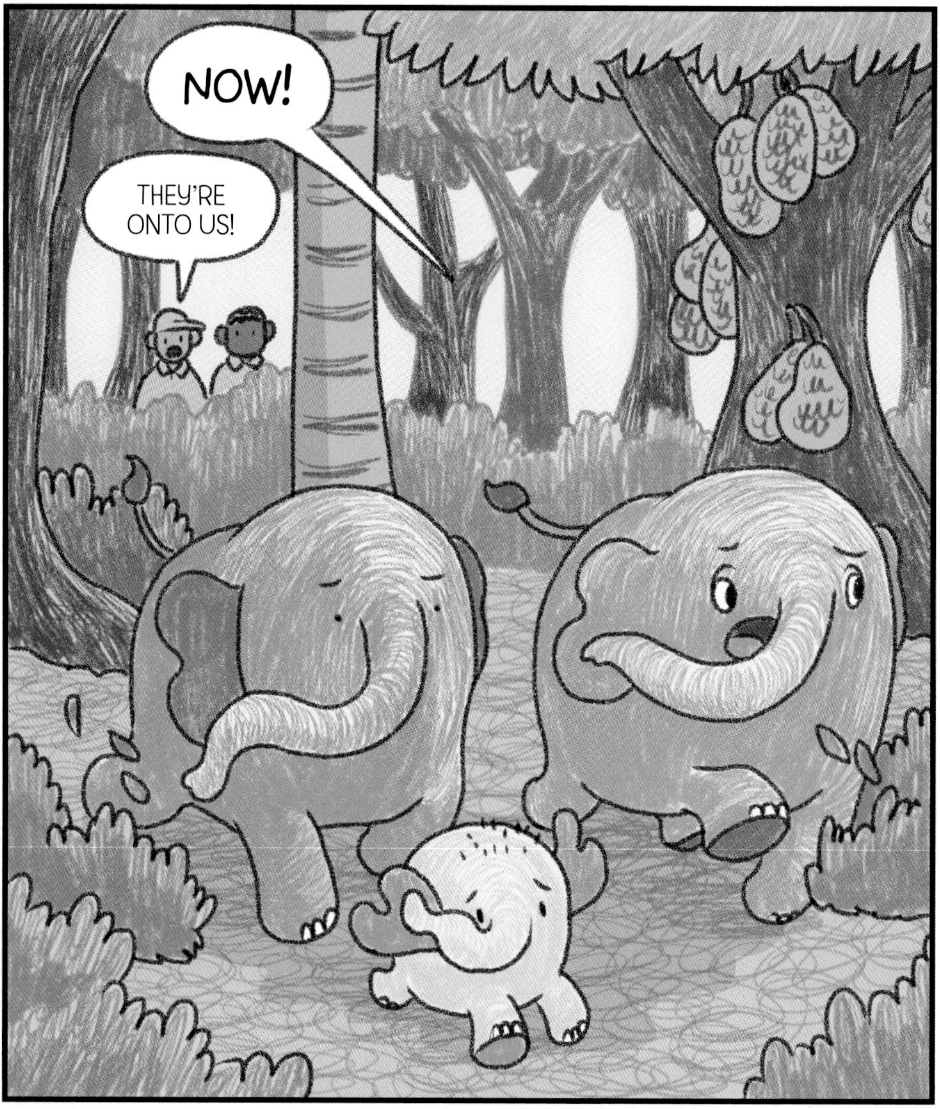
NOW!
THEY'RE ONTO US!

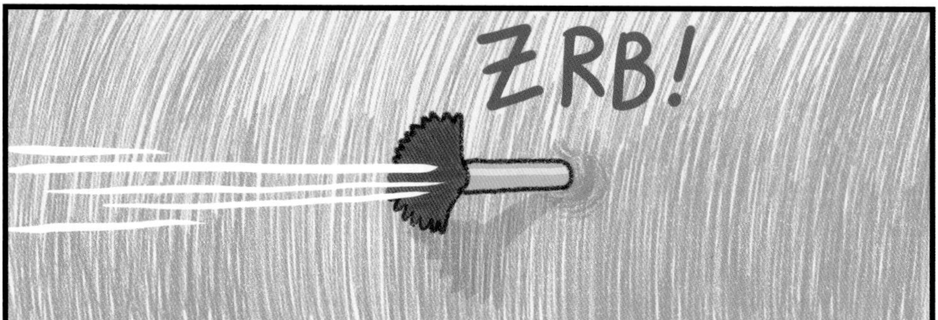
ZRB!

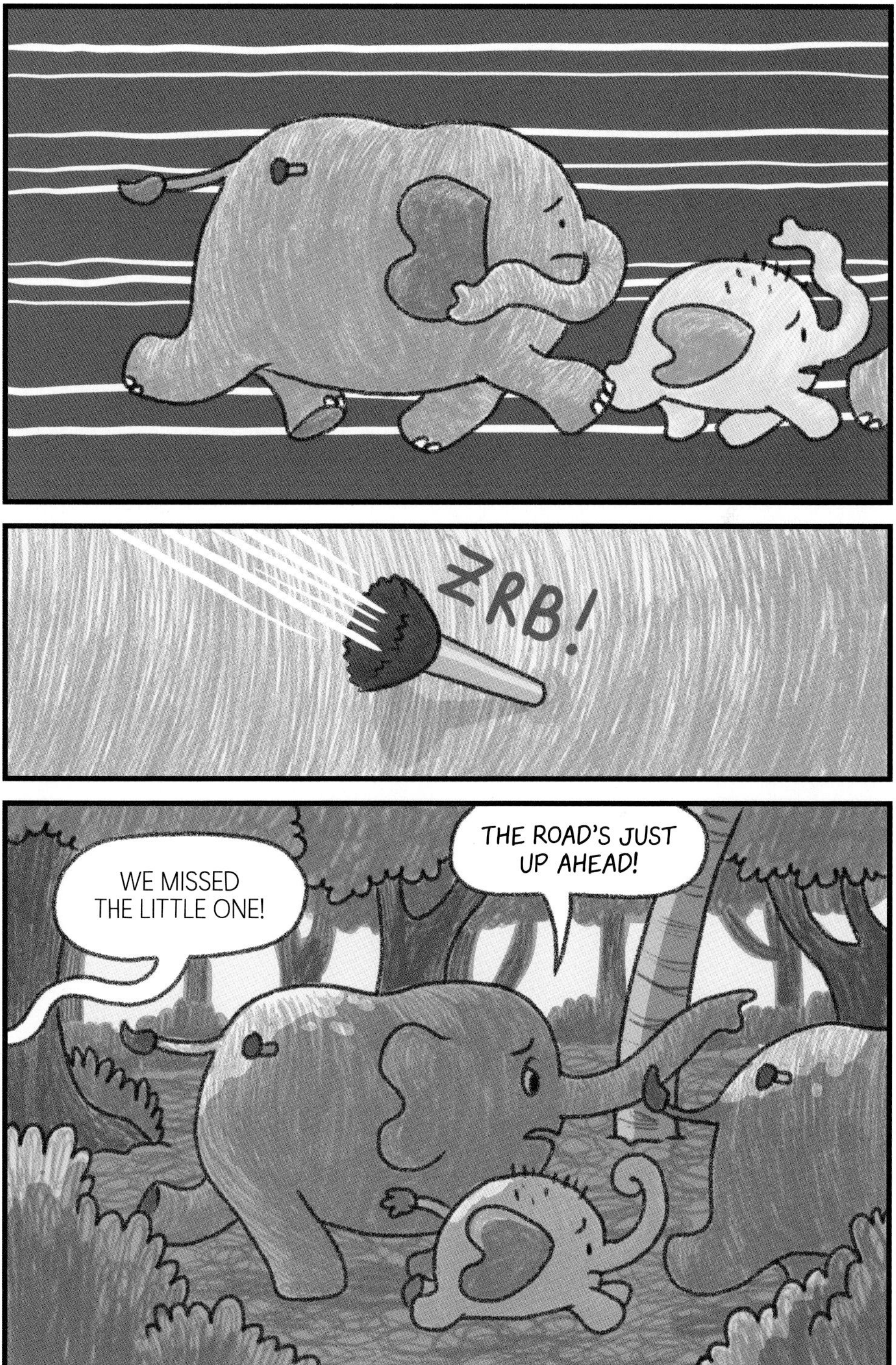
ZRB!
WE MISSED THE LITTLE ONE!
THE ROAD'S JUST UP AHEAD!

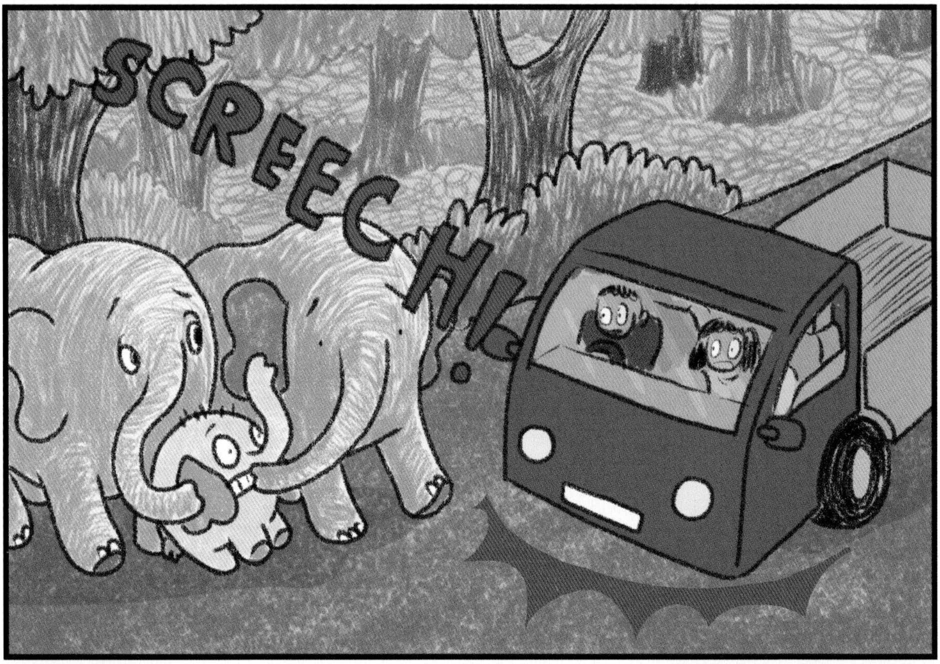
SCREECH!

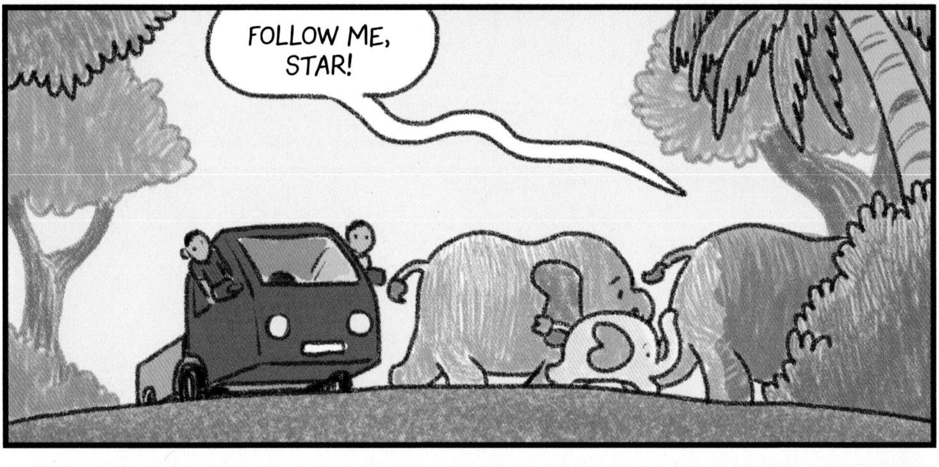
FOLLOW ME, STAR!

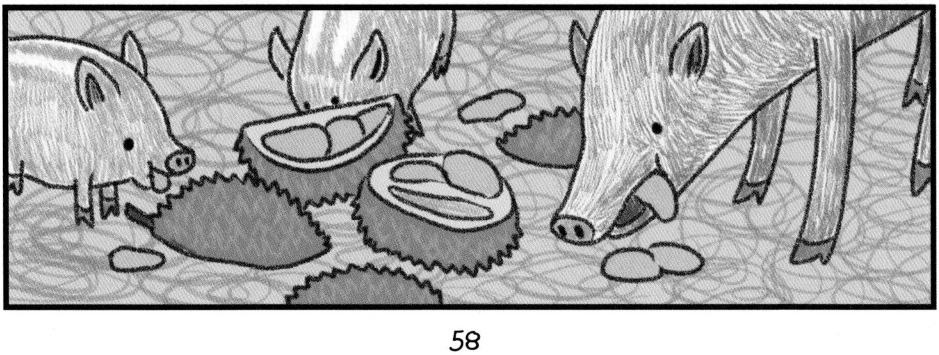

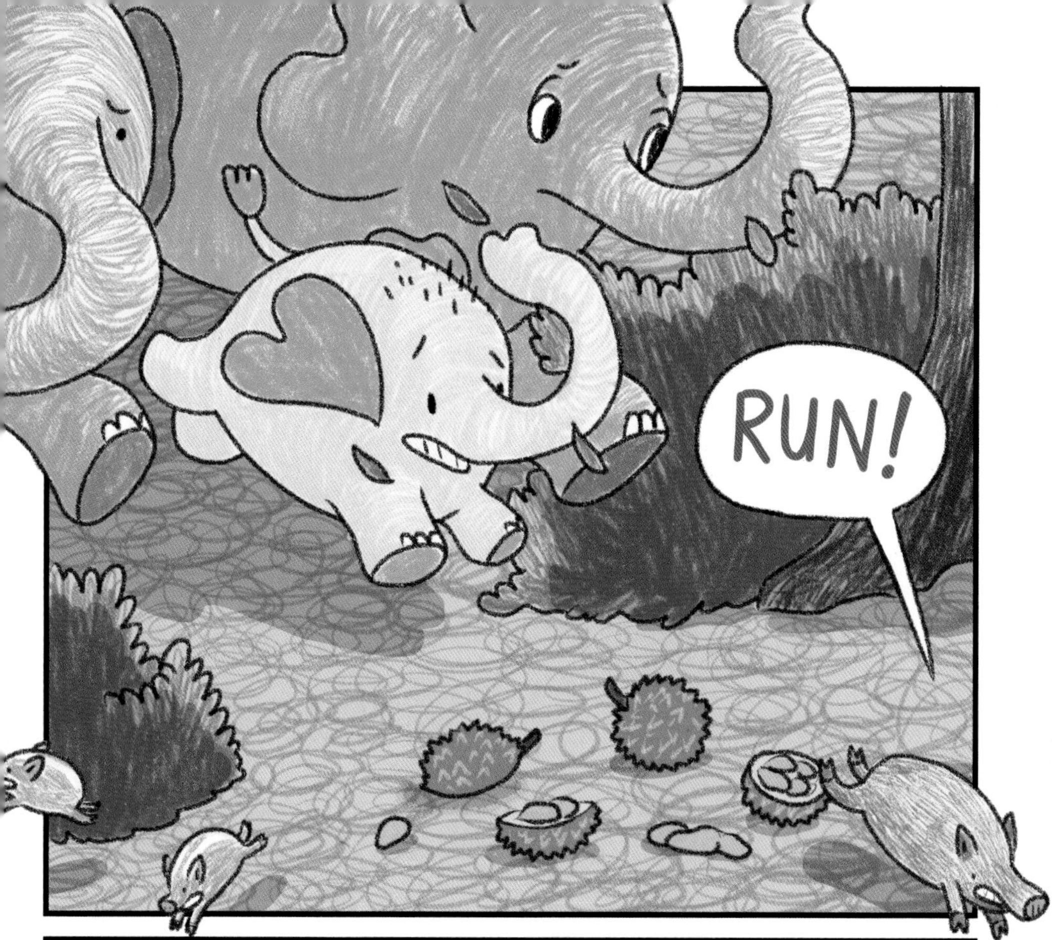
RUN!

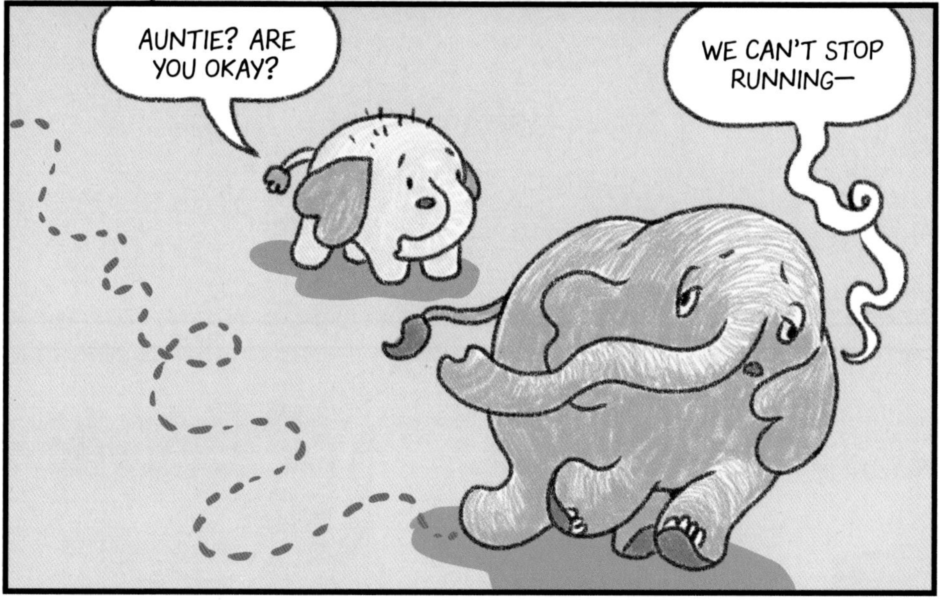
AUNTIE? ARE YOU OKAY?
WE CAN'T STOP RUNNING—

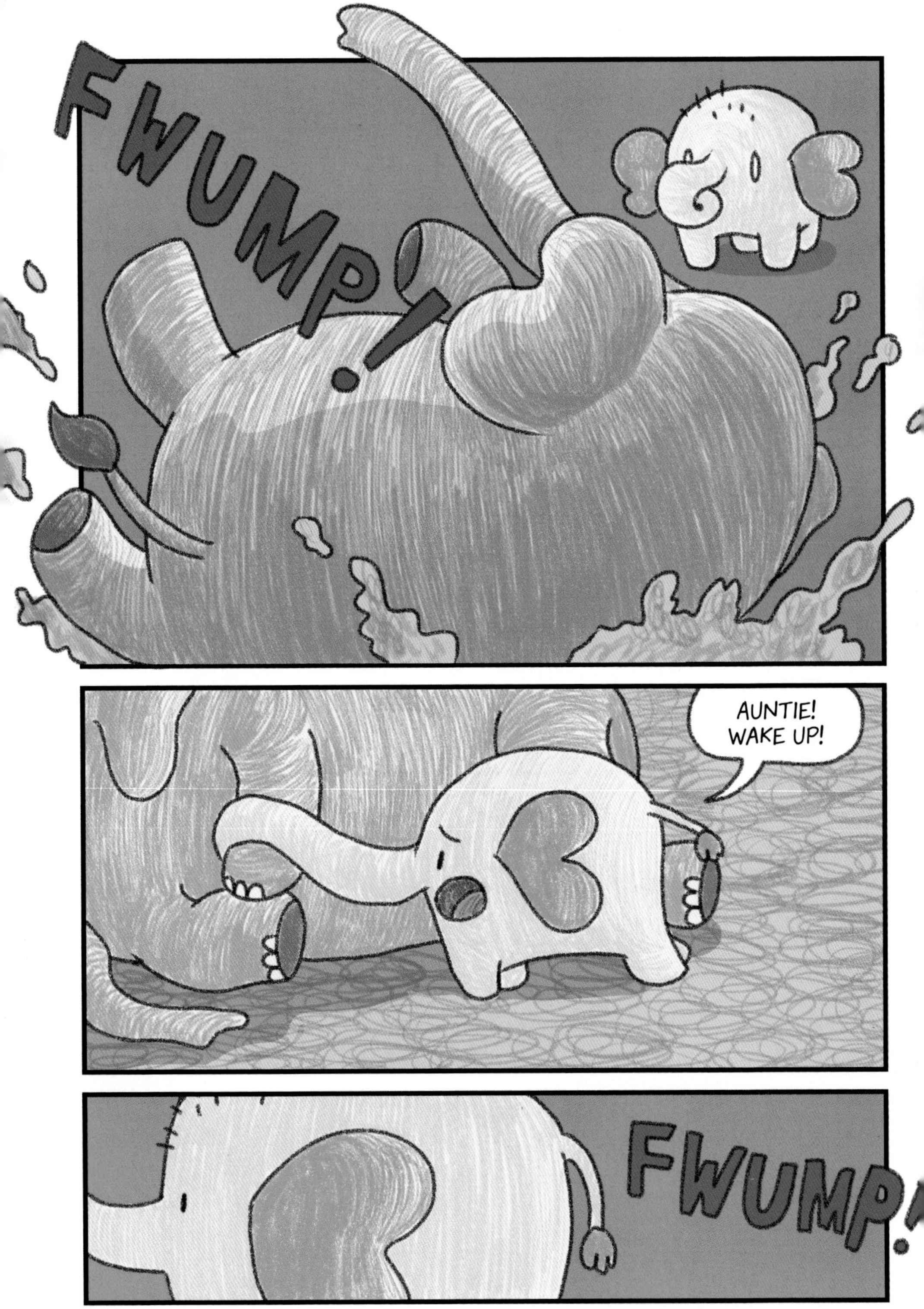
FWUMP!
AUNTIE! WAKE UP!
FWUMP!

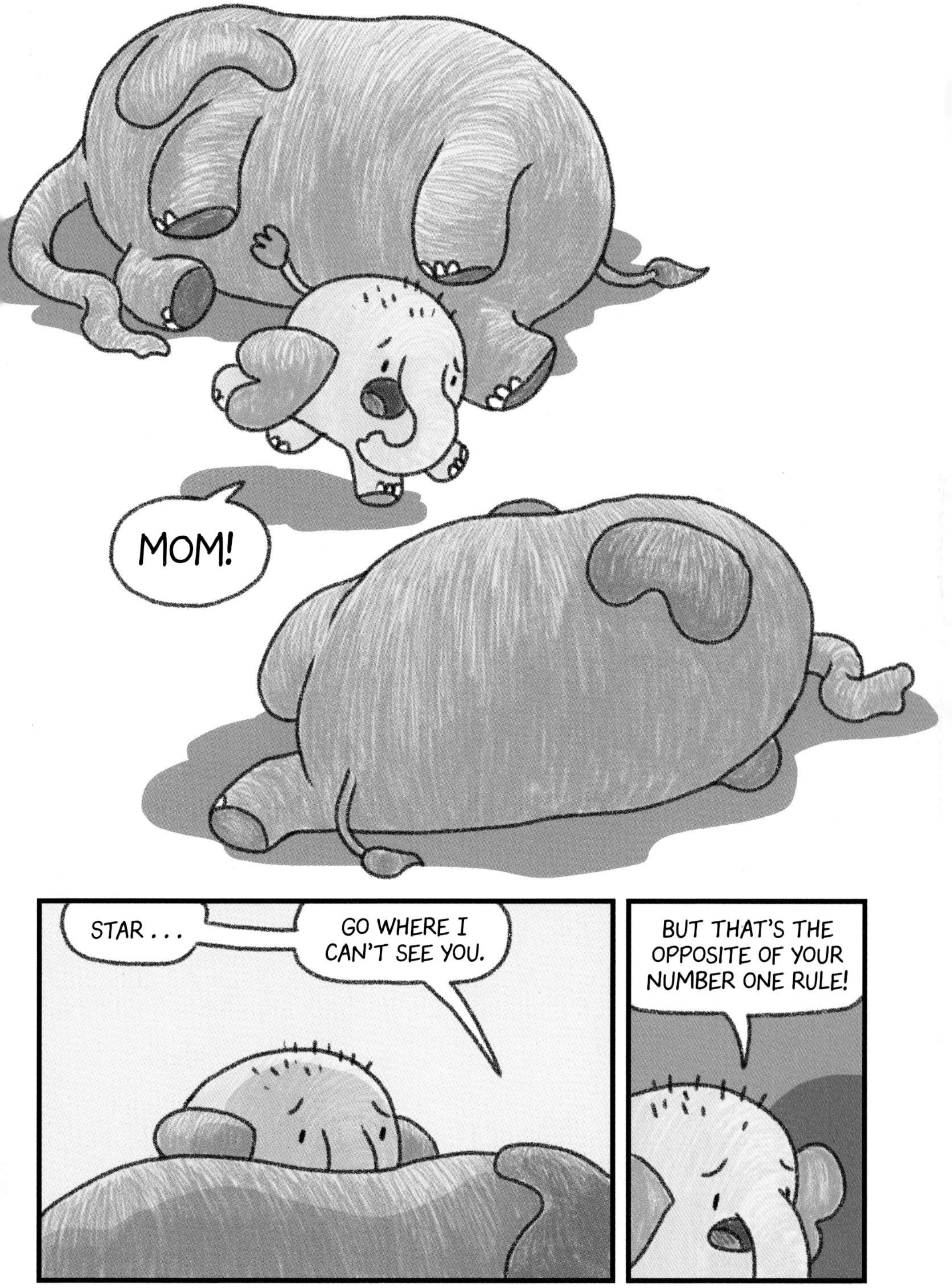
MOM!
STAR . . .
GO WHERE I CAN'T SEE YOU.
BUT THAT'S THE OPPOSITE OF YOUR NUMBER ONE RULE!

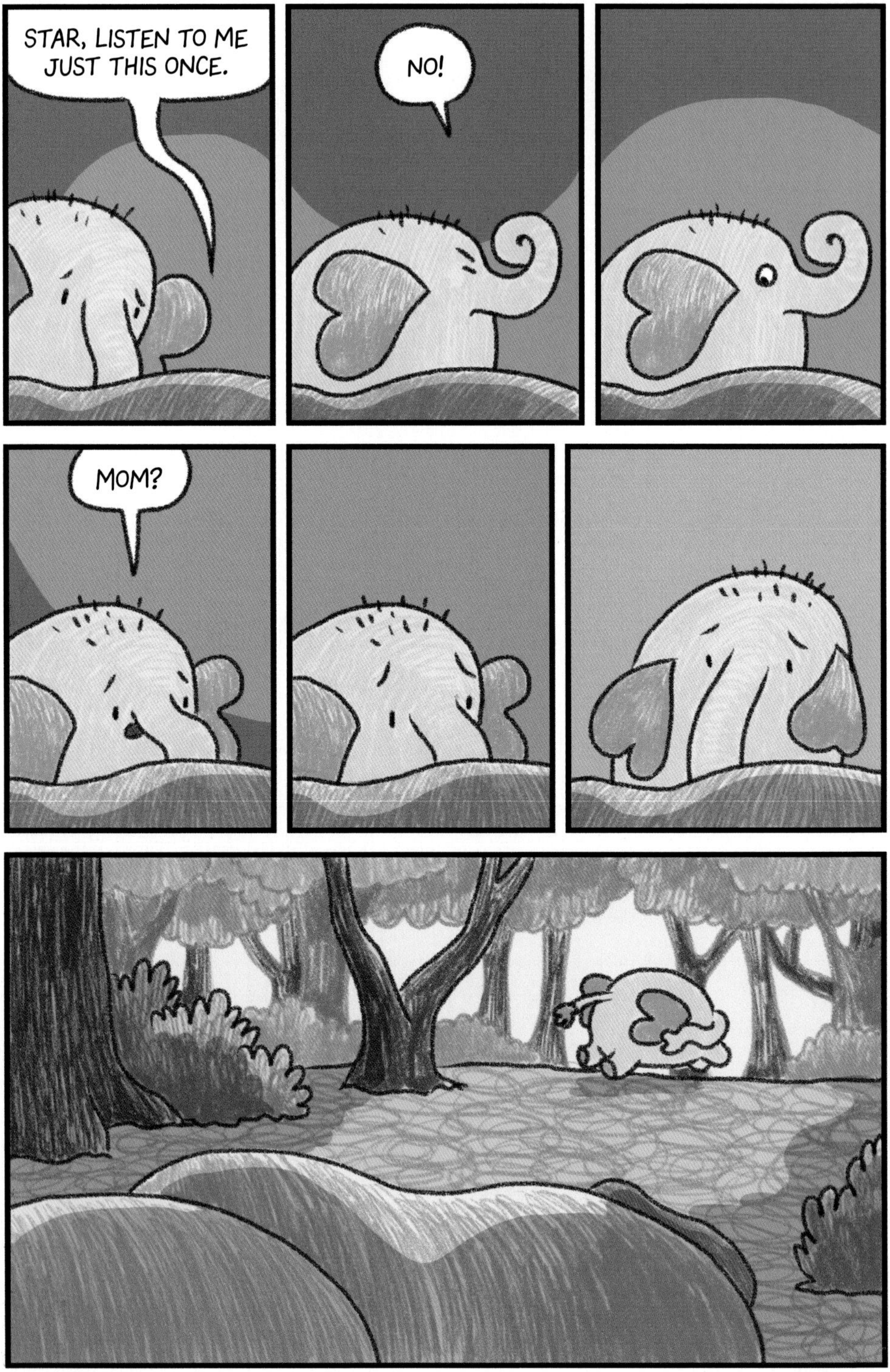
STAR, LISTEN TO ME JUST THIS ONCE.
NO!
MOM?

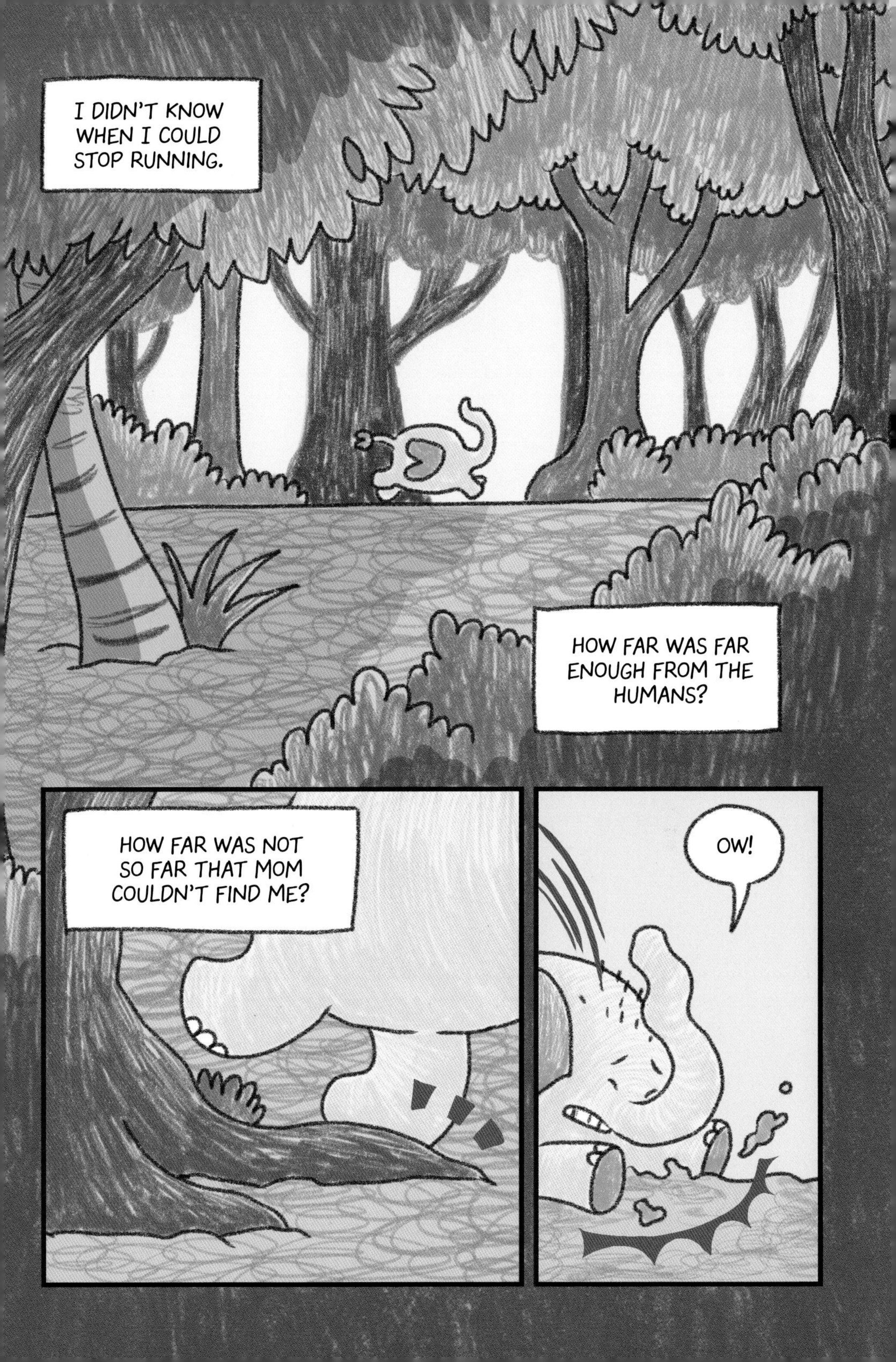
I DIDN'T KNOW WHEN I COULD STOP RUNNING.
HOW FAR WAS FAR ENOUGH FROM THE HUMANS?
HOW FAR WAS NOT SO FAR THAT MOM COULDN'T FIND ME?
OW!

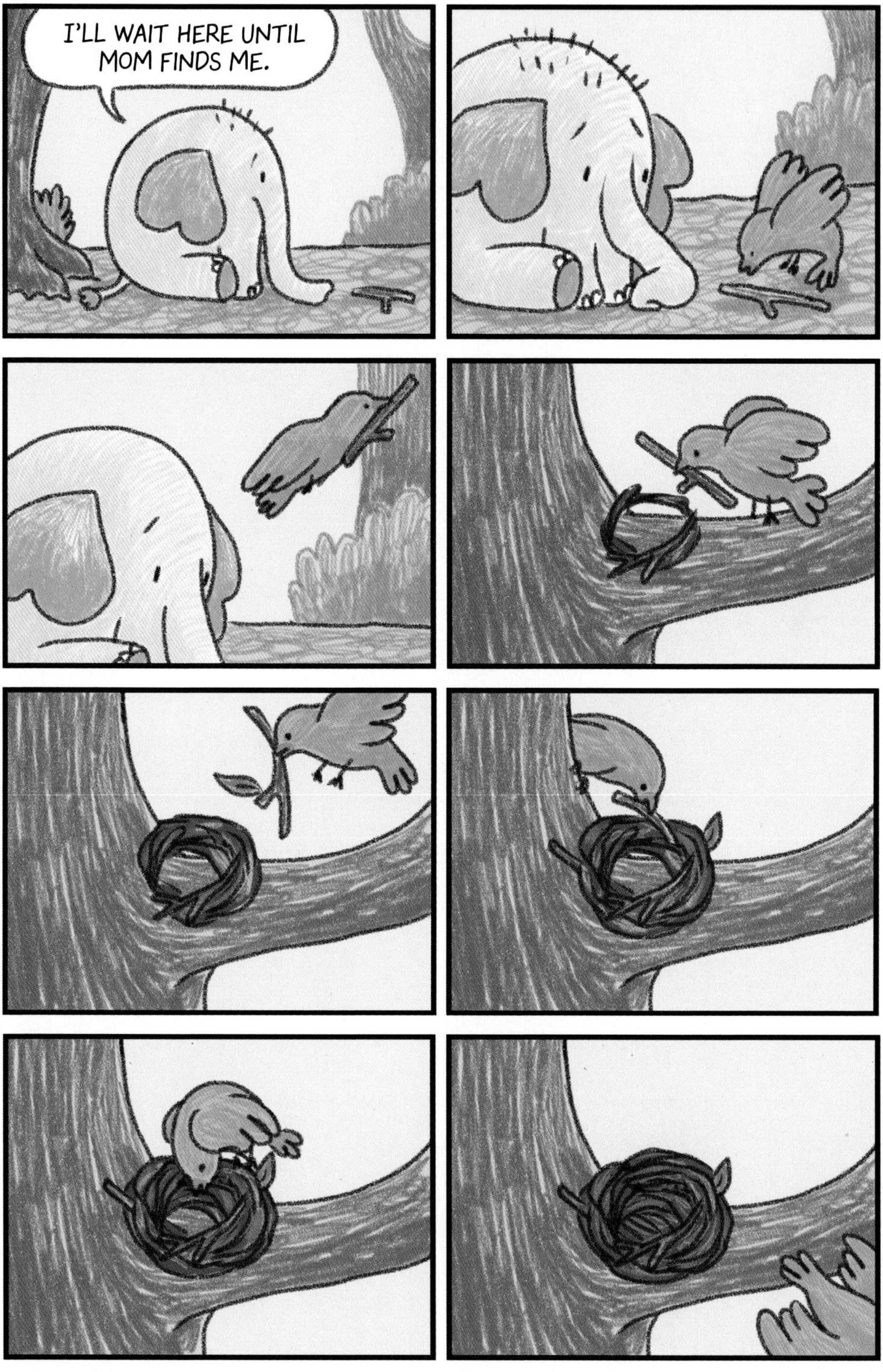
I'LL WAIT HERE UNTIL MOM FINDS ME.

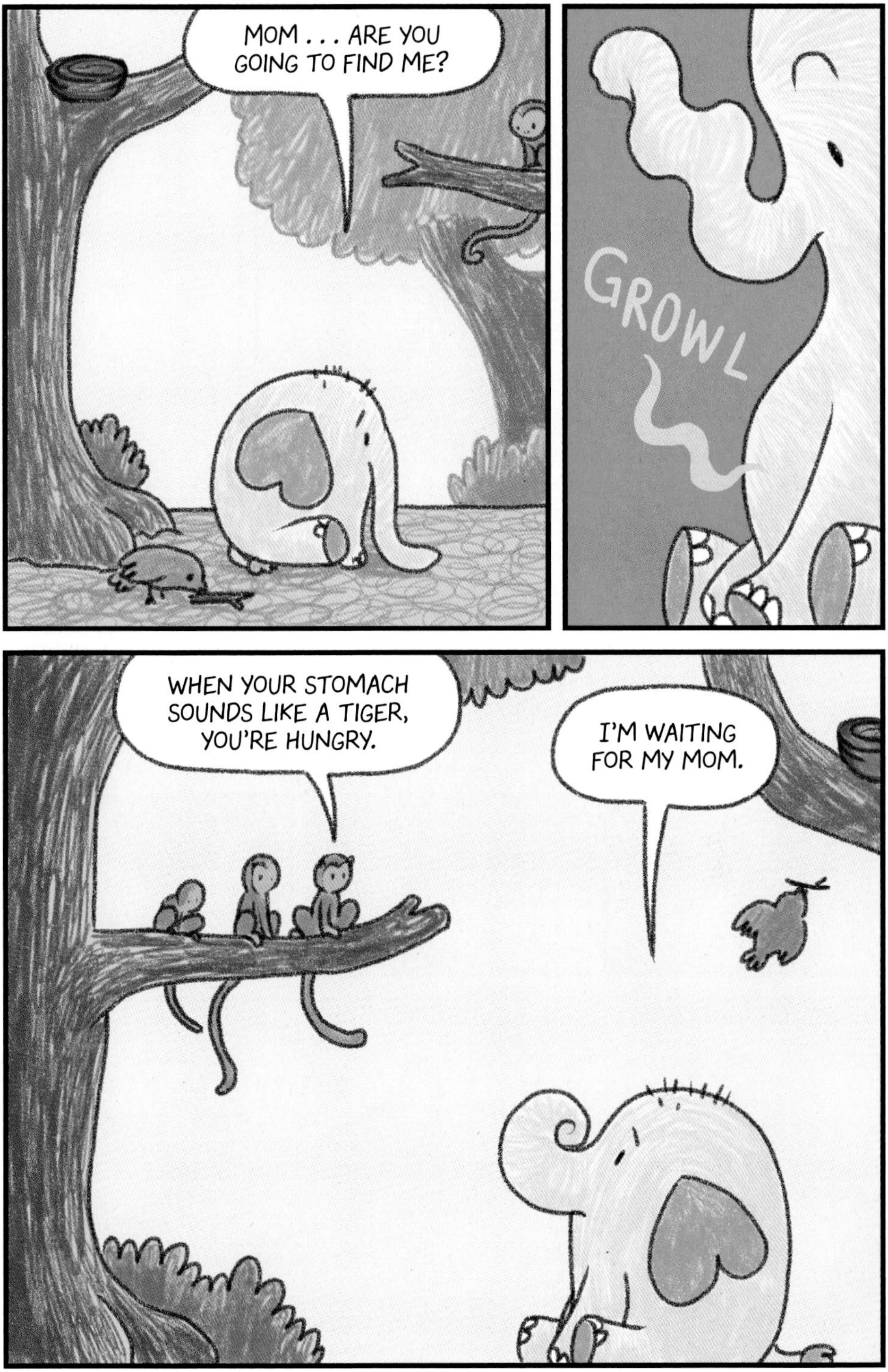
MOM . . . ARE YOU GOING TO FIND ME?
GROWL
WHEN YOUR STOMACH SOUNDS LIKE A TIGER, YOU'RE HUNGRY.
I'M WAITING FOR MY MOM.

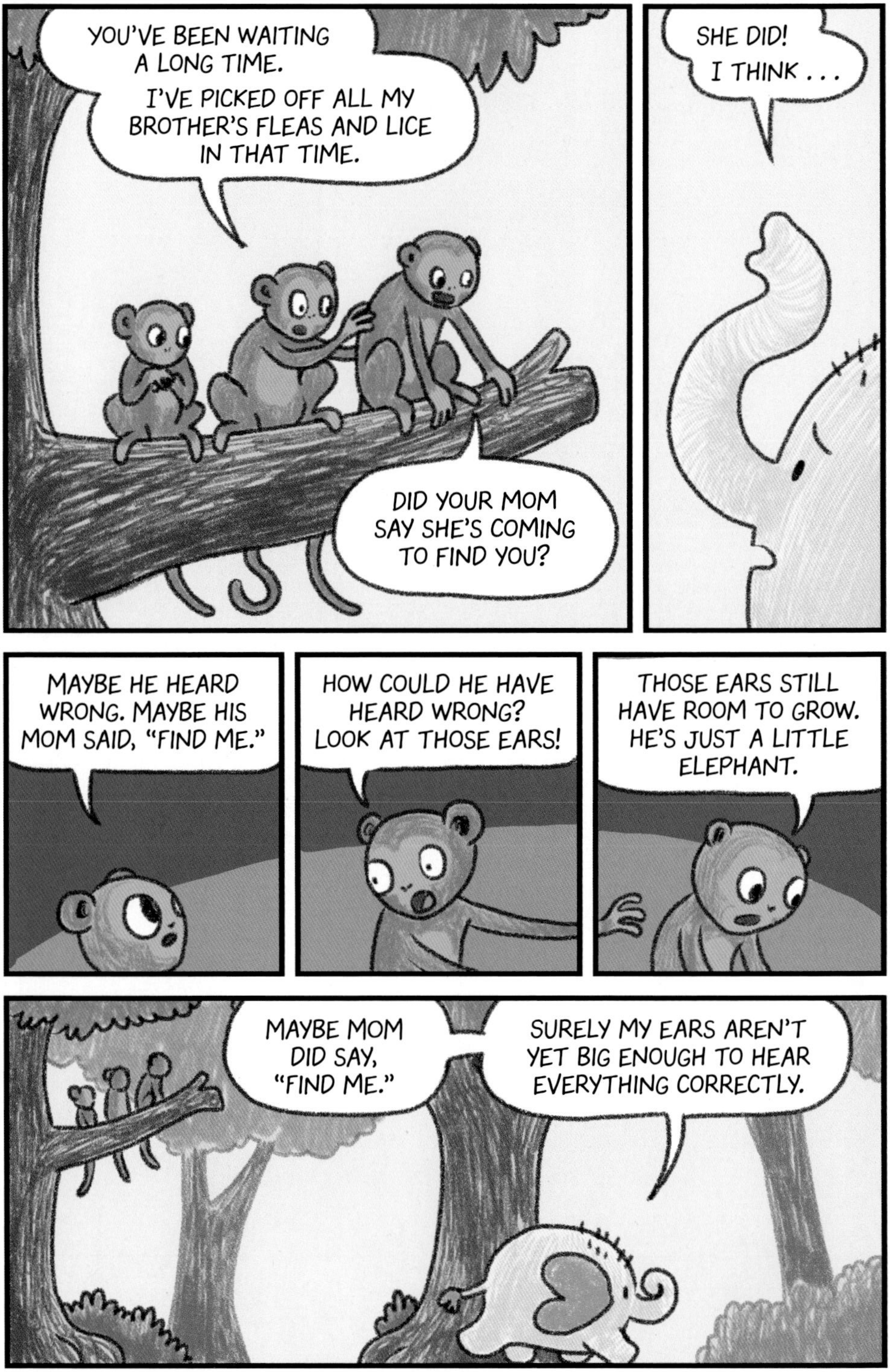
YOU'VE BEEN WAITING A LONG TIME.
I'VE PICKED OFF ALL MY BROTHER'S FLEAS AND LICE IN THAT TIME.
DID YOUR MOM SAY SHE'S COMING TO FIND YOU?
SHE DID! I THINK . . .
MAYBE HE HEARD WRONG. MAYBE HIS MOM SAID, "FIND ME."
HOW COULD HE HAVE HEARD WRONG? LOOK AT THOSE EARS!
THOSE EARS STILL HAVE ROOM TO GROW. HE'S JUST A LITTLE ELEPHANT.
MAYBE MOM DID SAY, "FIND ME."
SURELY MY EARS AREN'T YET BIG ENOUGH TO HEAR EVERYTHING CORRECTLY.

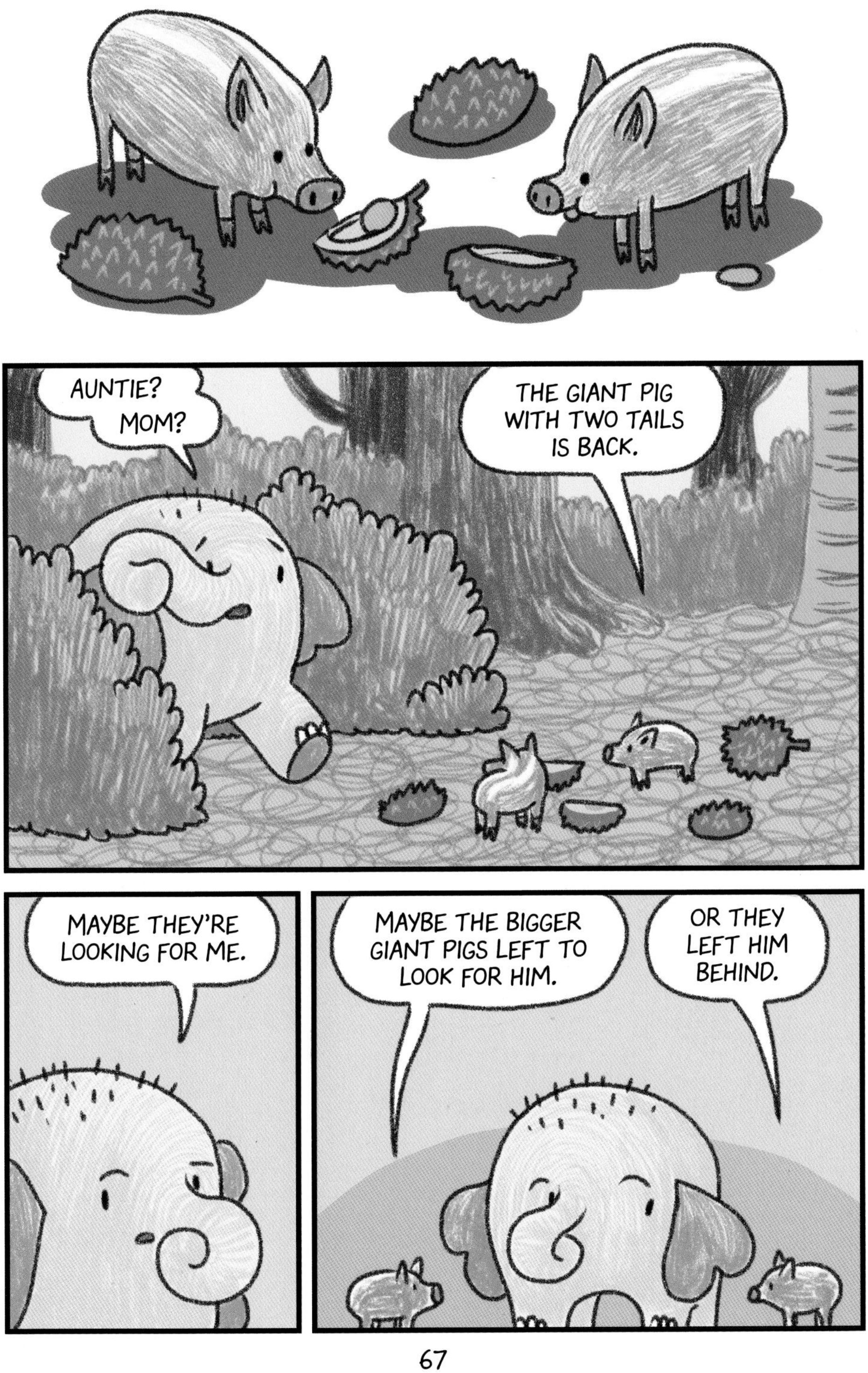
AUNTIE?
MOM?
THE GIANT PIG WITH TWO TAILS IS BACK.
MAYBE THEY'RE LOOKING FOR ME.
MAYBE THE BIGGER GIANT PIGS LEFT TO LOOK FOR HIM.
OR THEY LEFT HIM BEHIND.

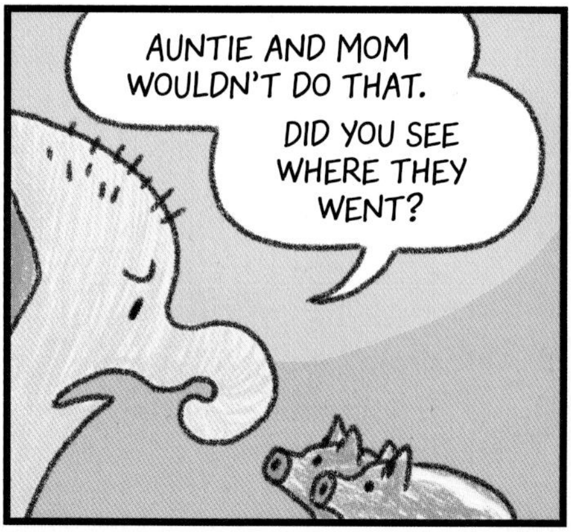
AUNTIE AND MOM WOULDN'T DO THAT.
DID YOU SEE WHERE THEY WENT?
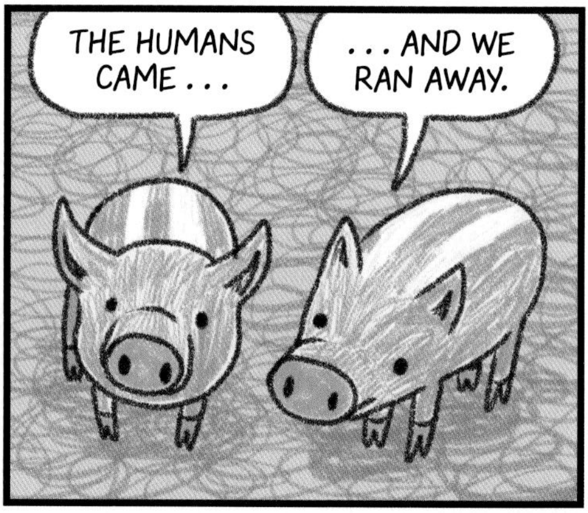
THE HUMANS CAME . . .
. . . AND WE RAN AWAY.
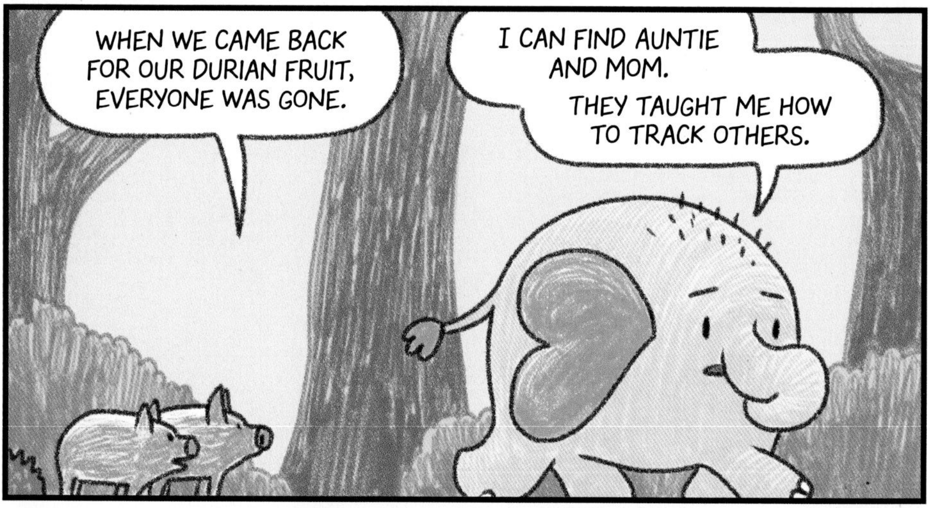
WHEN WE CAME BACK FOR OUR DURIAN FRUIT, EVERYONE WAS GONE.
I CAN FIND AUNTIE AND MOM.
THEY TAUGHT ME HOW TO TRACK OTHERS.
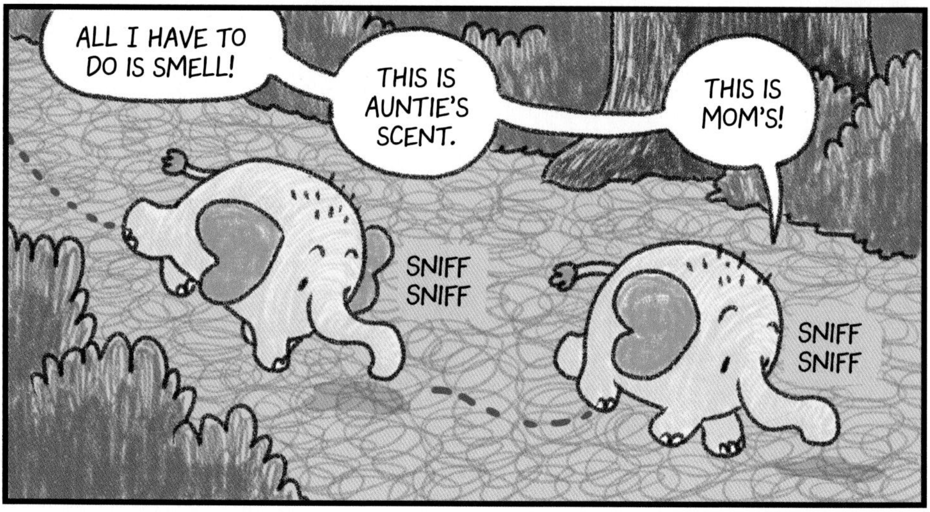
ALL I HAVE TO DO IS SMELL!
THIS IS AUNTIE'S SCENT.
THIS IS MOM'S!
SNIFF SNIFF
SNIFF SNIFF

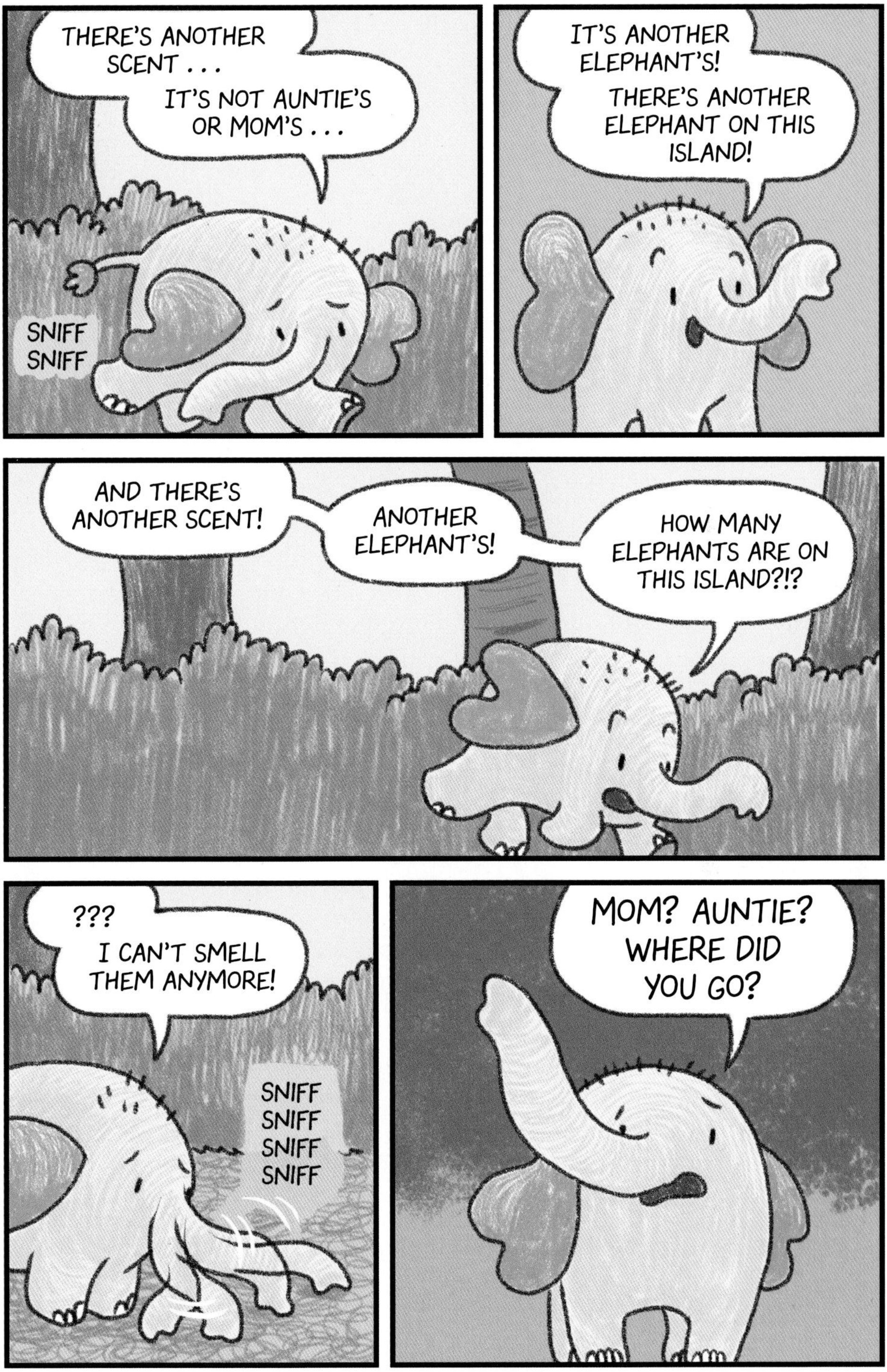
THERE'S ANOTHER SCENT . . .
IT'S NOT AUNTIE'S OR MOM'S . . .
SNIFF SNIFF
IT'S ANOTHER ELEPHANT'S!
THERE'S ANOTHER ELEPHANT ON THIS ISLAND!
AND THERE'S ANOTHER SCENT!
ANOTHER ELEPHANT'S!
HOW MANY ELEPHANTS ARE ON THIS ISLAND?!?
???
I CAN'T SMELL THEM ANYMORE!
SNIFF SNIFF SNIFF SNIFF
MOM? AUNTIE? WHERE DID YOU GO?

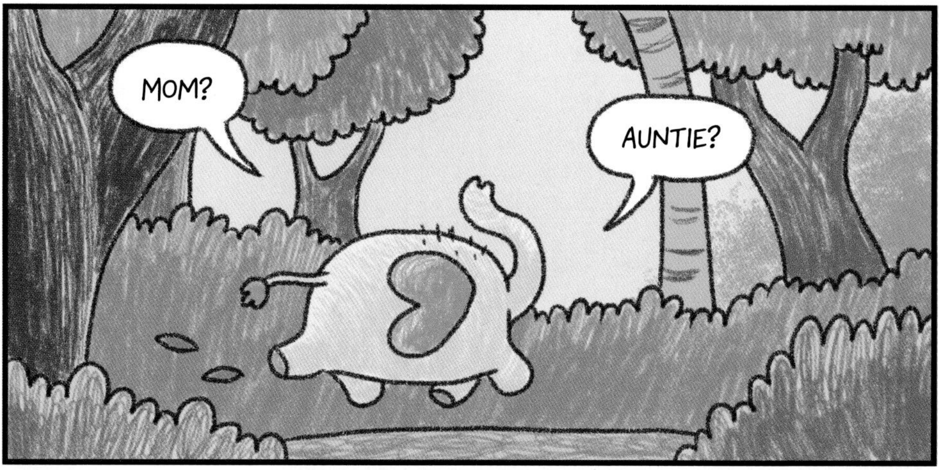
MOM?
AUNTIE?

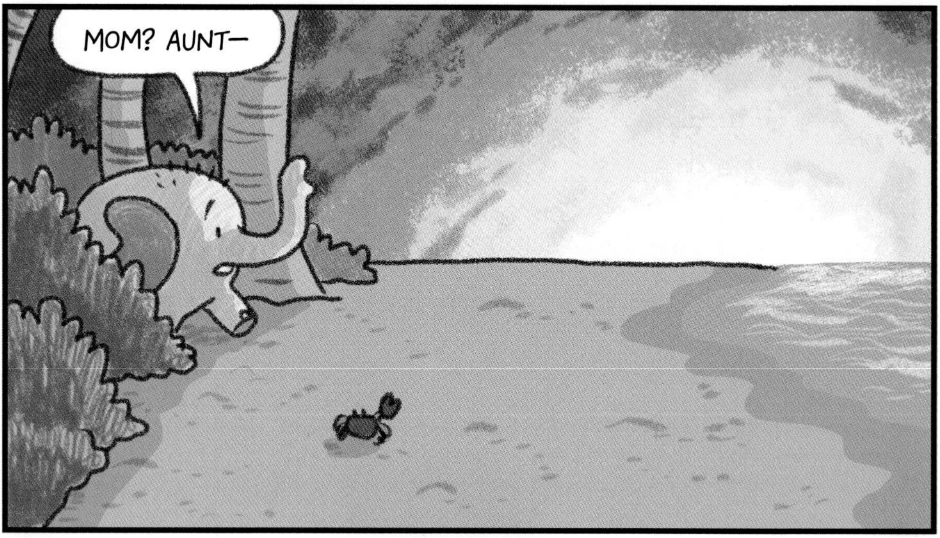
MOM? AUNT—

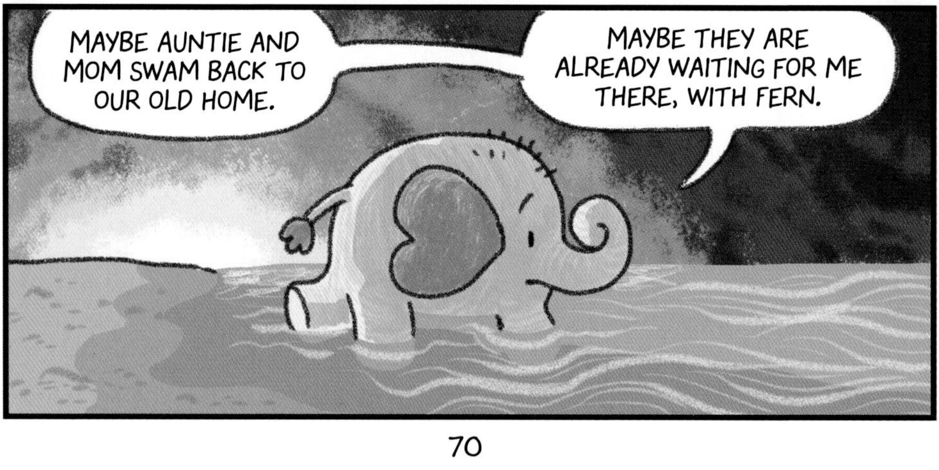
MAYBE AUNTIE AND MOM SWAM BACK TO OUR OLD HOME.
MAYBE THEY ARE ALREADY WAITING FOR ME THERE, WITH FERN.

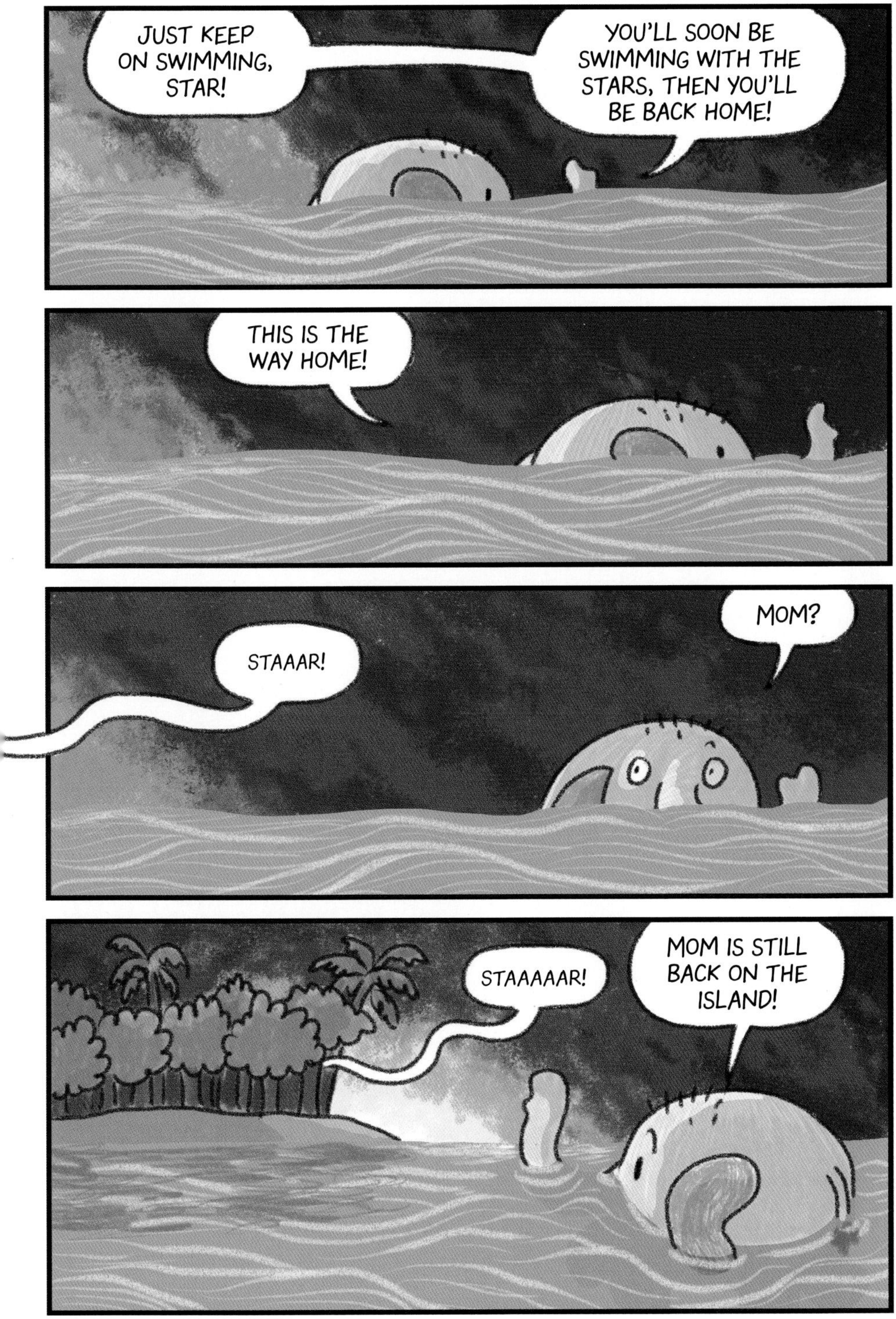
JUST KEEP ON SWIMMING, STAR!
YOU'LL SOON BE SWIMMING WITH THE STARS, THEN YOU'LL BE BACK HOME!
THIS IS THE WAY HOME!
STAAAR!
MOM?
STAAAAAR!
MOM IS STILL BACK ON THE ISLAND!

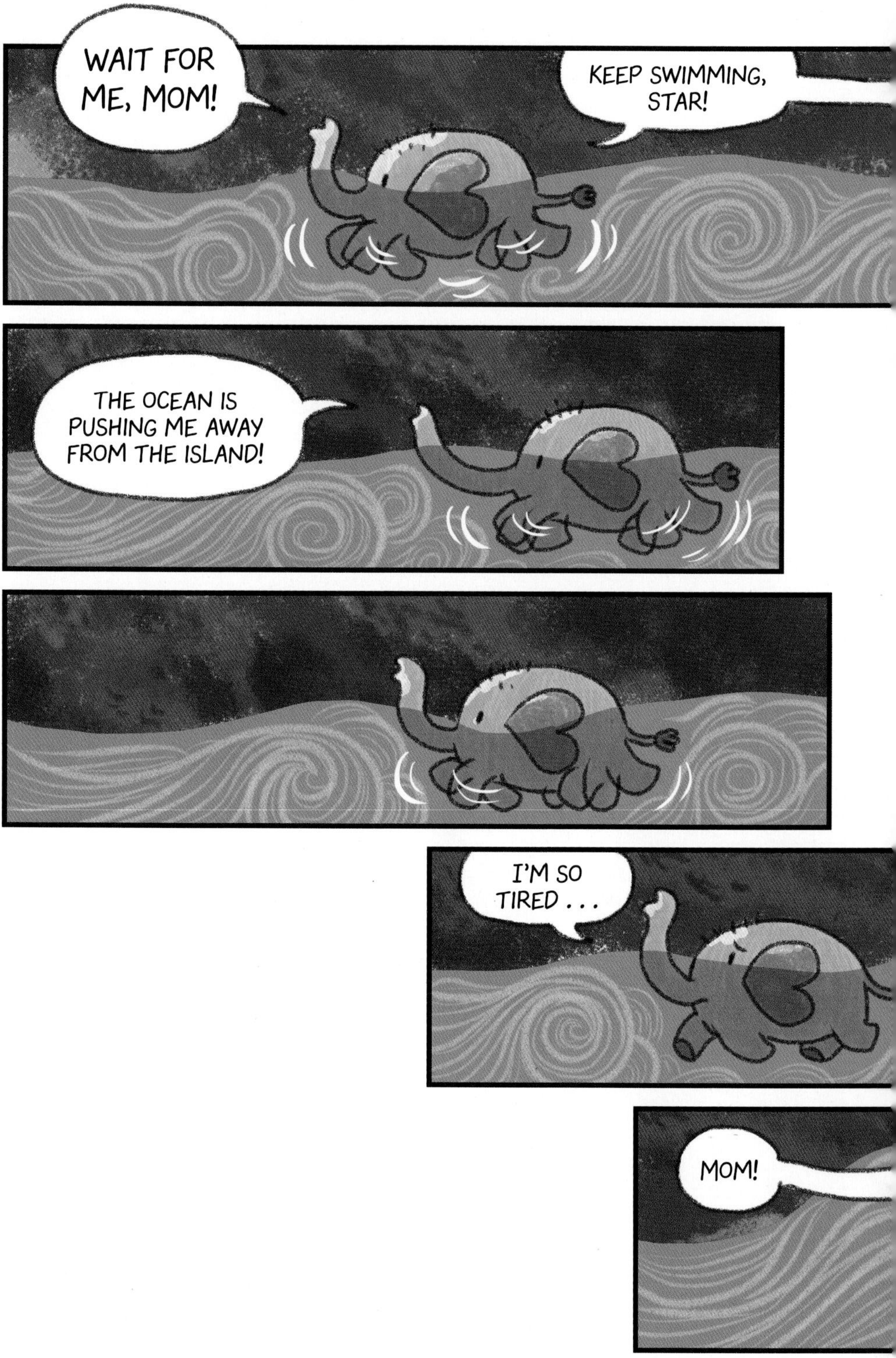
WAIT FOR ME, MOM!
KEEP SWIMMING, STAR!
THE OCEAN IS PUSHING ME AWAY FROM THE ISLAND!
I'M SO TIRED . . .
MOM!

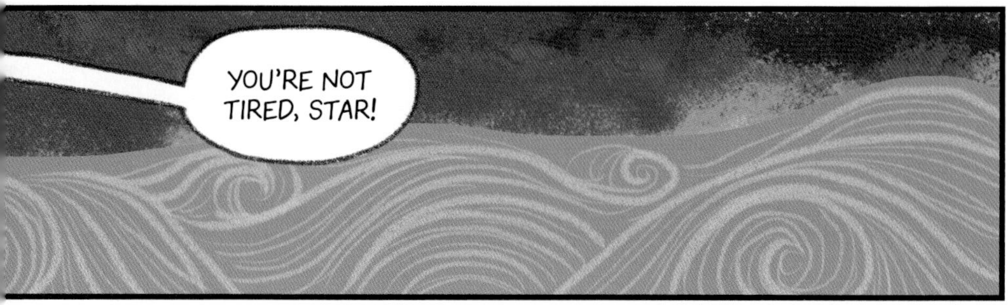
YOU'RE NOT
TIRED, STAR!

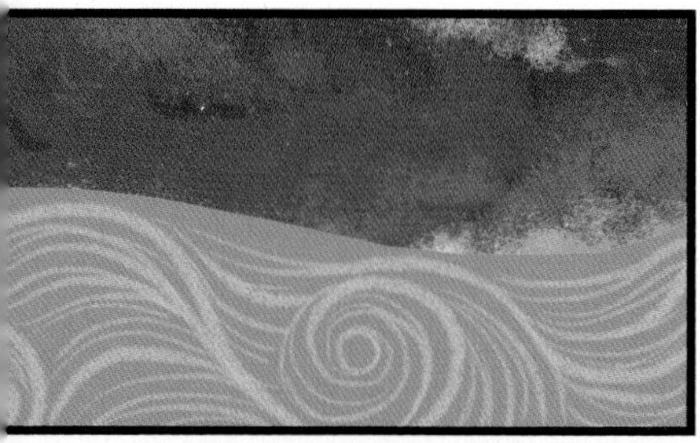

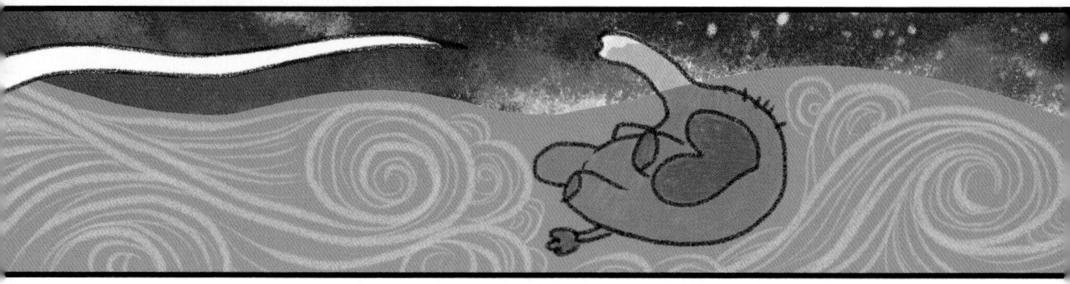

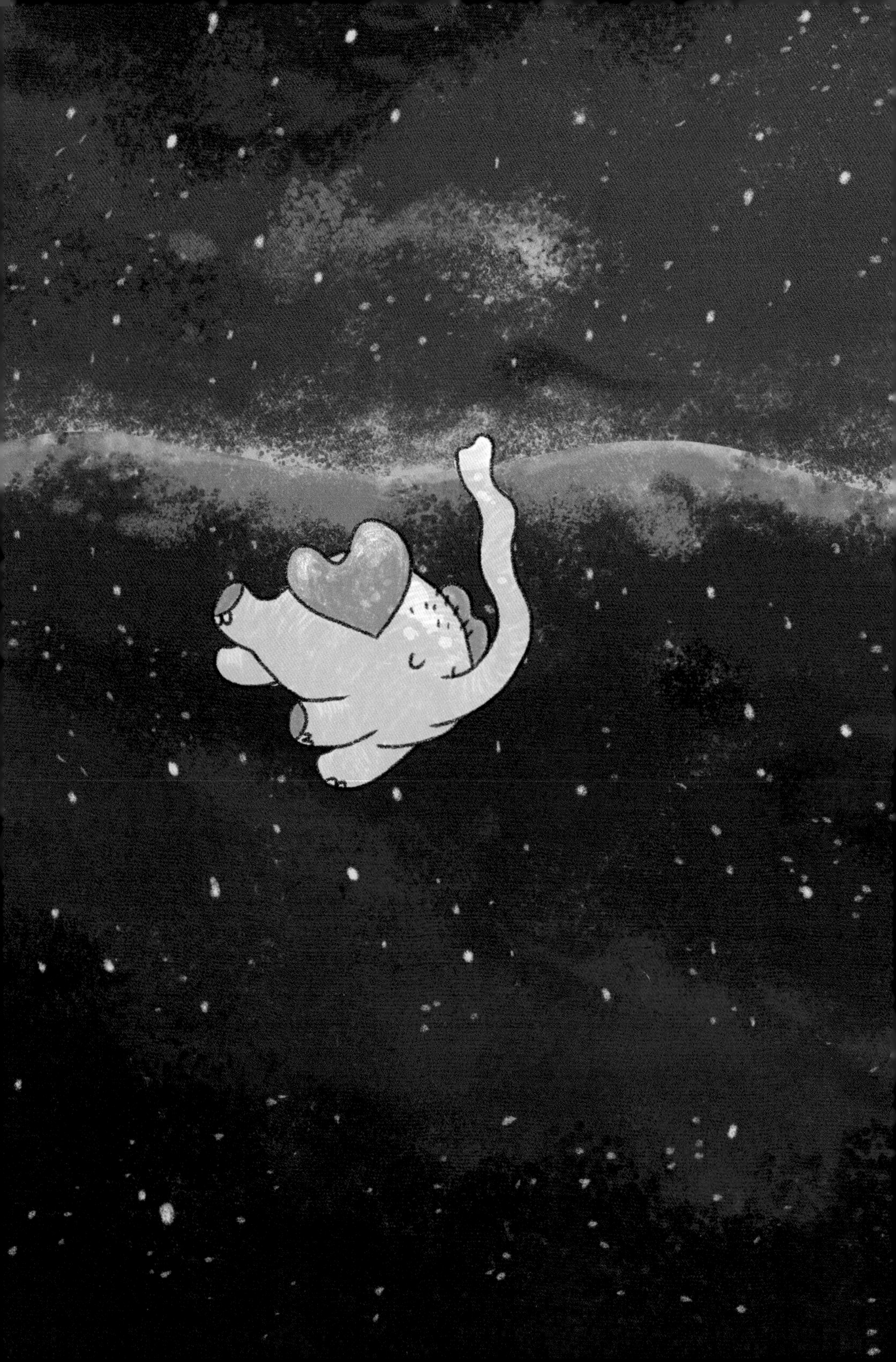

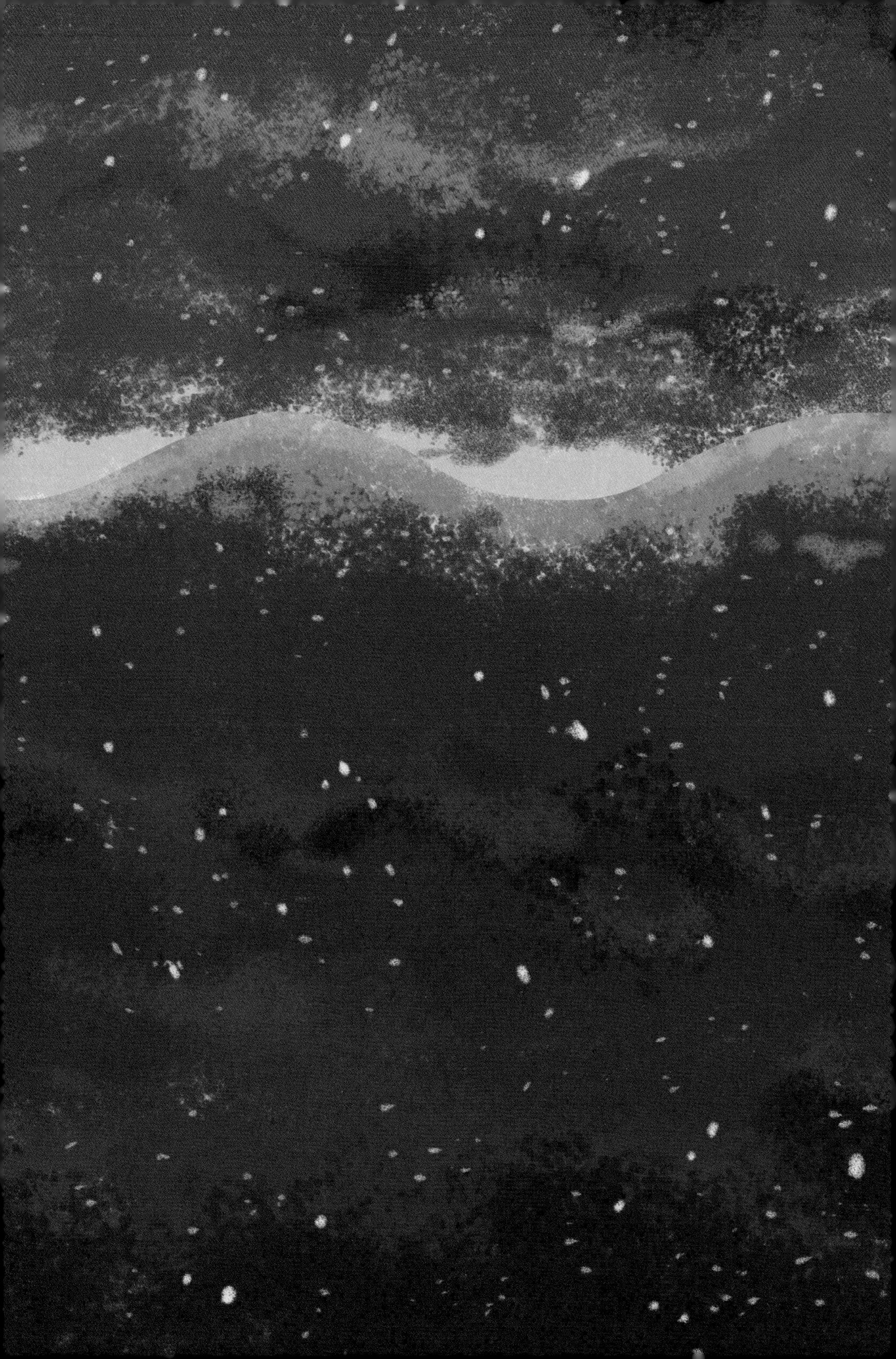

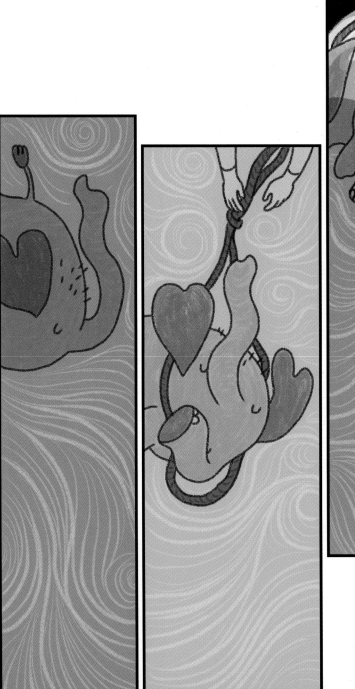

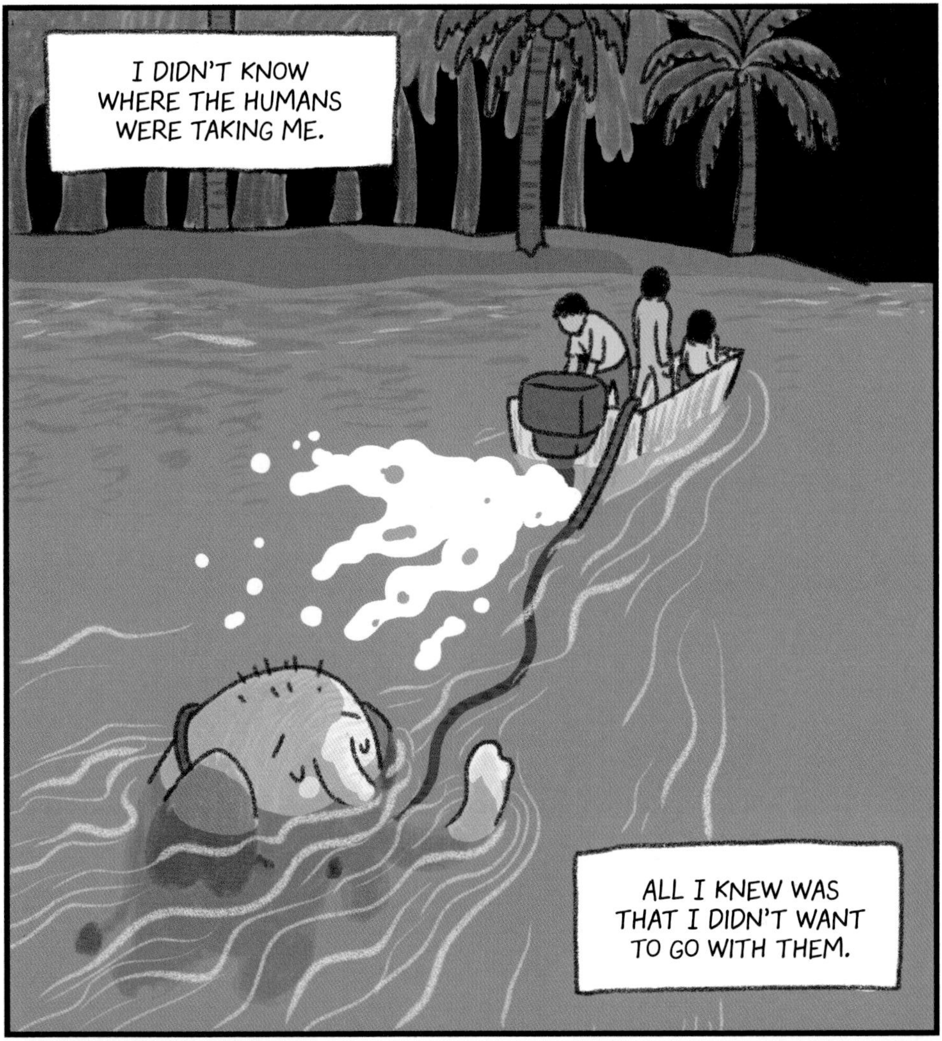
I DIDN'T KNOW
WHERE THE HUMANS
WERE TAKING ME.
ALL I KNEW WAS
THAT I DIDN'T WANT
TO GO WITH THEM.

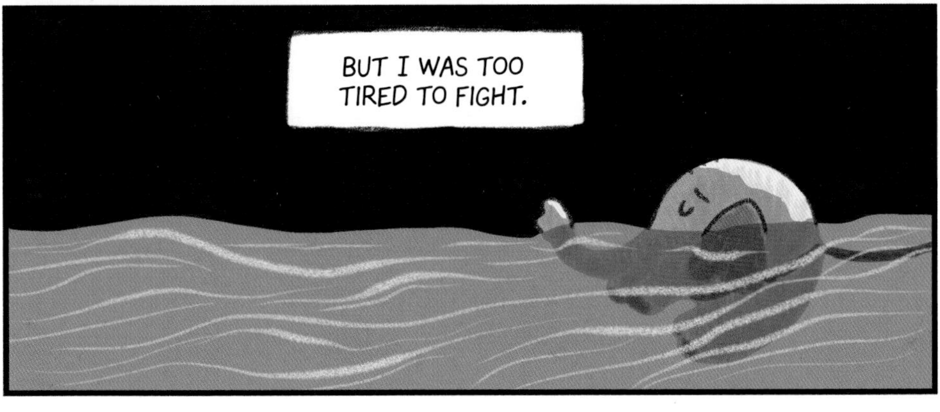
BUT I WAS TOO
TIRED TO FIGHT.

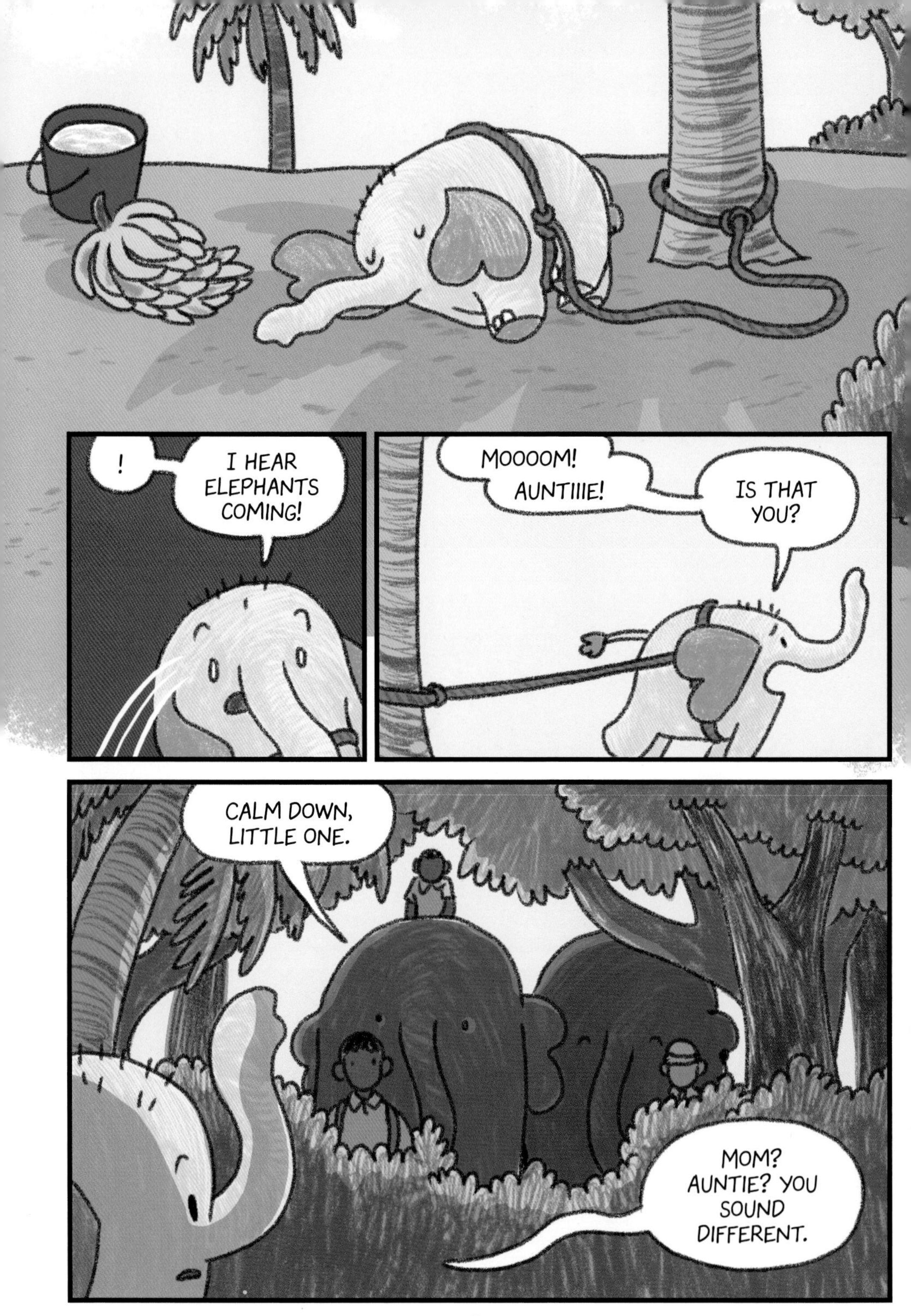
!
I HEAR ELEPHANTS COMING!
MOOOOM!
AUNTIIIE!
IS THAT YOU?
CALM DOWN, LITTLE ONE.
MOM? AUNTIE? YOU SOUND DIFFERENT.

ARE YOU THE TWO ELEPHANTS I SMELLED YESTERDAY?

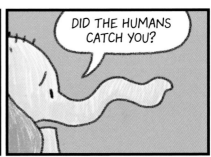

DID THE HUMANS CATCH YOU?

GET AWAY!

79

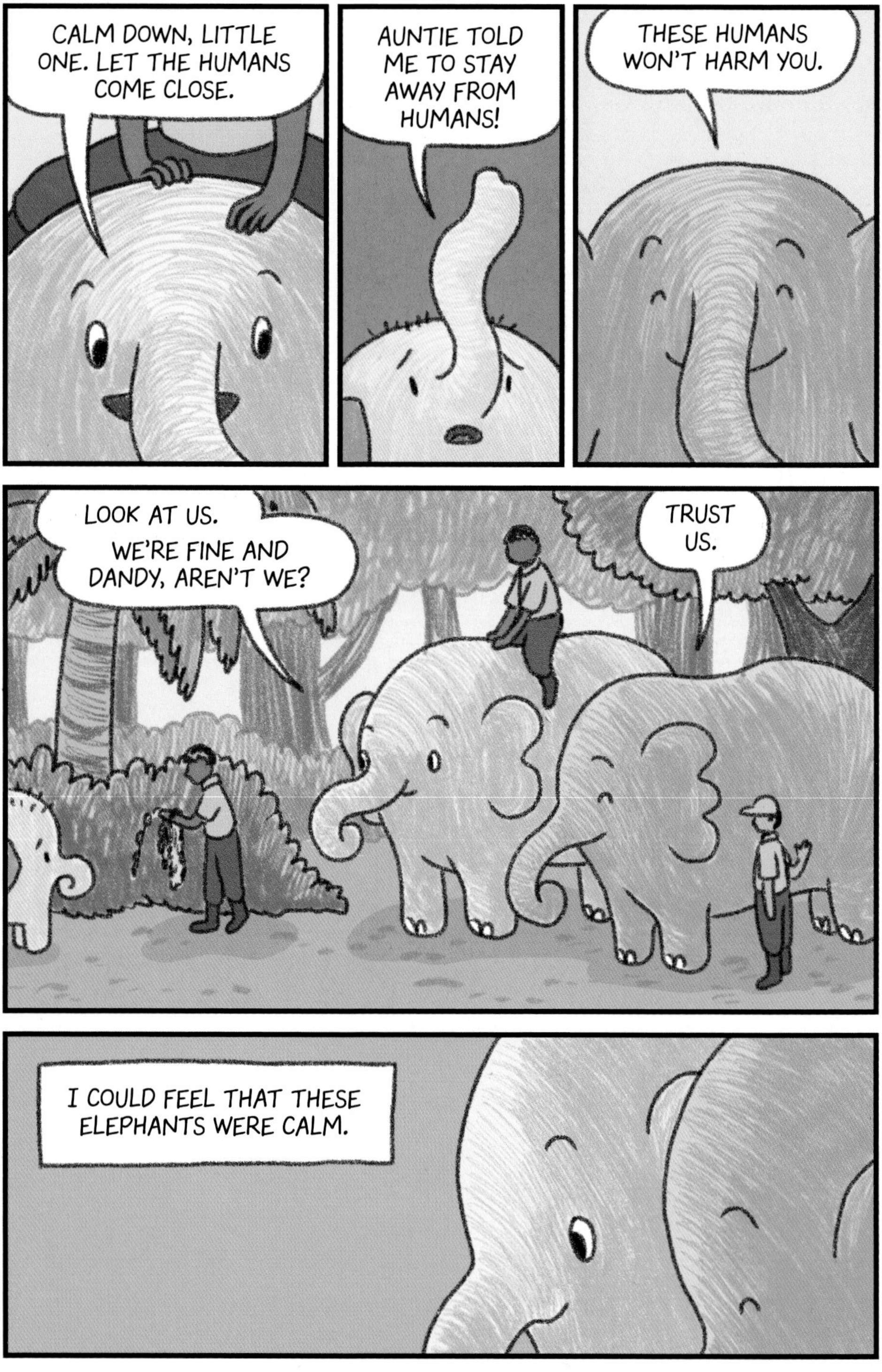
CALM DOWN, LITTLE ONE. LET THE HUMANS COME CLOSE.
AUNTIE TOLD ME TO STAY AWAY FROM HUMANS!
THESE HUMANS WON'T HARM YOU.
LOOK AT US.
WE'RE FINE AND DANDY, AREN'T WE?
TRUST US.
I COULD FEEL THAT THESE ELEPHANTS WERE CALM.

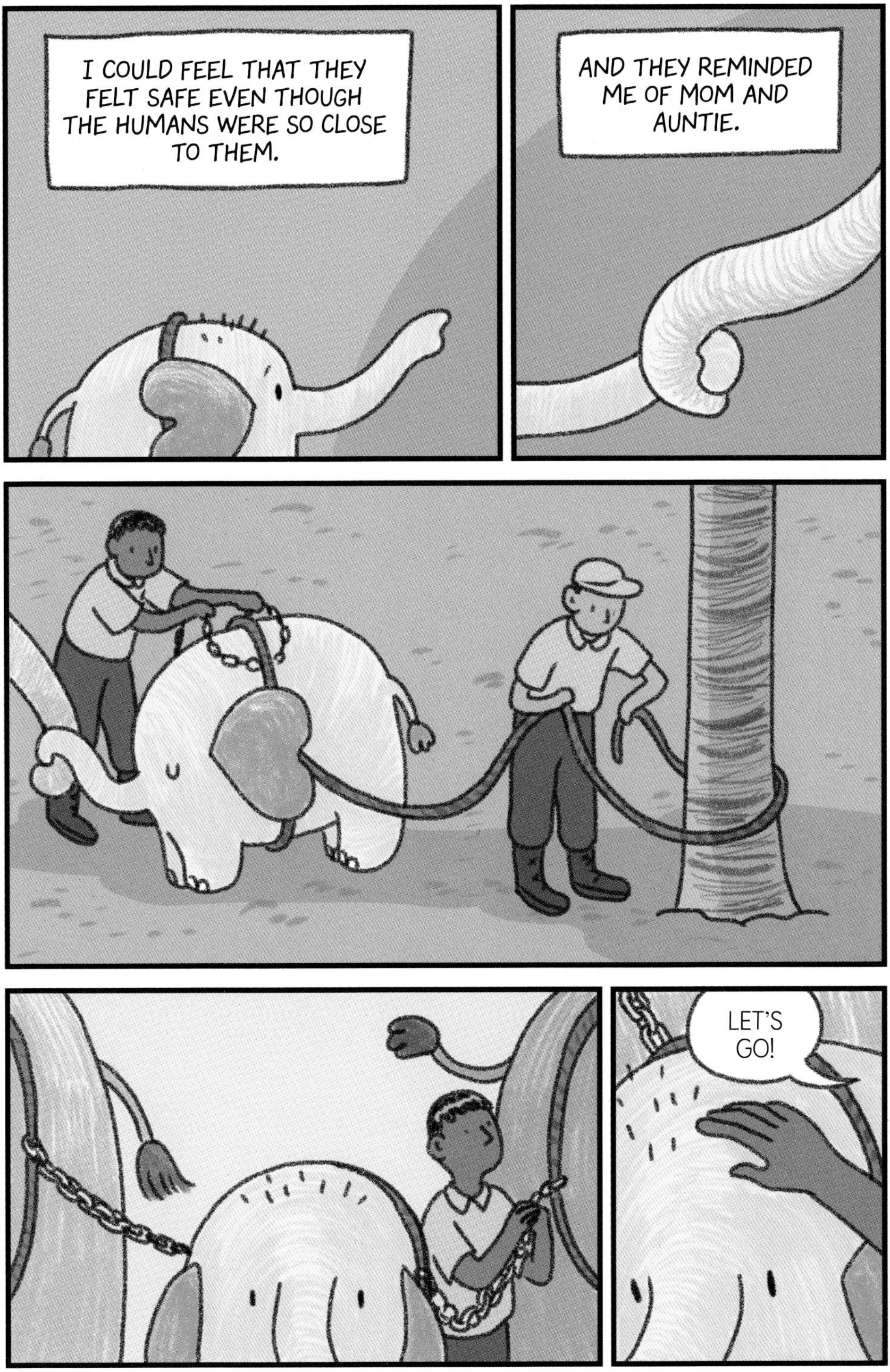
I COULD FEEL THAT THEY FELT SAFE EVEN THOUGH THE HUMANS WERE SO CLOSE TO THEM.
AND THEY REMINDED ME OF MOM AND AUNTIE.
LET'S GO!

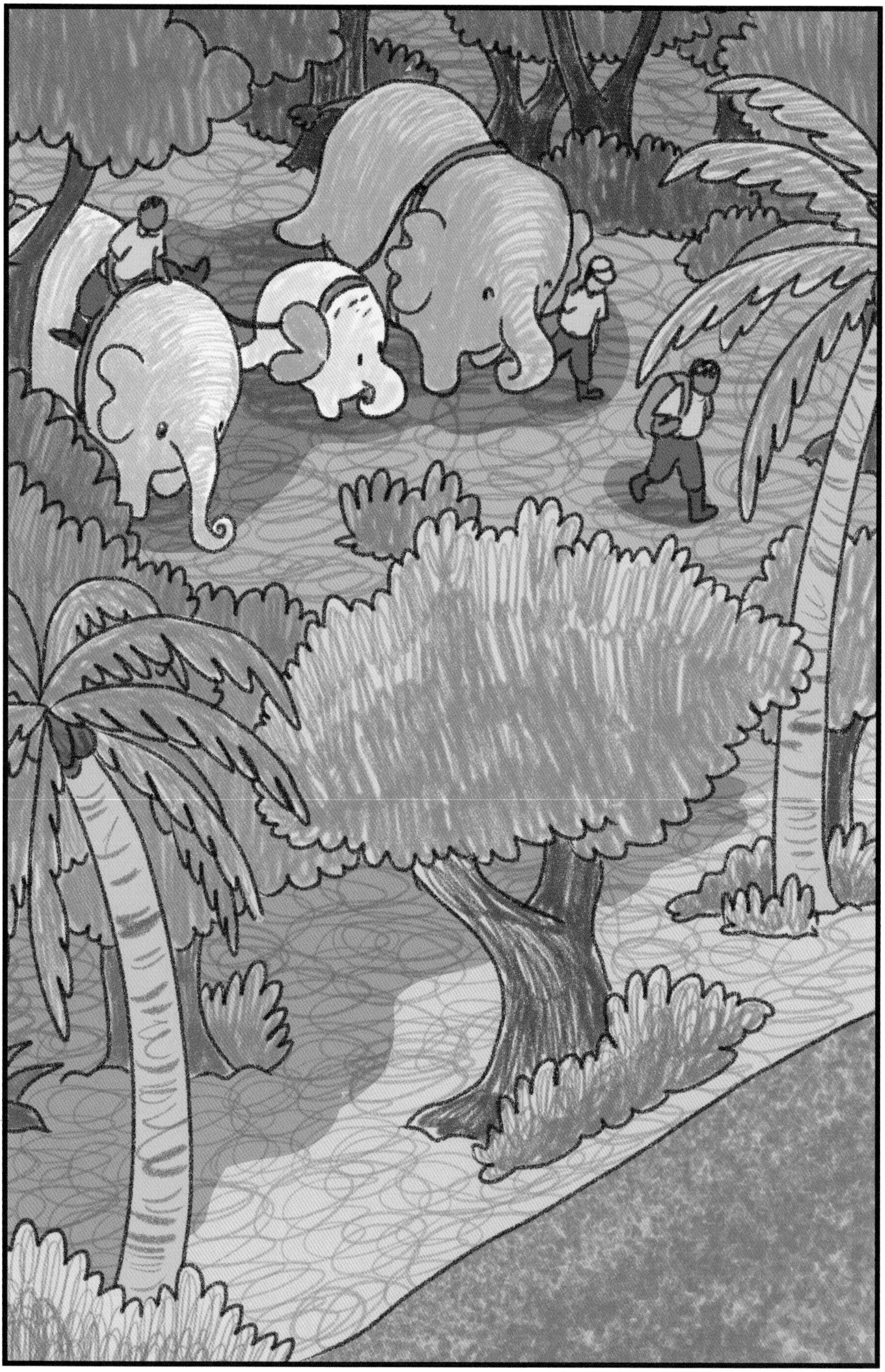

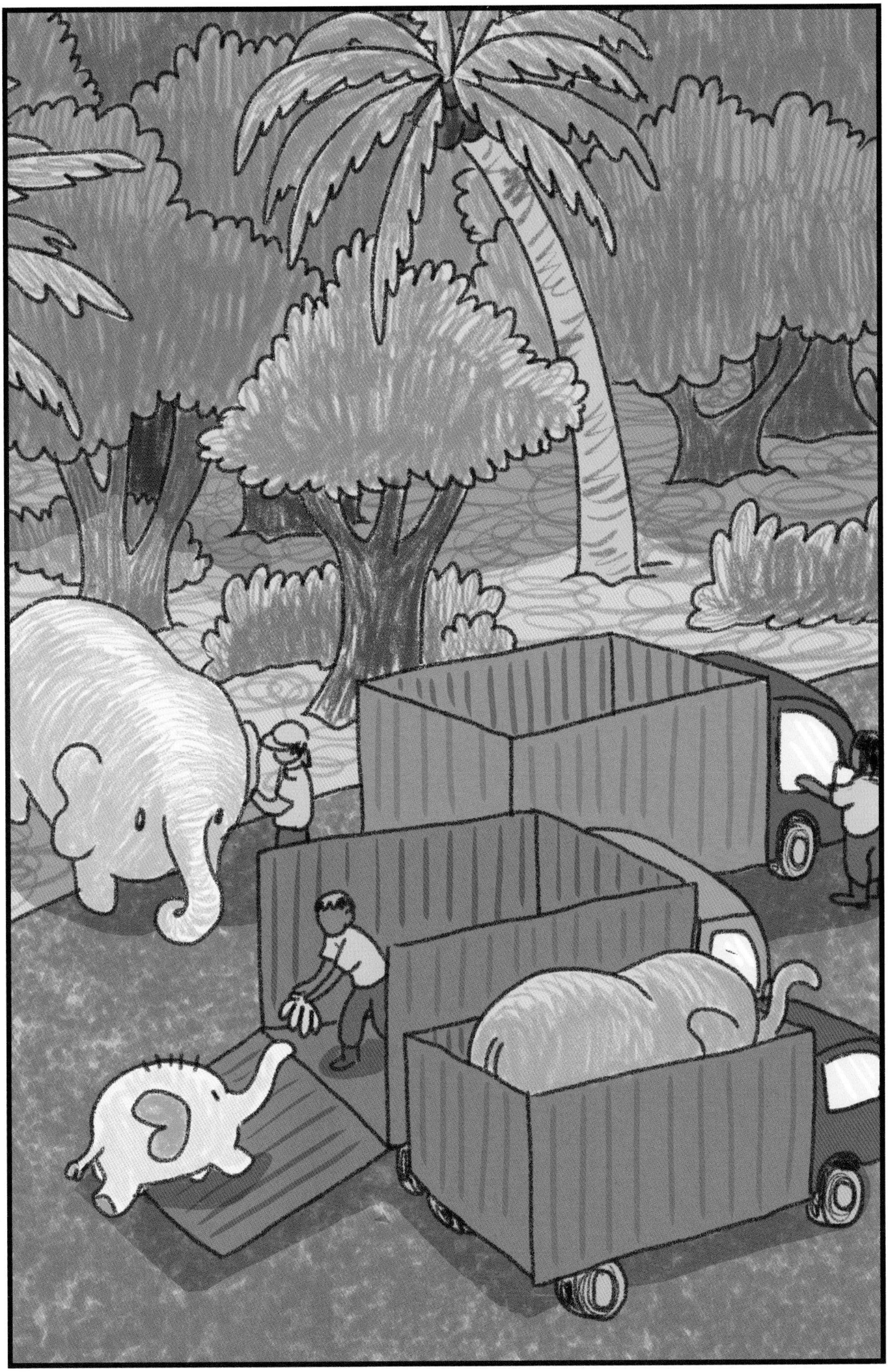

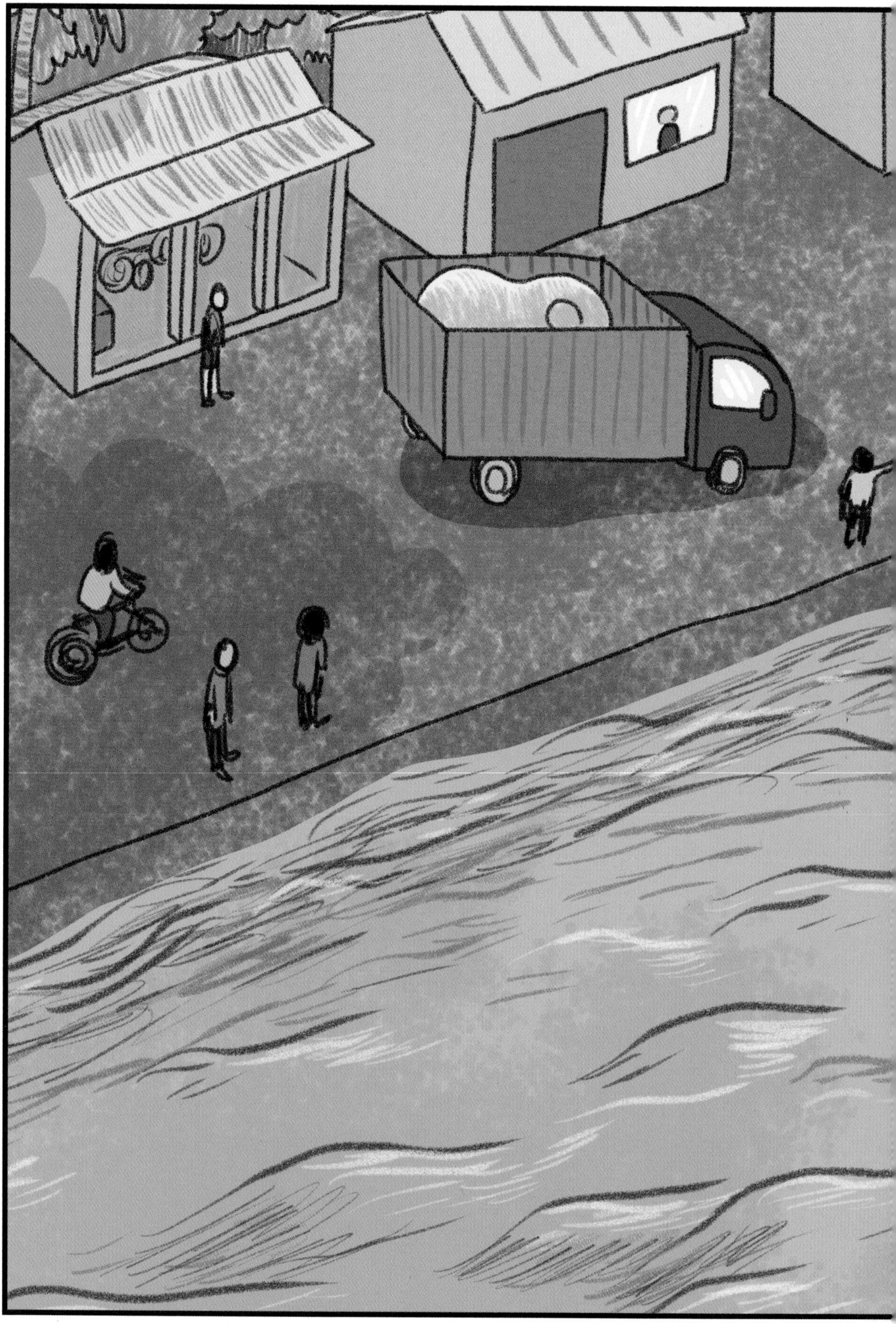

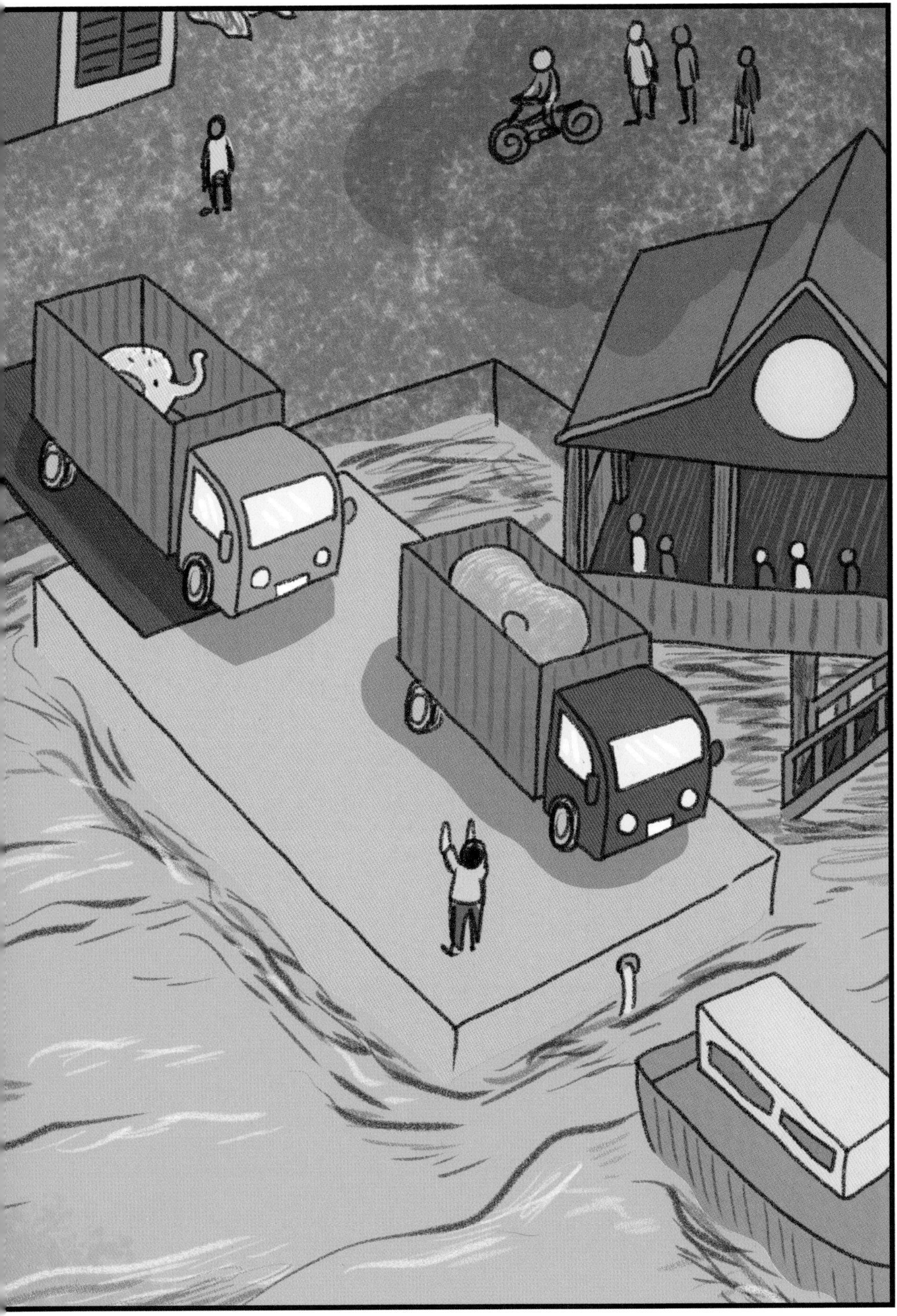

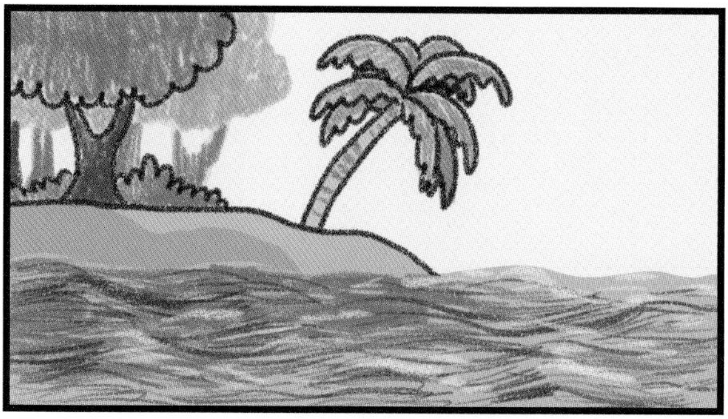

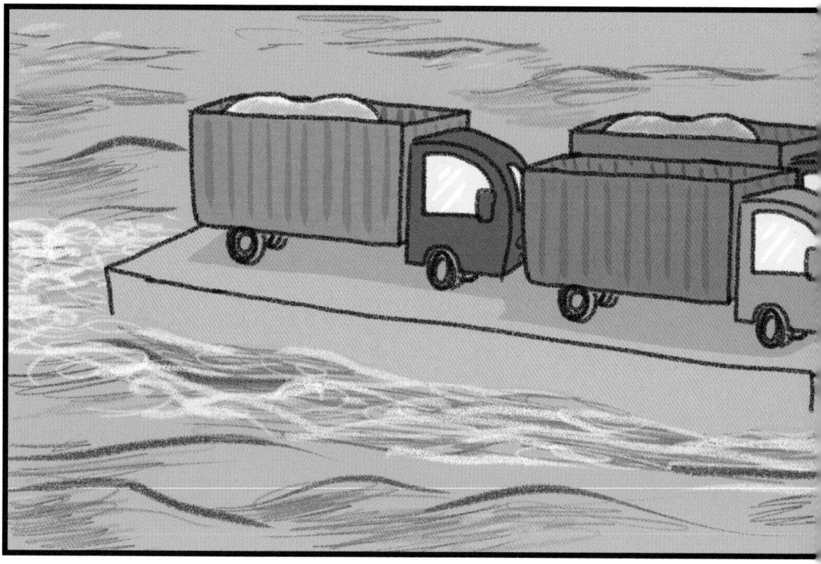

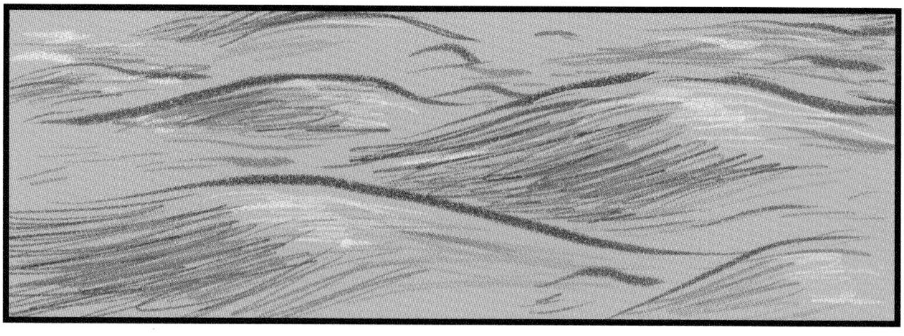

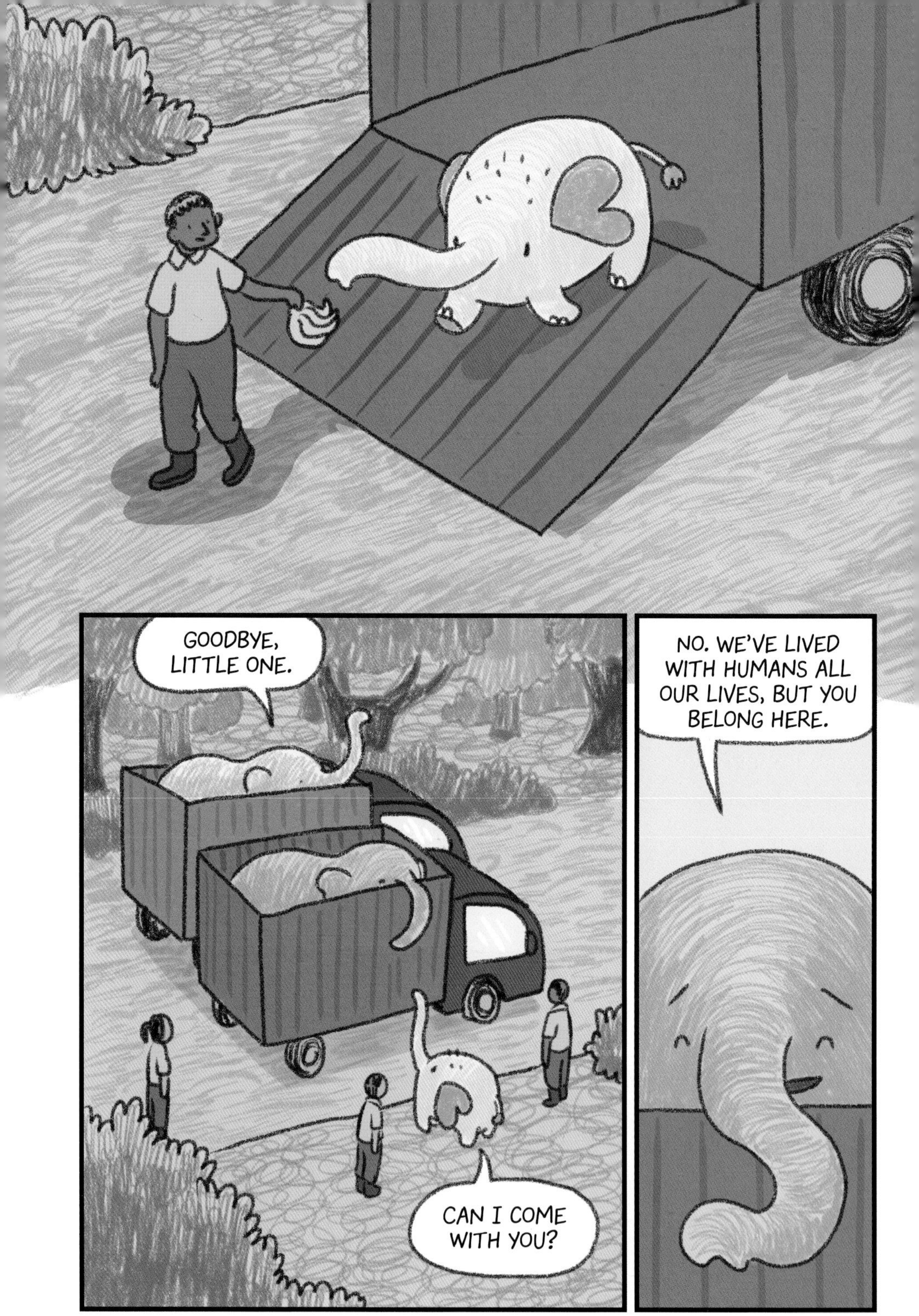
GOODBYE, LITTLE ONE.
CAN I COME WITH YOU?
NO. WE'VE LIVED WITH HUMANS ALL OUR LIVES, BUT YOU BELONG HERE.

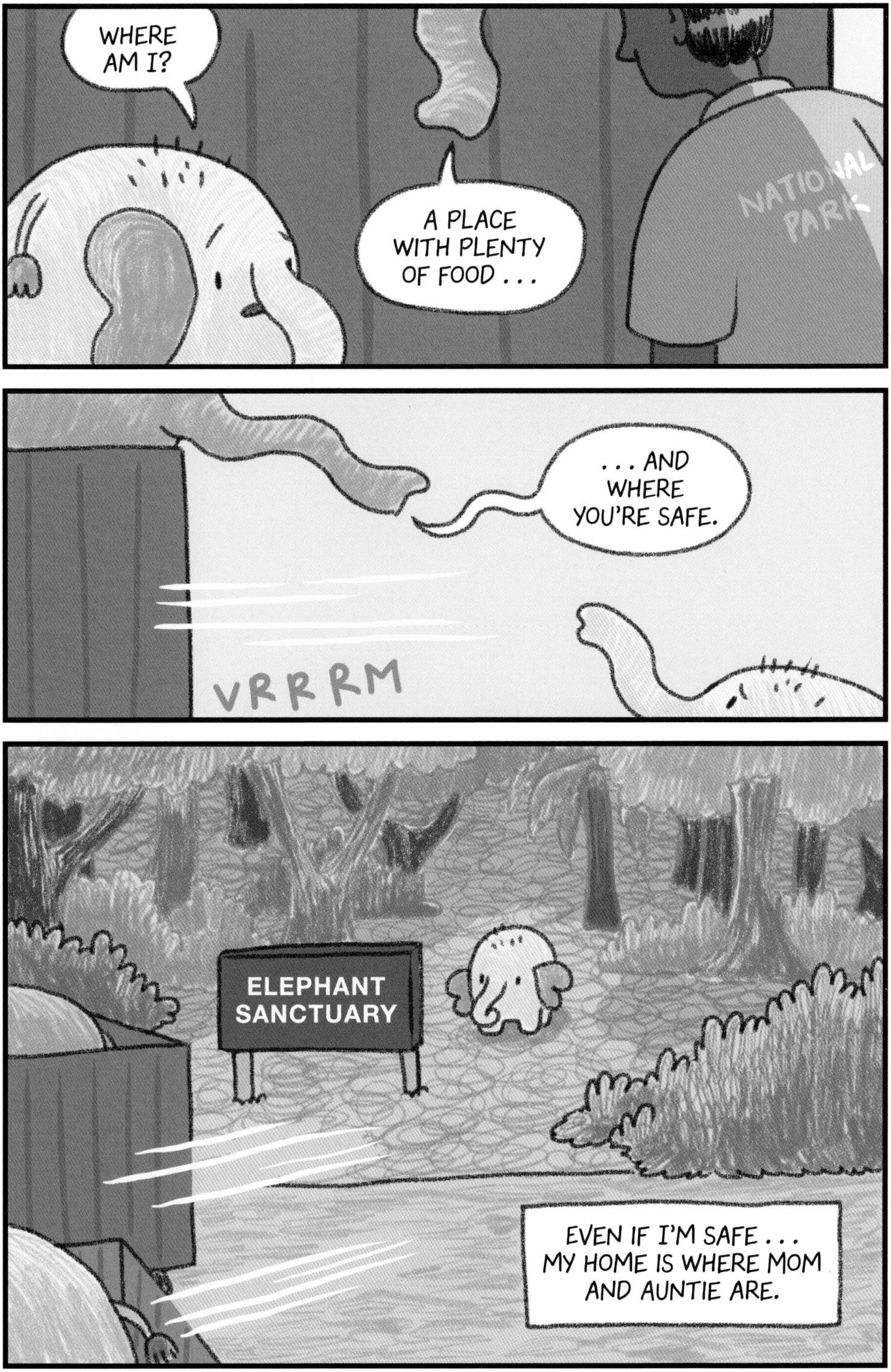
WHERE AM I?
A PLACE WITH PLENTY OF FOOD . . .
NATIONAL PARK
. . . AND WHERE YOU'RE SAFE.
VRRRM
ELEPHANT SANCTUARY
EVEN IF I'M SAFE . . . MY HOME IS WHERE MOM AND AUNTIE ARE.

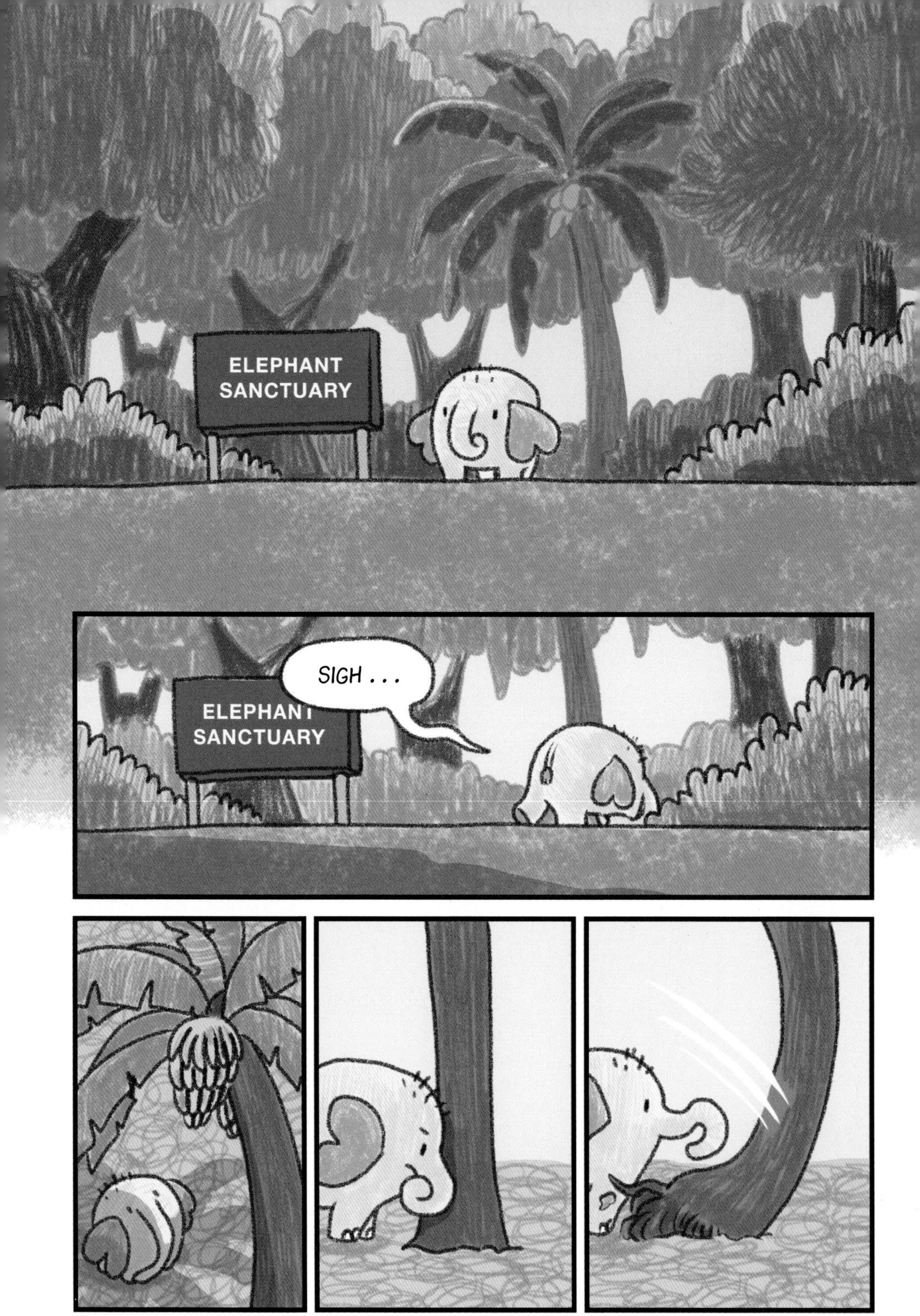
ELEPHANT SANCTUARY
ELEPHANT SANCTUARY
SIGH . . .

CRASH!

NOM NOM

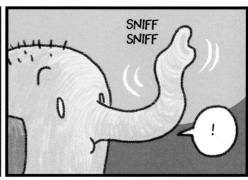

SNIFF SNIFF

!

THAT SCENT IS SO FAMILIAR . . .

STAR, YOU'RE FINALLY WHERE I CAN SEE YOU.

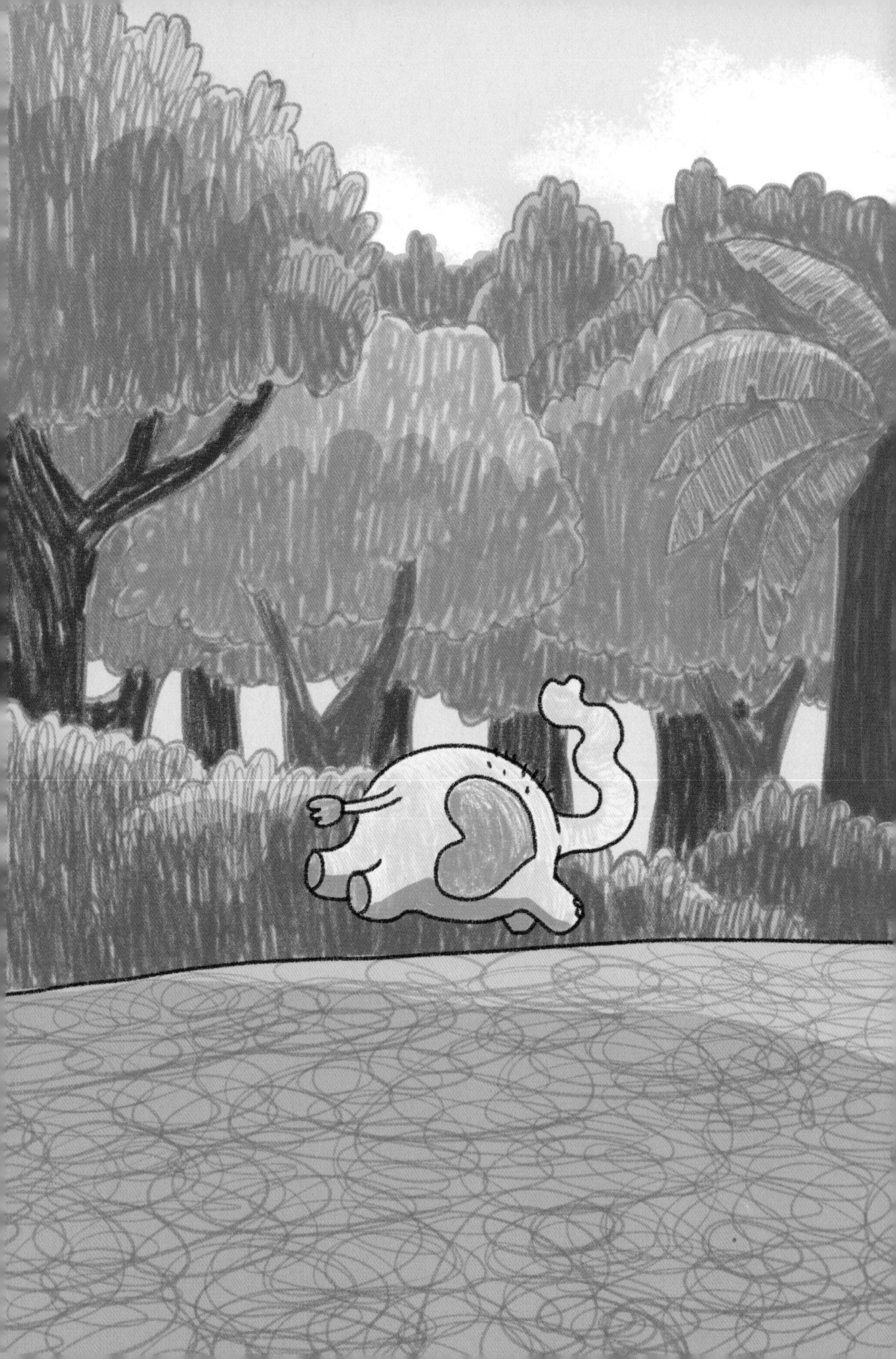

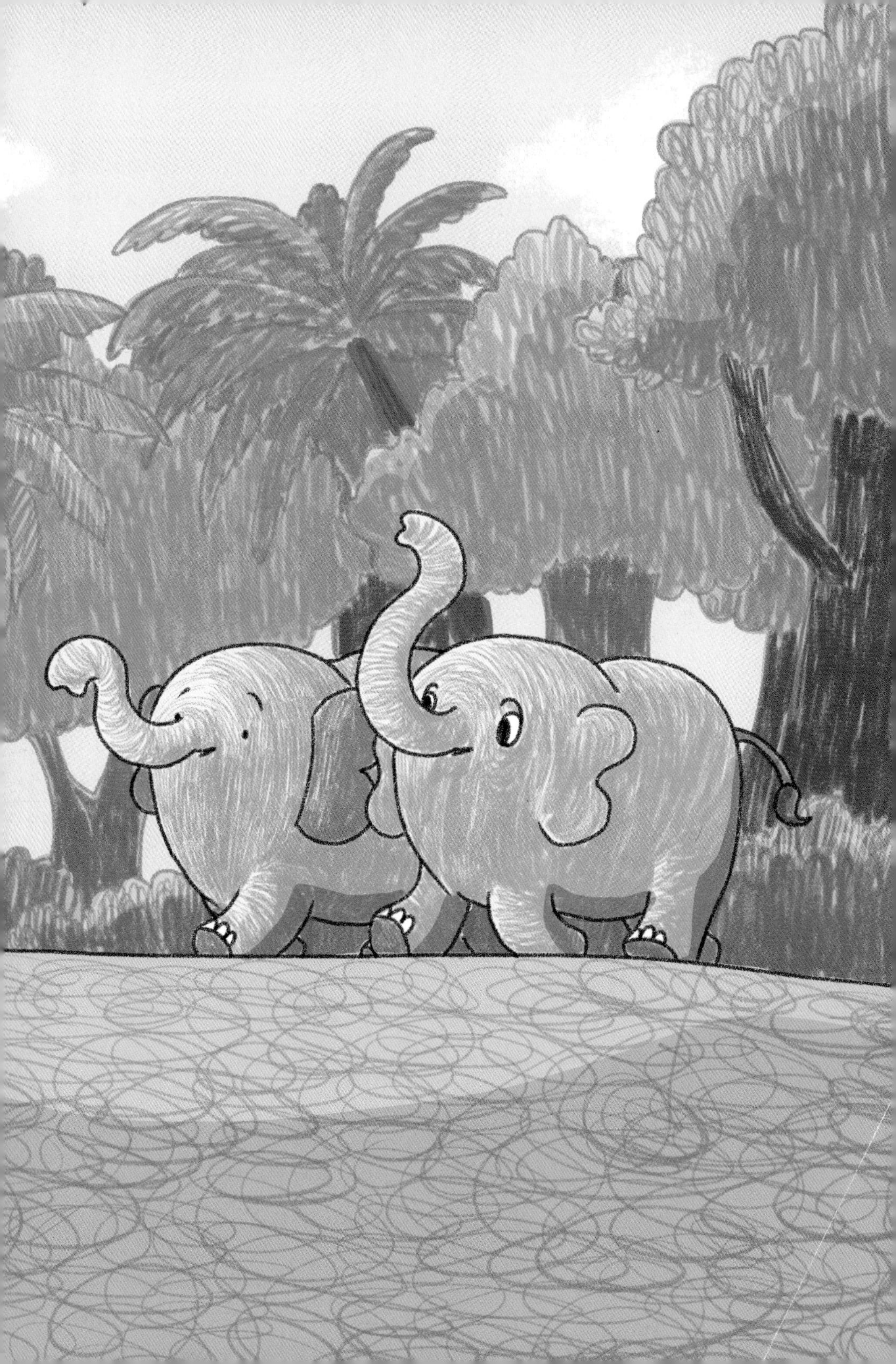

THE TRUE STORY BEHIND STAR'S ADVENTURE

IN 1990, THREE BULL ELEPHANTS IN MALAYSIA LOST THEIR HOME DUE TO DEFORESTATION.

DEFORESTATION HAPPENS WHEN TREES ARE CUT DOWN AND REMOVED FROM THE FORESTS.

THE SMALLEST ELEPHANT WAS SIX FEET TALL AT SHOULDER HEIGHT.

IN THIS BOOK, STAR RUNS INTO ME. BUT THIS DID NOT ACTUALLY OCCUR IN THE TRUE STORY BECAUSE ORANGUTANS LIKE ME LIVE FAR AWAY FROM THE THREE BULL ELEPHANTS' ORIGINAL HOME.

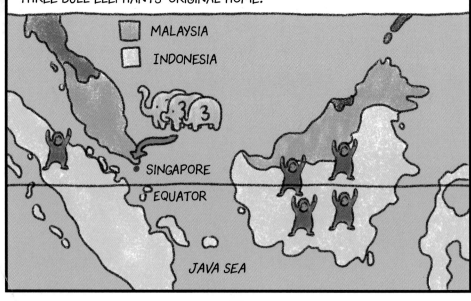

MALAYSIA

INDONESIA

SINGAPORE

EQUATOR

JAVA SEA

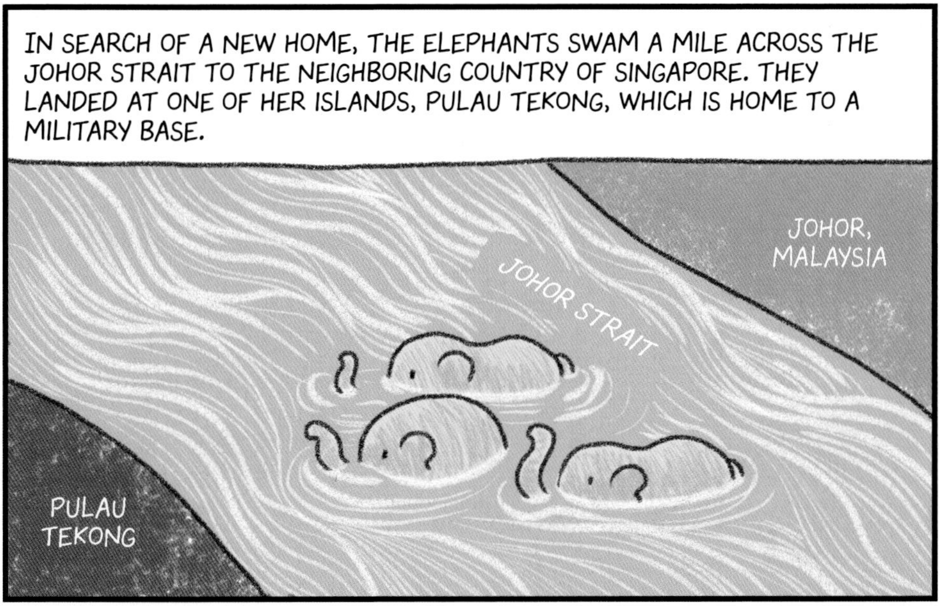
IN SEARCH OF A NEW HOME, THE ELEPHANTS SWAM A MILE ACROSS THE JOHOR STRAIT TO THE NEIGHBORING COUNTRY OF SINGAPORE. THEY LANDED AT ONE OF HER ISLANDS, PULAU TEKONG, WHICH IS HOME TO A MILITARY BASE.
JOHOR, MALAYSIA
JOHOR STRAIT
PULAU TEKONG

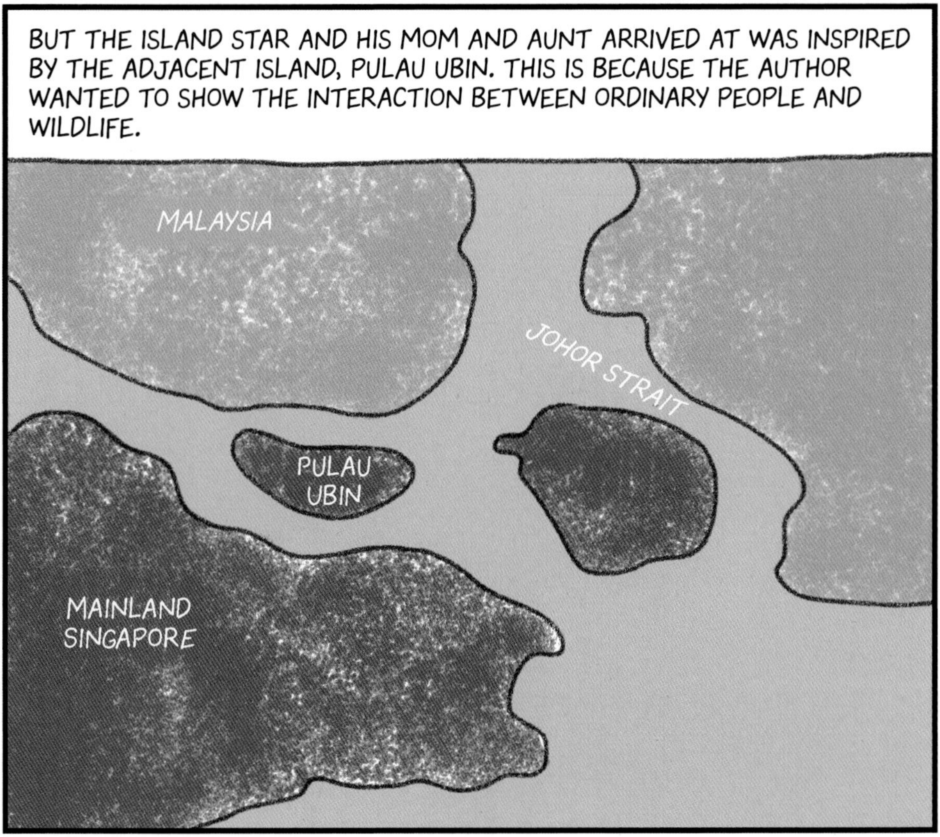
BUT THE ISLAND STAR AND HIS MOM AND AUNT ARRIVED AT WAS INSPIRED BY THE ADJACENT ISLAND, PULAU UBIN. THIS IS BECAUSE THE AUTHOR WANTED TO SHOW THE INTERACTION BETWEEN ORDINARY PEOPLE AND WILDLIFE.
MALAYSIA
JOHOR STRAIT
PULAU UBIN
MAINLAND SINGAPORE

THE THREE BULL ELEPHANTS WERE FIRST SPOTTED ON PULAU TEKONG ON MAY 29, 1990.

THEY WERE NOT SEEN AGAIN FOR ABOUT A WEEK, BUT THEY LEFT PLENTY OF EVIDENCE OF THEIR PRESENCE.

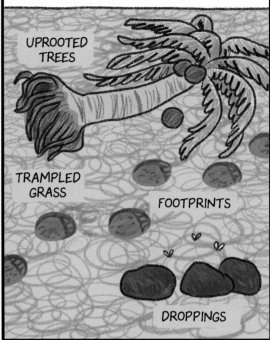

UPROOTED TREES

TRAMPLED GRASS

FOOTPRINTS

DROPPINGS

THE SINGAPORE ARMED FORCES WORKED WITH THE MALAYSIAN WILDLIFE DEPARTMENT AND THE SINGAPORE ZOO TO TRACK DOWN THE ELEPHANTS AND RELOCATE THEM TO ENDAU-ROMPIN NATIONAL PARK IN MALAYSIA.

OF COURSE, THE BIGGEST STARS OF THE WHOLE OPERATION WERE THE TWO TRAINED ELEPHANTS FROM THE NATIONAL ELEPHANT CONSERVATION CENTRE IN KUALA GANDAH, MALAYSIA.

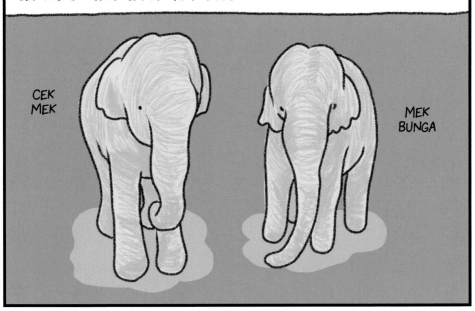

CEK MEK

MEK BUNGA

EVEN THOUGH I LIVE FAR AWAY FROM STAR AND HIS HERD, I MAKE AN APPEARANCE IN THIS BOOK BECAUSE ORANGUTANS LIKE ME ARE ALSO LOSING OUR HOMES DUE TO DEFORESTATION.

BUT WHILE ELEPHANTS MIGHT JOURNEY ACROSS WATER BODIES TO FIND A NEW HOME, I AM A POOR SWIMMER.

I'M A POOR SWIMMER, TOO!

99

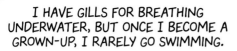

I HAVE GILLS FOR BREATHING UNDERWATER, BUT ONCE I BECOME A GROWN-UP, I RARELY GO SWIMMING.

STAR AND HIS HERD ARE GREAT SWIMMERS BECAUSE THEY HAVE TRUNKS FOR SNORKELING, AND THEIR LARGE BODIES MAKE IT EASIER FOR THEM TO FLOAT.

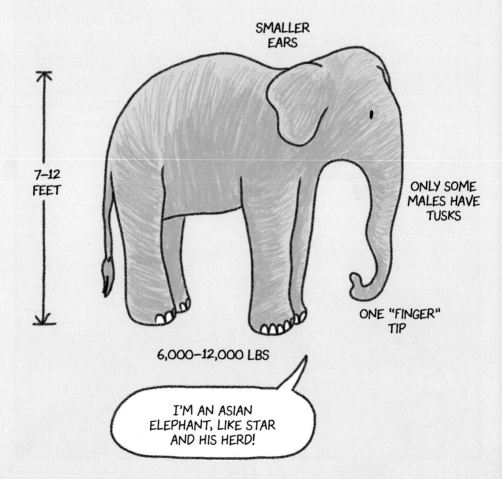

SMALLER EARS

7–12 FEET

ONLY SOME MALES HAVE TUSKS

ONE "FINGER" TIP

6,000–12,000 LBS

I'M AN ASIAN ELEPHANT, LIKE STAR AND HIS HERD!

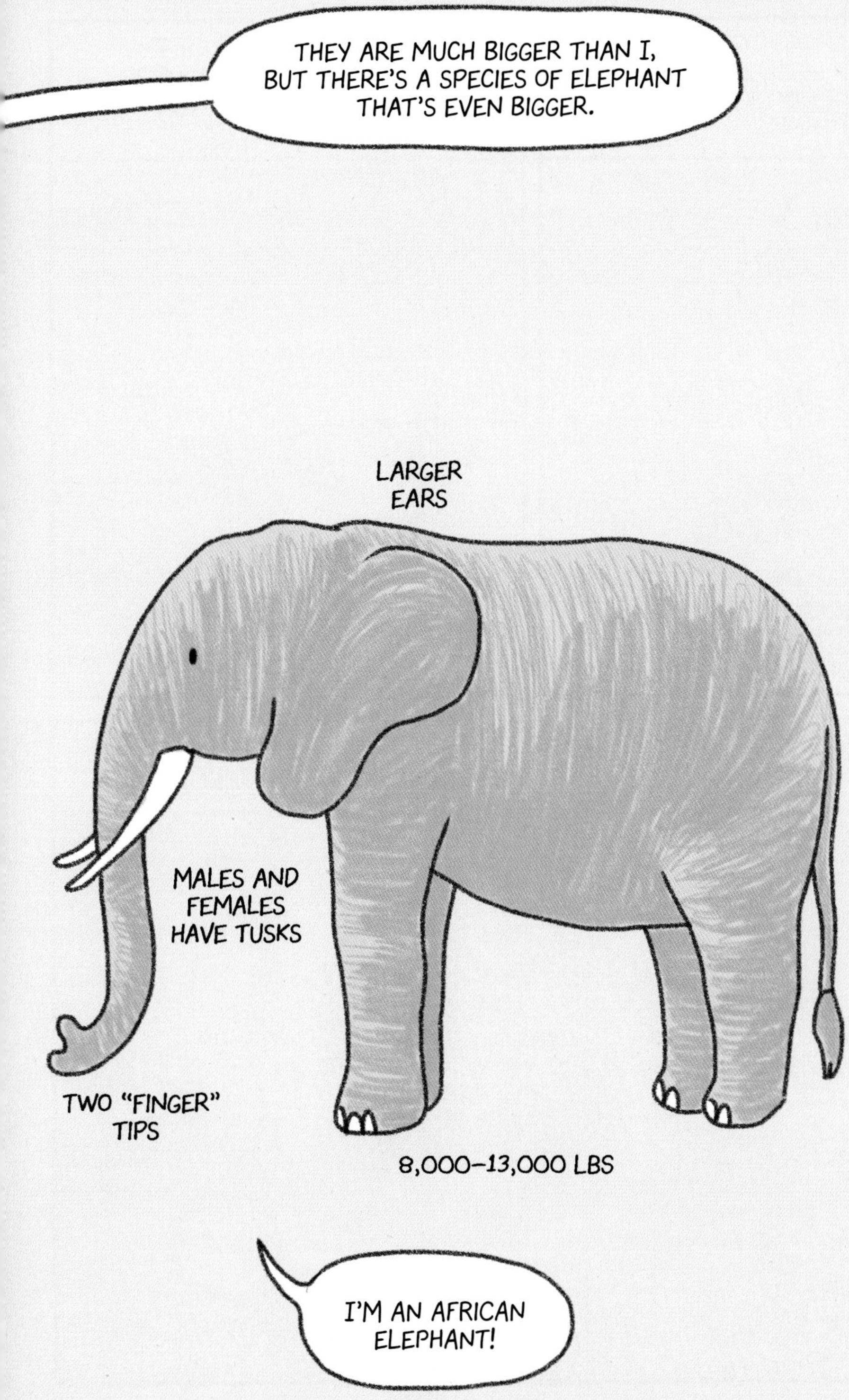
THEY ARE MUCH BIGGER THAN I, BUT THERE'S A SPECIES OF ELEPHANT THAT'S EVEN BIGGER.
LARGER EARS
8–13 FEET
MALES AND FEMALES HAVE TUSKS
TWO "FINGER" TIPS
8,000–13,000 LBS
I'M AN AFRICAN ELEPHANT!

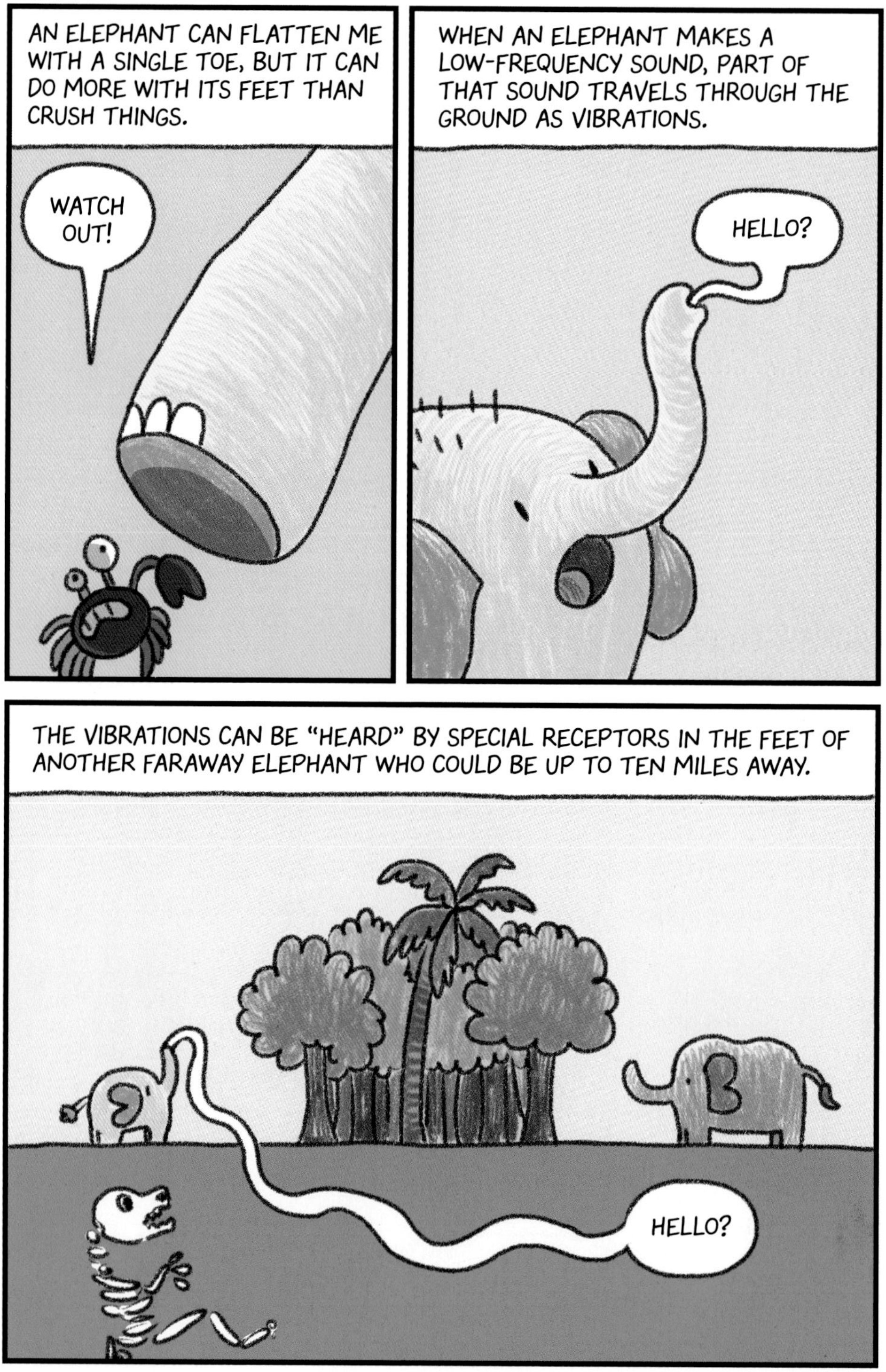
AN ELEPHANT CAN FLATTEN ME WITH A SINGLE TOE, BUT IT CAN DO MORE WITH ITS FEET THAN CRUSH THINGS.
WATCH OUT!
WHEN AN ELEPHANT MAKES A LOW-FREQUENCY SOUND, PART OF THAT SOUND TRAVELS THROUGH THE GROUND AS VIBRATIONS.
HELLO?
THE VIBRATIONS CAN BE "HEARD" BY SPECIAL RECEPTORS IN THE FEET OF ANOTHER FARAWAY ELEPHANT WHO COULD BE UP TO TEN MILES AWAY.
HELLO?

IN ADDITION TO THEIR EXCELLENT HEARING, ELEPHANTS ALSO HAVE A GREAT SENSE OF SMELL, WHICH THEY CAN EVEN USE TO "COUNT."

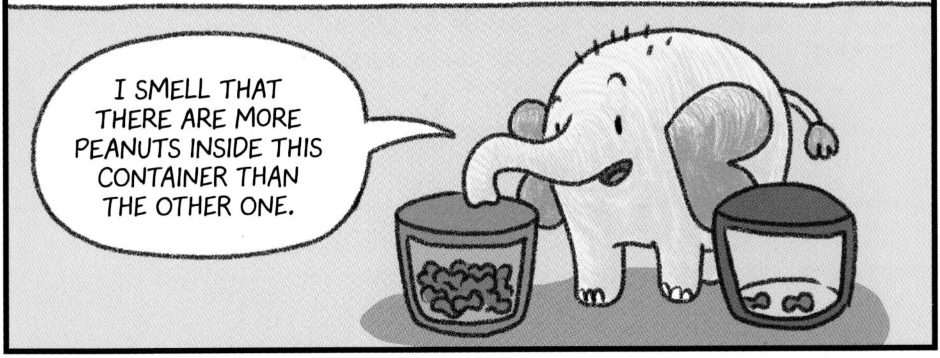
I SMELL THAT THERE ARE MORE PEANUTS INSIDE THIS CONTAINER THAN THE OTHER ONE.

ELEPHANTS ARE AWESOME, BUT THE BEST THING ABOUT BEING A FIDDLER CRAB IS THAT THERE'S NO GROWN-UP TO BOSS ME AROUND. YOU MIGHT NOTICE THAT STAR AND HIS MOM HAVE TO DO WHAT AUNTIE SAYS. THIS IS BECAUSE ELEPHANTS LIVE IN A MATRIARCHY, WHICH IS A SYSTEM WHERE A FEMALE ELDER IS THE LEADER OF THE GROUP.

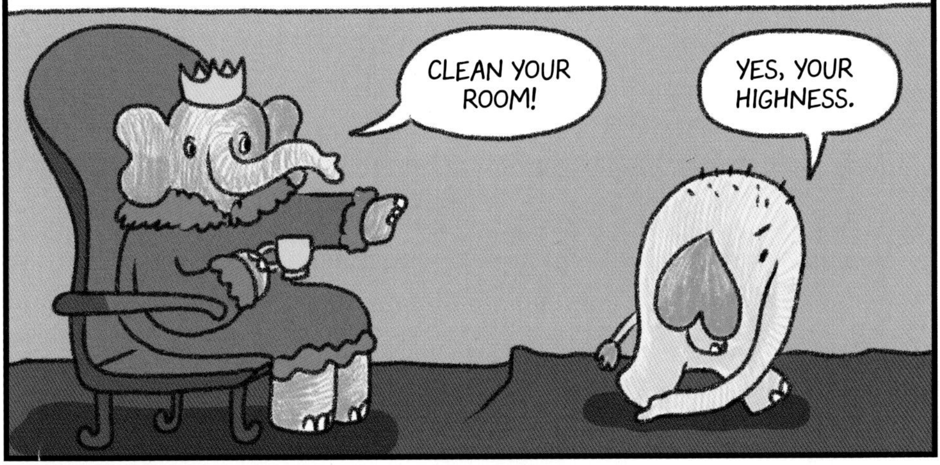
CLEAN YOUR ROOM!
YES, YOUR HIGHNESS.

BUT EVEN THOUGH LITTLE ELEPHANTS HAVE TO LISTEN TO THEIR MOMS AND AUNTS, THEY ARE ALMOST AS AWESOME AS FIDDLER CRABS.

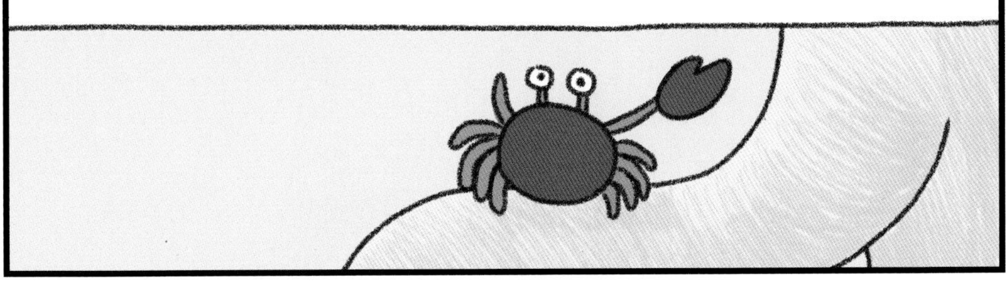

STAR!

TELL US HOW WE CAN HELP YOU AND YOUR FELLOW ELEPHANTS!

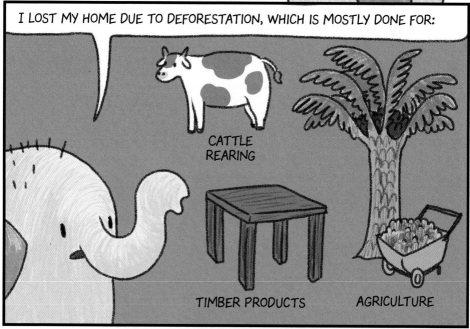

I LOST MY HOME DUE TO DEFORESTATION, WHICH IS MOSTLY DONE FOR:

CATTLE REARING

TIMBER PRODUCTS

AGRICULTURE

TO PROTECT ANIMALS LIKE ME, YOU CAN HELP REDUCE THE DEMAND FOR TIMBER PRODUCTS BY . . .

1. RECYCLING

2. CUTTING DOWN ON PAPER WASTE

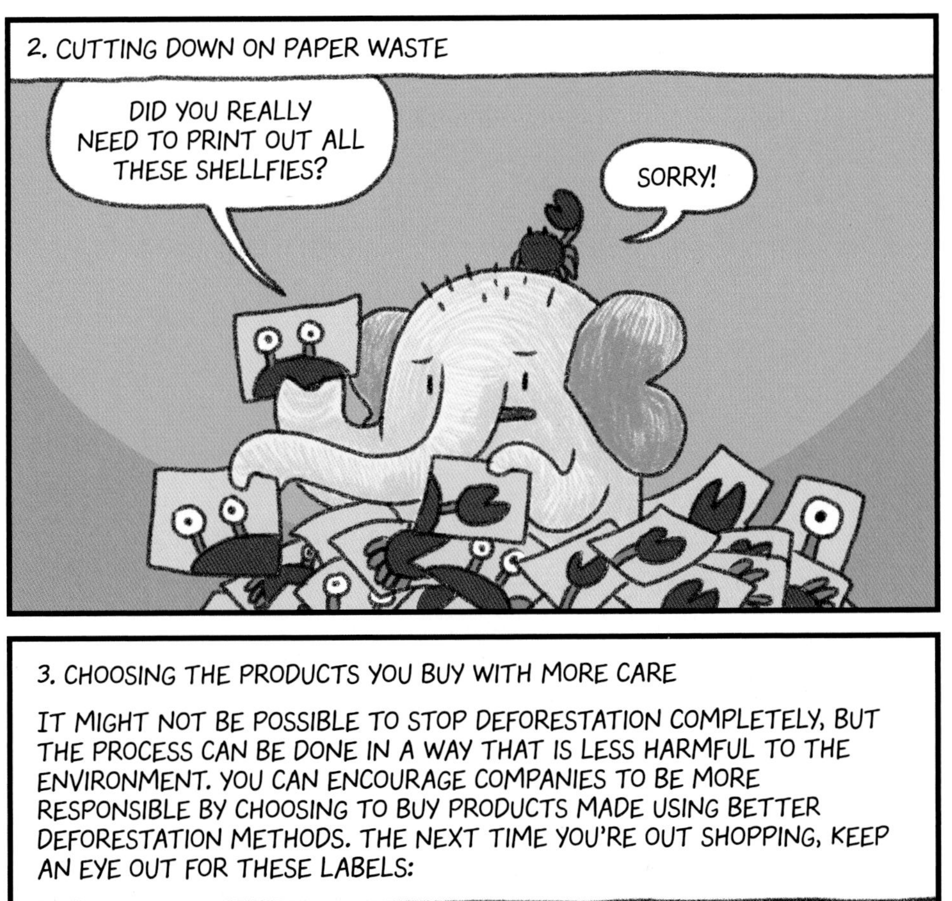
DID YOU REALLY NEED TO PRINT OUT ALL THESE SHELLFIES?
SORRY!

3. CHOOSING THE PRODUCTS YOU BUY WITH MORE CARE

IT MIGHT NOT BE POSSIBLE TO STOP DEFORESTATION COMPLETELY, BUT THE PROCESS CAN BE DONE IN A WAY THAT IS LESS HARMFUL TO THE ENVIRONMENT. YOU CAN ENCOURAGE COMPANIES TO BE MORE RESPONSIBLE BY CHOOSING TO BUY PRODUCTS MADE USING BETTER DEFORESTATION METHODS. THE NEXT TIME YOU'RE OUT SHOPPING, KEEP AN EYE OUT FOR THESE LABELS:

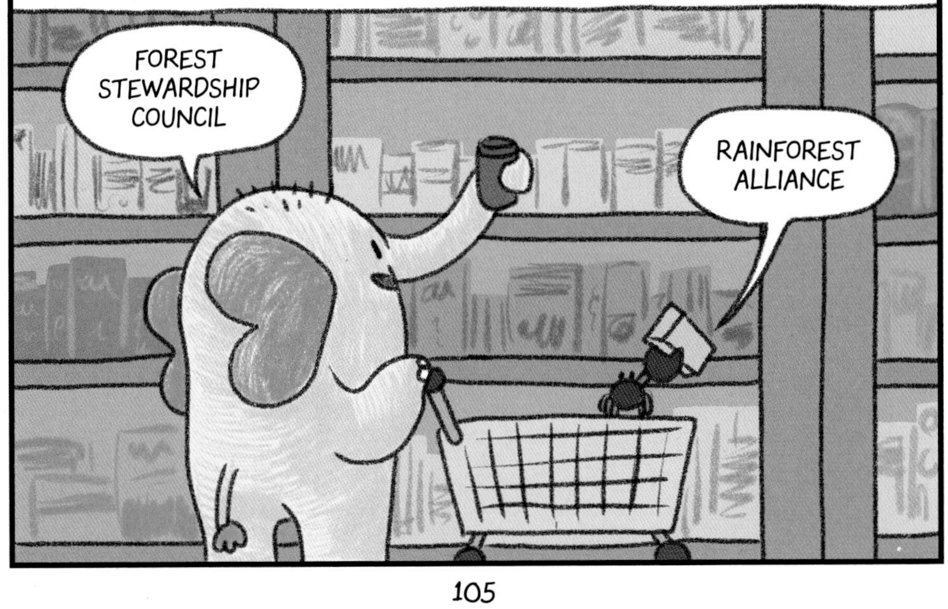
FOREST STEWARDSHIP COUNCIL
RAINFOREST ALLIANCE

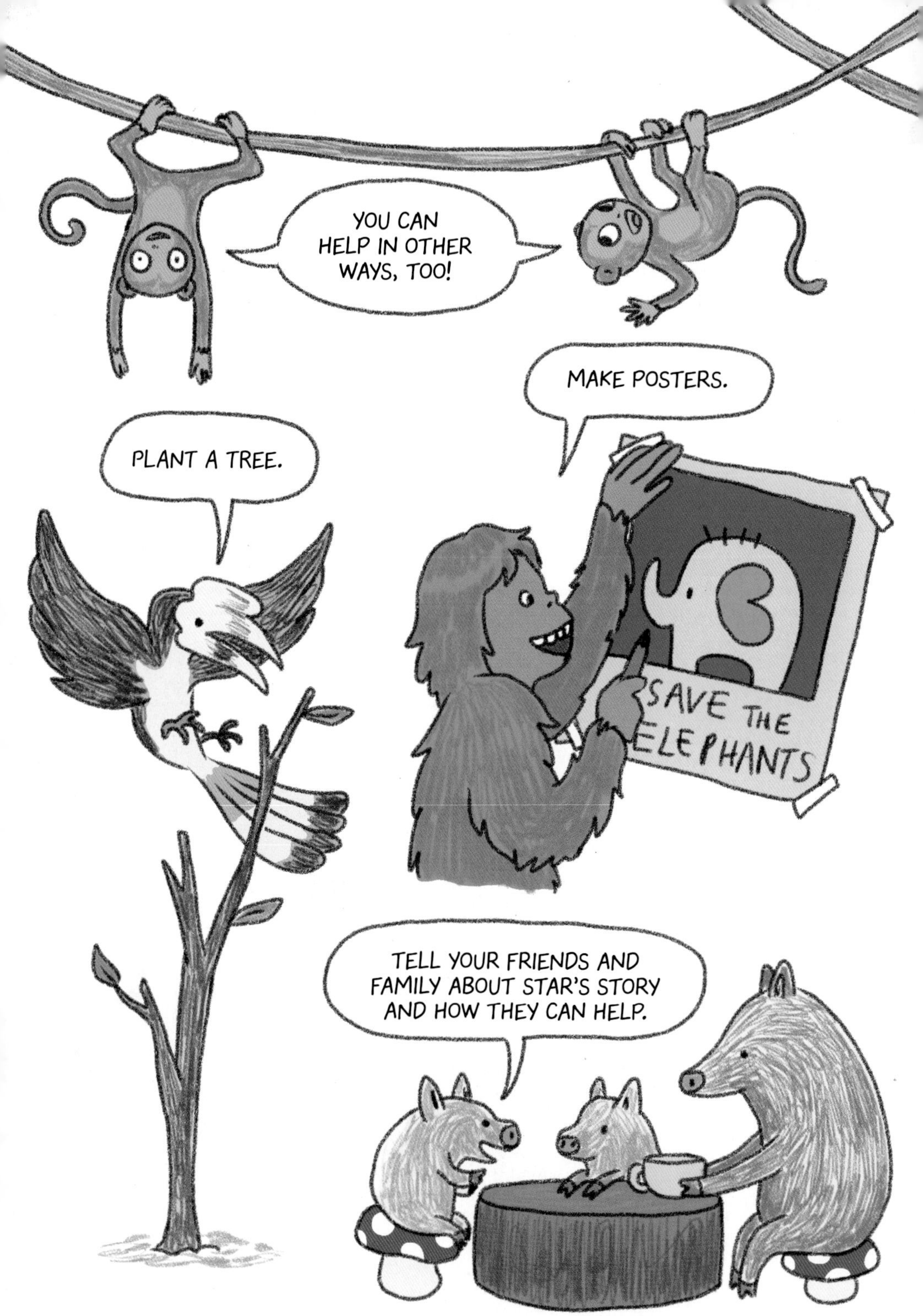
YOU CAN HELP IN OTHER WAYS, TOO!
MAKE POSTERS.
PLANT A TREE.
SAVE THE ELEPHANTS
TELL YOUR FRIENDS AND FAMILY ABOUT STAR'S STORY AND HOW THEY CAN HELP.

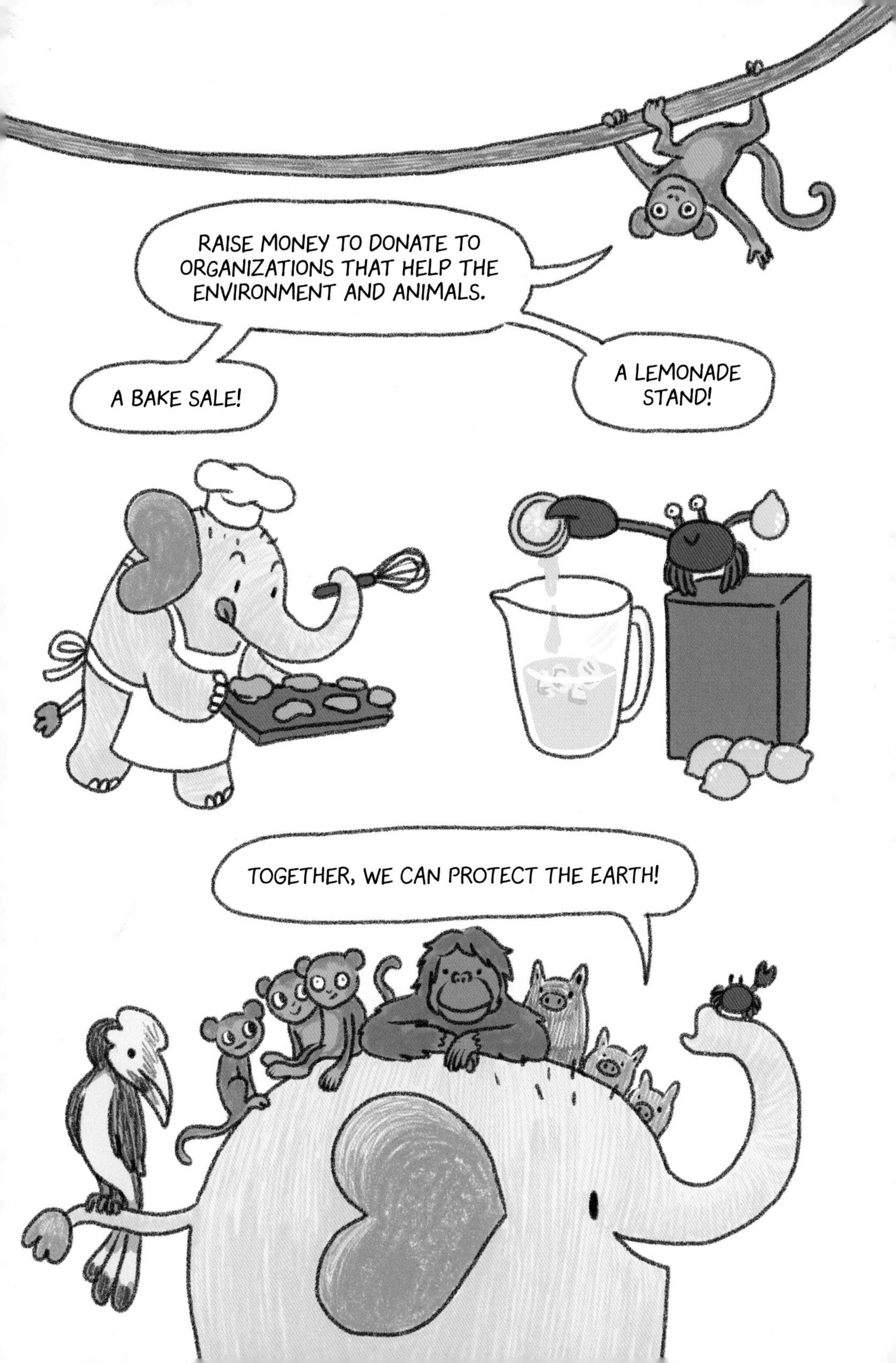
RAISE MONEY TO DONATE TO ORGANIZATIONS THAT HELP THE ENVIRONMENT AND ANIMALS.
A BAKE SALE!
A LEMONADE STAND!
TOGETHER, WE CAN PROTECT THE EARTH!

ARE YOU READY TO EMBARK ON ANOTHER EXCITING ADVENTURE?
CLIMB INTO THE WILDERNESS IN:

SURVIVING THE WILD

RAINBOW
THE KOALA

REMY LAI

REMY LAI was born in Indonesia, grew up in Singapore, and currently lives in Brisbane, Australia, where she writes and draws stories for kids with her two dogs by her side. She is also the author of the critically acclaimed *Pie in the Sky*, *Fly on the Wall*, and *Pawcasso*. **remylai.com**